MW00756705

MAX in the HOUSE of SPIES

ALSO BY
Adam Gidwitz:

A Tale Dark & Grimm
In a Glass Grimmly
The Grimm Conclusion

The Inquisitor's Tale:
Or, The Three Magical Children and Their Holy Dog

The Unicorn Rescue Society series:

The Creature of the Pines

The Basque Dragon
WITH JESSE CASEY

Sasquatch and the Muckleshoot
WITH JOSEPH BRUCHAC

The Chupacabras of the Río Grande
WITH DAVID BOWLES

The Madre de Aguas of Cuba
WITH EMMA OTHEGUY

The Secret of the Himalayas
WITH HENA KHAN

OPERATION KINDERSPION

MAX in the HOUSE of SPIES

Adam Gidwitz

DUTTON CHILDREN'S BOOKS

TOP SECRE

SECRET

DUTTON CHILDREN'S BOOKS
An imprint of Penguin Random House LLC, New York

First published in the United States of America by Dutton Children's Books,
an imprint of Penguin Random House LLC, 2024

Copyright © 2024 by Adam Gidwitz
Photograph on page 302 from the collection of Patricia Lewy
Photograph on page 302 from the collection of Michael Steinberg

Visit us online at PenguinRandomHouse.com.

Library of Congress Cataloging-in-Publication Data is available.

ISBN 9780593112083
1st Printing

Printed in the United States of America

LSCH

Edited by Julie Strauss-Gabel
Design by Anna Booth
Text set in Maxime Regular

To Mama and Papa

And in memory of their dear friends,
Jorja Fleezanis and Michael Steinberg

Between the truth and my mother, I choose my mother.

— Albert Camus (sort of)

MAX in the HOUSE of SPIES

To understand the story that follows, you have to remember a few things. Actually, you have to *forget* a few things. You have to forget everything that you know about World War II, about Nazi Germany, and about the Holocaust. This tale begins in the summer of 1939, and the characters in it—many of whom were real people—did not know that World War II was about to begin. And they certainly didn't expect the Holocaust to occur, with its death camps and gas chambers. It's hard to believe it now, but to average people in England and Germany in 1939, the mass murder of six million Jews, and millions of others, was quite literally unimaginable.

Even so, in 1939, life for Jews in Germany was brutal and frightening. Which is why many left, and why some of those who couldn't leave resorted to sending their children far away from home . . .

CHAPTER
One

Once there was a boy who had two immortal creatures living on his shoulders.

This was the fourth most interesting thing about him.

The first most interesting thing about Max—that was his name—was that he was a genius. He could make a working radio from the junk at the bottom of a trash can, and he could usually predict what someone was going to say ten minutes before they said it.

The second most interesting thing about Max was that, when he was eleven years old, his parents sent him away from Germany, where he was born and grew up, to England. All by himself. Even though he'd never been there, didn't know anyone there, and barely spoke any English.

The third most interesting thing about Max was that, when he got to England, he fell in with spies. Real, honest-to-goodness spies. A lot of them.

And the fourth most interesting thing about him was that he had two immortal creatures living on his shoulders.

But that's probably what you have the most questions about, so let's start there.

The two immortal creatures appeared the day his parents sent him to England.

His family had been arguing about it for weeks. Their small Berlin apartment shook as Max had stomped from the living room to his bedroom to the kitchen and back again, shouting things like:

"You *can't* make me go!"

"Everything is *fine*! Who cares about the stupid Nazis?! They don't matter!"

"What if you *need* me?!"

And, more quietly, alone in his room, *"What if I need you?"*

But no matter what Max said, his parents had refused to change their minds. His mother had held him at the train station against her soft stomach, while his small, thin father had stroked Max's hair. They'd waved as the train pulled out, taking Max and the 198 other Jewish children to Holland and the ferry. Max hadn't waved back. He'd just stared at them and thought, *How could you do this?*

The 198 children had left the train station in Holland and boarded a steam-powered ferry. With a blast of its foghorn, the ship had pushed out into the North Sea, bound for England.

Thirty-one minutes later, Max had fallen asleep.

This might be a little surprising. But after a trauma—something really awful that happens to you—your brain often makes you fall asleep right away. Maybe to help you process the trauma. Or maybe because your brain is scared of more traumas, and figures you won't have to experience them if you're asleep. Whatever the reason, it happens a lot. And it happened to Max.

So he fell asleep thirty-one minutes into the ferry ride.

Thirty-two minutes into the ferry ride, he heard a voice in his ear.

"Max. *Max!*"

Max jerked awake and looked around.

"Max, you are drooling."

Max quickly wiped his mouth.

Wait. Who said that?

He looked to either side of him. He was sitting on a bench in the belly of the steamship. There were other kids on other benches. Some boys were sleeping, leaning against each other, not too far away. A girl had her face buried in a handkerchief, sitting across from Max. But the voice had been right next to his ear. And it had *not* sounded like a kid's voice.

"What'd you wake him up for?" said another voice, very near his other ear.

"He was drooling. It was disgusting! I thought he would want to know!"

Max spun from side to side. *Where were these voices coming from?*

"You think he doesn't have bigger problems than drooling

in his sleep? The poor kid just lost his country, his home, his parents. You can't let him drool a little?"

Now Max was staring at his left shoulder. His eyes came into focus.

Crouching there was a tiny man with a bulbous nose, thinning hair, twinkling eyes, and a sour smile.

"Hiya," he said.

Max screamed and fell off the bench.

The sleeping boys woke up with a start and looked around to see what the commotion was. The girl across the way lowered her handkerchief and glared through wet eyelashes at Max.

"No need to scream." This was coming from Max's right shoulder. He turned . . . and saw *another* tiny man, who looked exactly like the first. This tiny man said, "We are not going to hurt you."

"He's not worried we're going to *hurt* him," said the little creature on Max's left shoulder, who Max would later learn was called Stein. "He's worried he's going insane."

"You are not going insane," said the creature on Max's right shoulder, who Max would later learn was called Berg. "We are really here! Sitting on your shoulders!"

Berg spoke with an antique German accent, like something out of a storybook.

Stein sounded more like a vaudeville comedian.

Max looked desperately to the children on the other benches. They were staring at him.

"Don't worry," said Berg. "They cannot see us. Or hear us."

"Just like we can't hear you! Say something!" Stein demanded.

Max said, "I'm dreaming."

"Nope!" Stein said. "Not a dream!"

Max put his butt on his bench. He eyed both of these tiny men warily, his gaze flitting between them. Then he said, "I'm gonna go back to sleep. Since this is a dream, when I wake up for real, you're going to be gone."

"I wouldn't count on it," said Berg.

"Yeah, not gonna happen," added Stein. "Sorry, kid."

Max did not believe them. His eyelids were so heavy they closed themselves.

Max slept the remaining seven hours and fourteen minutes of the journey to England.

He dreamed of his parents sitting on the threadbare sofa in their living room, listening to the radio Max had built for them, the way they always did after Max's father got home from work: Papa's eyes closed behind his wire-rimmed spectacles, his head resting against the cushions; Mama twisting her long hazelnut hair up away from her neck and smiling proudly at Max, who was on the rug leaning against their knees. But in the dream, instead of the symphonic music the radio station usually played, the wireless set was illogically making announcements about the ferry ride. Still, the dream should have made Max happy. But instead it filled him with an emotion he did not have a word for. Maybe the word was *longing*. Or maybe it was *guilt?*

But why should Max feel guilty? He hadn't *chosen* to leave.

Then the ferry's foghorn blew three blasts to the boats in Harwich Port, and Max woke with a start.

He rubbed his eyes. The children around Max were peering out of portholes, gazing at the industrial coastline of shipyards and cargo docks. Wondering what the next days, weeks, and months would hold for them. Wondering how they would like their new foster families. And wondering when their parents would be joining them in England.

Not knowing that very few of their parents would be joining them in England.

At least, Max thought, *that weird dream about the creatures on my shoulders is over—*

"*There's* our sleeping beauty!" shouted Stein, grinning at Max.

"You drooled again! It was gross!" added Berg.

Never mind.

CHAPTER

Two

Now, Max was smart enough to know that Stein and Berg couldn't *really* be on his shoulders. They were figments of his imagination. Products of the terrible trauma of being separated from his parents and his homeland. They had to be.

Nonetheless he decided, for the moment, to play along.

"So where did you *come* from?" Max asked the creatures.

"I come from Germany!" said Berg. "Or, what people now call Germany. It's had lots of different names since the beginning of time. 'Ugg.' 'Flurp.' 'The Holy Roman Empire.' But no matter what you call it, I am a spirit of that land! Some people refer to me as a *kobold*."

Max had heard of kobolds in fairy tales. They were what we, in English, might call hobgoblins—little creatures that cause mischief, like hiding your keys under the couch or raising the toilet seat in the middle of the night so in the morning when you sit down you fall in.

"I, on the other hand," said Stein, and then he added, "uh, other shoulder, I guess . . . am a spirit of the Jewish people. I *also* cause mischief. Usually by sticking myself to someone and making their life miserable. It's my speciality. My kind have had lots of names since the beginning of time, but these days people tend to call me a *dybbuk*."

Max had heard of dybbuks, too. They were supposed to be evil spirits, who possessed people and tormented them. He had always expected them to look scary.

Neither Stein nor Berg looked scary. They looked like little old men. Balding. With round noses and round bellies. Nearly identical.

"So, are you twins or something?" Max said, squinting at one and then the other.

"Yeah, you could say that," said Stein.

"No! Of course not!" said Berg at exactly the same moment.

The dybbuk and the kobold frowned at each other.

"Look," said Stein to Berg, "we were born at the same moment, one instant before the end of the Sixth Day of Creation. Made by the same Holy Hand. And we look identical. Doesn't that make us twins?"

"Well, not really, since an infinity of other creatures like us were created at the same instant. Thousands of other kobolds and dybbuks. Not to mention all the goblins, hobgoblins, gnomes, leprechauns, duendes, jumbies, dokkaebi . . ." Berg got a faraway look on his face. "Is there a word for an infinite number of twins? Two is twins . . . Eight is octuplets . . . So infinity would be . . . ?"

"Infinets?" Stein suggested.

"Besides," Berg went on, "Stein and I are not identical. He is ugly. I, on the other hand"—Berg paused dramatically—"am *hideous*." He hid his face in the crook of his tiny arm.

Stein said, "You're dramatic is what you are."

"So . . ." Max asked, "*why* are you sitting on my shoulders?"

Stein replied, "I don't know what *he's* doing here"—he pointed a warty thumb at Berg, who was still hiding his face—"but I'm hitching a ride out of Germany. I don't know if you read the news, but have you heard of these guys called *the Nazis*? Maniacs? Love a clean uniform? Hate pretty much everything and everyone else?"

Berg looked up. "I'm doing the same thing, obviously!" He turned to Stein. "But I didn't expect to see *you* here!"

Of all the things that Max had trouble believing at this moment, one struck him as *most* unbelievable: "Wait, you both just *happened* to choose *me* to hitch a ride on? What about all these other kids?" He gestured around at the benches of the ferry. "Are all their shoulders crowded with spirits, too?"

Stein and Berg looked around. "Hey! There's Frank!" Stein exclaimed. "Hey Frank! Good to see ya!" He turned back to Max. "Just Frank."

Max was trying to see Frank. He couldn't. "There's a spirit over there named *Frank*?"

Berg said, "We call him Frank. His true name is unpronounceable. Even by us."

"It's a very small part of God's true name, actually," Stein declared.

"Very small," agreed Berg. "More like the punctuation."

Max said, "God's true name has punctuation?"

Berg slapped his hand over his mouth. "We've said too much."

"But," Stein went on, "to answer your question, I don't know how we both ended up on your shoulders. I guess you're just lucky."

Berg was staring off into the distance. "I felt . . . *drawn* to you, somehow. Like it was my destiny to find you . . ."

Stein shifted uncomfortably. "Yeah, actually . . . me too."

Max look back and forth and back again between the two little creatures. Then he said, "So is this a *haunting?* I'm possessed by evil spirits now?"

"No!" Berg said. "I never think of it as a *haunting!*"

"It's more . . . an *annoying,*" said Stein. "And *heckling. Heckling* is a speciality of mine. It's what I was put on Earth to do." Then he added, "I think."

Berg murmured, "Yah, God never really *explained* anything to us. Just . . . made us and sent us on our way." He perked up. "But I'm *pretty* sure my purpose is to *bother* people. Bothering people is the only thing that brings a slight ray of sunshine to this landscape of never-ending darkness. For example, while you were sleeping, I tied that boy's shoelaces together." Berg started to snicker as he nodded toward a boy a few benches away who had somehow managed to sleep through the blasting of the ferry's foghorn. His shoelaces were indeed tied together. "It is going to be very funny when he gets up and falls on his face, no?"

"Love it." Stein chuckled.

Max sighed and stood.

"What are you doing?" demanded Berg.

Max went over to the sleeping boy and gently shook him. The boy woke with a start.

Max pointed to his shoelaces. "Careful."

The boy sat up blearily and mumbled, "How did that happen?" He hurried to untie them without another word to Max.

"Hey, you're no fun!" Berg complained.

"If you're always this way," Stein agreed, "this is going to be a very boring lifetime."

Max said, "You mean you're going to be on my shoulders for the *rest of my life*?" The boy fixing his laces apparently didn't hear Max say this. Somehow. As if this conversation was happening on some different plane of reality.

"Don't worry," Berg reassured him. "I plan to return to Germany as soon as the Nazis leave. Which should happen pretty soon. Three hundred years? Five hundred years at the very most."

"Yeah," Stein agreed, "you humans can't focus on anything for more than a few centuries. You're like toddlers."

The ferry collided with the dock and the doors opened. A wet gray sky framed the backs of eager, frightened children.

Max took in the scene. Seagulls called. A child wept. Berg hocked up some phlegm from deep in his throat.

Max murmured, "This is going to be terrible, isn't it?"

"Oh, Maxy," said Stein, "you have no idea."

CHAPTER
Three

Max waited on the dock in the drizzling rain as the grown-ups got everything sorted. Most children were being taken to the train station, where they'd continue on to London. Others were being picked up by their foster families right here.

Max had been told he'd be living in London, so he figured he'd be going with the children to the station. But when he tried to follow the train group, a young woman with a clipboard hustled over and steered him toward the waiting families.

"Here it comes . . ." Stein said. "The big moment . . ." And then, in a radio-game-show voice, he said, "Who is Max's *new family?*"

They're not my new family, Max thought. *I'm just staying in their house for a little while.*

He scanned the people who were waiting. There were elderly couples, smiling kindly at all the children, waiting to see which one would go home with them. There was a big family, with four children of their own already—two of whom were chasing each other and shrieking. There was a young priest.

Back home in Berlin, Max's upstairs neighbor was a Lutheran pastor who was very calm and very kind. Living with the priest might not be too bad.

But then Max saw who was there for him. There was no room for confusion.

A man in a black cap and matching suit held a sign: MAX BRETZFELD.

The woman with the clipboard led Max over to him. She said, "Mr. Montagu, I presume?"

The man with the sign snapped, "Certainly not! I am Mr. Ken, the Montagus' chauffeur."

The woman with the clipboard looked very confused. "Mr. Montagu didn't come himself?"

Mr. Ken frowned. "I can't explain the behavior of the lordly class. And it's not *Mr.* Montagu, it's *Lord* Montagu, thank you very much. It's not for me to question, nor you neither." Mr. Ken pivoted. "Are you Master Max?"

Max swallowed and shrugged. He'd never been called "Master" anything.

"Right, then. Where are your bags?"

Max had a small duffel with him, containing everything he owned. He held it up.

Mr. Ken raised his eyebrows and said nothing.

After filling out some paperwork, Mr. Ken led Max to an enormous black car. The inside was nicer than Max's family's apartment.

The three hour drive began in total silence.

Well, it was total silence for Mr. Ken.

Stein and Berg wouldn't shut up.

"I have never been to England," said Berg.

"Me neither," replied Stein.

"It looks as barren and worthless as Germany," said Berg.

"You sweet-talker. I bet you say that about all the countries."

Max stared out the window at the wet, gray, industrial Midlands of England. He couldn't believe he was here.

He'd never left Germany.

He'd never traveled without his parents.

He'd never even spent a night away from them.

Now he was on his way to live with a *lord*? Did Lord Montagu live in a mansion? A *castle*? Did he have a family? Or would it just be Lord Montagu and Max alone in some spooky manor house?

Well, he wouldn't be *alone*. "So," Max said, "you're *really* here, sitting on my shoulders?"

"What is *real*? What is *here*? What is *your shoulders*?" Berg wondered aloud.

Max ignored Berg. "Let's test it."

Stein furrowed his thick little brows. "You're going to *test* whether we're *really* here? How?"

Max said, "It's simple. You tell me something that I could not *possibly* know. Then I'll check if it's true by asking Mr. Ken, or looking it up in a book at Lord Montagu's castle . . . or manor, or whatever. If you can tell me something that is true that I could not possibly have known myself, that'll prove that you're not just figments of my imagination."

Stein and Berg made faces like they were trying very hard to follow Max's logic. Then Stein said, "Yeah, I guess that makes sense. You just thought of that? Just now?"

"Yes," said Max. "Why?"

"Smart kid," said Stein.

Berg said, "I still don't get it."

But Stein was ready to start the test: "All right, I got one."

Max took a deep breath. He was either about to learn that he was going insane, or that there were more things in heaven and earth than were dreamt of in his science textbooks.

"Okay," said Stein. "Ready?"

"Ready," said Max.

"The last guy whose shoulder I lived on was car-obsessed. Talked about them all the time. You know much about cars, Maxy?"

"No," said Max. "Pretty much nothing. My family doesn't own a car."

"Perfecto. So this guy worked at BMW. He was always talking about how their cars were way faster than English cars, even though the English ones had more horsepower. It turns out a Rolls-Royce has *twice* the horsepower of a BMW. Did you know that, Max?"

Max shook his head. "No. I had no idea."

"Why are we talking about cars now?" Berg asked.

Stein said, "Max is going to ask Mr. Ken if I'm right—that Rolls-Royce cars have twice the horsepower of BMW cars. If they do, that proves we're not just figments of Max's imagination."

"Wow," said Berg. "High stakes for you, huh, Max?"

Max took a deep breath.

Would he have to reassess his mental stability? Or *everything* else?

"Excuse me, Mr. Ken?" Max said.

Mr. Ken kept his eyes on the road and grunted, "Gotta use the toilet, Master Max?"

Max blushed. "No sir." His English was only so-so, so he thought carefully as he tried to construct his question: "Is this car faster than a BMW car, or slower?"

Mr. Ken's face lit up. "You want to know whether this Rolls-Royce Phantom can outrace one of your puny German BMW roadsters? Well, let me tell you, young man. This English beauty has a hundred and sixty horsepower. Your little BMW has got eighty horsepower. Do you hear that? One sixty versus eighty! And yes, maybe the Phantom is more than twice the weight of the BMW, but that's where English engineering comes in, isn't it? Because . . ."

Mr. Ken kept talking, and Max could feel the car accelerating—as if Mr. Ken had something to prove. But the acceleration was not the cause of the sudden lurch in his stomach.

"A hundred and sixty is twice as much as eighty, isn't it, Max?" said Stein.

Max couldn't believe it.

It seemed that there were two immortal creatures on his shoulders.

For real.

Max interrupted Mr. Ken's monologue about English car-making to ask if he could pull over.

Once the car came to a stop, Max thrust his door open and puked all over the side of the road.

CHAPTER
Four

Number 28 Kensington Court was not a manor, or a castle.

It was a stately brick town house on a street of stately brick town houses, just around the corner from Kensington Palace— which was where the royal family stayed when they wanted to be in the *stylish* part of London.

And Lord Montagu did not live alone. At the moment, Max stood in the luxurious foyer of 28 Kensington Court, on carpet as thick as his mattress in Berlin, surrounded by the curious faces of the Montagu family, peering at him with a mix of apprehension, anxiety, and hope.

He should have been glad—to be in such a beautiful place, surrounded by a warm, welcoming family. But all he could think of was his parents, in their small apartment, in a working-class neighborhood called Kreuzberg.

They were probably eating dinner right now. Without him.

An elegant woman extended her hand and said, "How do you do, Max? I am Mrs. Montagu."

Max mustered up a sentence in his shaky English: "It is good to meet you, Mrs. Montagu." She smiled.

Next she introduced her two boys, David, who was exactly Max's age, and Anthony, who was a year younger but seemed far younger than that.

There were three men left to be introduced—and while they looked wildly different from one another, something about their eyes and their mouths made it clear they were brothers.

The oldest brother stepped forward first. He wore a perfectly tailored navy suit and introduced himself as Stuart Montagu. "Welcome to our home, Max."

Max took a risk: "Thank you for inviting me to stay in your home, *Lord* Montagu."

Everyone broke out laughing.

Max froze.

"Oh boy, now you've done it," said Stein.

"What did he do?" Berg asked.

"No idea, but it's done."

His tall, lordly host smiled. "Mr. Montagu will do fine, Max."

Next, the second brother introduced himself as Uncle Ewen. Ewen had a face as long as a battleship's deck and he was almost entirely bald. He explained that he didn't live at 28 Kensington Court, but he'd come over because he was *very* keen to meet Max. When he shook Max's hand, he smiled with one side of his mouth, as if he knew a secret and he thought Max might know it, too.

Max whispered to Berg and Stein, "*Why is he smiling at me like that?*" The creatures just shrugged their little shoulders.

The last of the three brothers was Uncle Ivor, who was the physical opposite of Uncle Ewen. Instead of Ewen's battleship face, Ivor's was like a full moon, with two smaller full moons (his glasses) over his eyes, and black hair tousled atop his head like an ocean on a windy night. He grabbed Max's hand between two plump palms and pumped it up and down like he was hoping to get water to pour out of Max's mouth. "Glad to meet you, young Max! Glad to meet you! Do you play table tennis, by any chance?"

Max did not, nor did he find out, just then, why Uncle Ivor would ask him that. Because Uncle Ewen was already leading Max into a gilded parlor, to a very large gift, wrapped in yellow-striped paper that nearly matched the walls. The entire Montagu family gathered round.

"Now, I know it must be *deucedly* uncomfortable being in a new country, away from everyone and everything you know," Uncle Ewen said to Max.

Is it that obvious? Max wondered. Apparently it was.

Ewen was explaining how he'd been in touch with the refugee group that got Max out of Germany through his official capacity working for the British government, and how he'd learned that Max liked radios.

This was incorrect.

Max did not like radios. Max *loved* radios.

Moments later, Max was tearing the yellow-striped wrapping paper off a radio set. He recognized it instantly as a Murphy model A46. It was large and expensive and *beautiful.*

"Uncle Ewen thought you might like to have it in your room," Mrs. Montagu said gently.

Max looked at them all in disbelief. No one got to have their *own* wireless set, in their *room.* That would be like a child owning a car.

"Are you sure?" he said.

Uncle Ivor threw his head back and laughed. "Don't be a fool, Max! Ask again and they might change their minds!"

"Can I show Max where his room is?" little Anthony asked. Mrs. Montagu said that was fine, as long as Anthony didn't run. Anthony ran anyway.

Max followed Anthony up the curving staircase with the polished wooden banister to an enormous bedroom with a four-poster bed and a marble fireplace.

"I've only seen bedrooms like this in films," Max murmured. Anthony smiled at him.

Uncle Ewen had carried the wireless set upstairs after them and now put it down on a small table near Max's bed. Then he stepped back, the rest of the family waited by the door, and Max reverentially approached the rounded, polished wood of the radio. Max picked up the yellow cotton-covered power cord and plugged it into a wall socket. Slowly, the wireless hummed to life.

A syrupy woman's voice rose from the gray grille cloth, singing: *Land of hope and glory . . .*

"Ugh!" Uncle Ivor exclaimed. "Vera Lynn! Turn the dial!"

Mr. Montagu objected: "Don't insult England's most beloved singer, Ivor! She was just voted 'Sweetheart of the British Army'! It said so in the *Times!*"

Max was momentarily frozen by this fraternal disagreement—until he noticed Uncle Ewen turn his back to Mr. Montagu and roll his eyes. Max hid a grin and changed the station.

The wireless's dial was marked not only with the numbers of radio frequencies, but also with the name of the city where the station assigned to that frequency was located. Vera Lynn was playing on the London Regional station.

Max turned the knob and a fuzzy broadcast in French buzzed through the speakers, coming all the way from Strasbourg, in eastern France.

Max turned the knob a bit more, and waited.

Static.

The dial said "Berlin."

He turned the knob again. Wales came through clearly. Scotland did, too.

The Scots were also playing Vera Lynn. A different song. "God almighty, she's a plague!" Ivor exclaimed.

But the rest of the Montagus were complimenting Ewen for picking such a marvelous wireless set.

And it was. On the stations broadcasting nearby, the sound was impeccable. Round and warm and loud as you please.

Almost as good as the one Max had built himself. Which was still back in Berlin. With his parents.

Max turned stiffly to Ewen Montagu. "Thank you for this kind gift. I am very pleased with it."

Everyone smiled at him.

Except for Ewen. Ewen's heavily lidded eyes studied Max carefully.

As if he thought, maybe, Max was hiding something.

Which Max was.

CHAPTER
Five

The family sat down for a late supper at the long dining room table under a branching chandelier.

The table was laid with fine silver and ornate china and cups that seemed to be made not of glass, but of crystal. Even the water glasses. All of which was strange enough for Max, having grown up eating from chipped porcelain and cracked cups at a small table in his family's kitchen.

Max's mother was probably cleaning those dishes now, while his father rested on the small sofa in the living room, his eyes closed. Max wondered if they missed him.

Suddenly, Max was pulled back to London by something more shocking than anything he had yet witnessed—more shocking than a mansion, or an English lord, or even Stein and Berg.

Mr. Montagu produced a book of matches from his inner jacket pocket and handed them to Mrs. Montagu. Mrs. Montagu lit two candles in silver candlesticks. And then she and Mr. Montagu and Ewen and Ivor and David and Anthony said:

"Baruch atah Adonai . . ."

Max felt suddenly lightheaded.

The Montagus were *Jewish*?

You would think that Max would have suddenly felt more comfortable, realizing that he was in a Jewish home, seeing the soft, familiar glow of the Shabbat candles. That he would have opened his mouth and sung the blessing, too . . .

But he didn't. He felt *worse.*

"Come on!" Stein encouraged Max. "Sing along! You gotta know this one!"

But Max simply watched the Montagus hold their glasses aloft for the blessing over the wine (or grape juice, for the children). And when the challah was passed around, a shiny braided loaf much longer and more perfect than anything Max's mother had ever baked, Max didn't even take any. He just sat there, unmoving. Finally, David had to pass the challah over him to Anthony, as the Montagus stared at this sullen, ungrateful child who had plopped himself down in the middle of their lives.

"You're being ridiculous, Max!" Berg scolded him. "Even I wouldn't behave *this* badly."

But the worst moment, for Max—worse than the shock that the Montagus were Jewish and no one had bothered to tell him; worse than sitting there like a warty kobold and *knowing* that he was sitting there like a warty kobold—was when they said the *motzi*, the prayer over the challah.

The prayer concludes with the words *hamotzi lechem min ha'aretz.*

Except when the Montagus said *hamotzi*, they made their

voices really high and cute. It sounded like *haaaa-mote-ZEE!* And the children smiled.

Max frowned so hard his stony face nearly shattered.

"What is your *problem?*" Berg hissed at Max.

"I think he's trying to poop," Stein replied.

"Here? In the *good* chairs?"

Max growled words only Berg and Stein could hear: "That's how *my* family says the *motzi.*"

The Montagus had broken into a few small conversations, when suddenly Max said, "Excuse me."

A half dozen curious faces turned toward him. He had already prepared the English in his head: "Thank you for inviting me to stay with you."

Mrs. Montagu broke into a wide, genuine smile. Mr. Montagu nodded approvingly. Uncle Ivor winked at Anthony. David went back to eating his challah. Only Uncle Ewen seemed to be waiting for whatever Max would say next. Which was: "When will I be allowed to go home, please?"

The smile slid off Mrs. Montagu's face. Mr. Montagu developed identical sets of frown lines on his chin and forehead. Uncle Ivor looked at his plate. Anthony looked hurt. David also appeared to want to know the answer to this question.

Uncle Ewen said, "We don't know, Max. It could be rather a long time."

Max had prepared a follow-up question: "When will my parents be able to come to England?"

Anthony and David glanced around at the grown-ups, expecting some sort of answer. But all the adults were looking at their plates now. Except for Uncle Ewen, who kept eye contact with Max. Ruefully, he said, "I imagine that could be rather a long time, too."

Max nearly stood up right then, walked up the curving carpeted staircases to his room, and slammed the door so hard the walls of the house shook.

But he didn't.

Instead, as the Montagus awkwardly tried to resume their conversations, tried to ignore the little refugee sitting at their table, tried to forget the policies of the government they had elected, that refused to let adult Jews enter England, Max picked up his napkin and casually placed it over the knife that lay to the right of his dinner plate.

When Mrs. Henshaw, the housekeeper, slid a filet of sole onto his dish, Max put his napkin onto his lap, like everyone else. Ivor had gained the attention of the other adults, telling a story about an eccentric Russian he had met at a coffee shop. No one noticed that the knife was now resting on Max's knees.

Ivor and the Russian had argued about who was more evil, Adolf Hitler (the dictator of Germany) or Joseph Stalin (the dictator of Soviet Russia). The Russian in the coffee shop had argued that it was Stalin. Ivor had told him it was Hitler by a mile. Mr. Montagu and Ewen both jumped in loudly. Max slid the knife into the pocket of his brown corduroy pants.

"Max . . ." said Berg. "What are you doing?"

Max didn't reply.

Berg said to Stein, "Did you see Max just put a *weapon in his pocket?*"

"I certainly did," said Stein. He jerked his warty nose around the table. "And somehow none of these *nudniks* noticed a thing."

A short while later, as Mrs. Henshaw was clearing the plates and Uncle Ewen was explaining that Hitler and Stalin were practically allies now—that one had prisons called "concentration camps" and the other prisons called "gulags" and they were both terrible places to die—Max leaned toward Mrs. Montagu and asked, "May I go to my room, please?"

All conversation ceased. Mrs. Montagu said, "But Max, there's still pudding. Wouldn't you like some pudding?"

Max kept his face very still when he said, "No thank you. I am tired and I would like to go to my room, please."

Uncle Ivor and Uncle Ewen exchanged glances. Mr. Montagu and Mrs. Montagu did, too. Anthony asked, "Can *I* have Max's pudding?"

After a space, Mrs. Montagu said, "Of course you may go to your room, Max." She smiled. With her mouth but not her eyes.

Max carefully stood up, putting his hands on his thighs as if standing up were an effort—but really to prevent the knife from digging into his leg.

Then he slowly walked up the curving staircase, one step at a time.

From the dining room, the whole Montagu family watched in silence.

CHAPTER
Six

Max closed the door to his room.

"WHY DID YOU STEAL THAT KNIFE?!" Berg demanded.

"I can't tell if he's a thief, or if he's planning a murder," Stein added.

Max took the knife out of his pocket.

"WHAT ARE YOU GOING TO DO NOW?" Berg wailed. "You're making me stressed, Max. It's supposed to be the other way around!"

Max studied the edge of the knife. He ran his finger down the blade, testing how sharp it was.

Stein mumbled, "I don't want to see what happens next."

Max walked . . .

. . . to the radio set.

He turned it around.

After checking that it was unplugged, Max inserted the knife into the head of a screw at the corner of the case and began to loosen the screw.

"*Ohhhh,*" said Berg.

"I totally thought he was gonna kill somebody," said Stein.

Max gingerly removed the case of polished wood and mesh.

What was revealed Max found more beautiful than just about anything in the world.

It was a small city of cylindrical towers, of wiry streets, and of blue rivers of metal running between them all. Max set to work as the kobolds watched from his shoulders.

Max unscrewed this, opened that, adjusted the other thing, unspooled a length of copper wire from inside one of the cylinders, and sawed it off with the table knife. Then he jammed it into a crack in the molding behind the little table and ran it up the wall so it reached higher than his head. Then he reassembled the wireless set.

He stared at it for a moment. He adjusted the dial.

Finally, he took the yellow cloth-covered power cord and plugged it back into the wall.

Suddenly, someone spoke to him from Berlin.

As clearly as if they were broadcasting from Kensington Palace, just around the corner.

Max exhaled and collapsed on the giant downy bed.

The voice emanating from the wireless set belonged to the newsman Hans Fritzsche. "The most trusted voice in Germany," they called him. Hans Fritzsche was explaining, in his polished, convincing style, that the Third Reich was the model modern nation now that they had dispensed with democracy, where the people *supposedly* ruled, but in fact where fat bankers and Jews made all the decisions. Like in England.

As Max lay on pillows softer than he had ever imagined pillows could be, he realized that Hans Fritzsche was talking about the Montagus. They were English Jews. In fact, Mr. Montagu, in addition to being a lord, owned a bank.

Max had heard about these English bankers and rich Jews for his whole life. Whenever his teacher in school blamed the "Jewish conspiracy" for anything, Max would always wonder which Jews were part of this conspiracy. *Max* obviously wasn't. And his parents certainly didn't seem to be. It was rare that a Nazi ever explained *which* Jews were supposedly to blame for ruining Germany's economy, *which* Jews had tried to subjugate Germany like some destitute colony, *which* Jews were bringing the whole world to the edge of war . . . but when they did, it was always the rich Jews of England.

It was the Montagus. And people like them.

Max didn't know whether the Montagus were responsible for all that or not. It didn't *seem* likely.

But then he stopped wondering about it because Dr. Joseph Goebbels came on the air. Goebbels was Minister for Public Enlightenment and Propaganda. He was always on the radio, shouting into the microphone. Tonight, his speech was particularly terrifying: "I will remind you what our Supreme Leader Adolf Hitler has so wisely said: if there is another war in Europe,

it will not lead to the destruction of Germany, but to the anni-
hilation of the Jewish race in Europe!"

"I can't stay here," Max said to Berg and Stein, switching
off the wireless.

"What?" Berg cried.

"Look at this place! You think you could do better?" Stein
demanded. "You want to go live with that priest you saw at the
ferry? Trust me, the food will be a lot worse."

"No," said Max. He put a pillow over his face. "I have to get
home."

Stein and Berg fell silent.

"You can't mean that," said Stein.

"Going back there would be madness," Berg agreed.

"Especially after everything your parents must have done to
get you *out,*" Stein reminded him.

Max said it again: "I have to get home." He threw the pillow
from his face to the floor. "*Why* would they send me away?"

Stein said, "Maxy, listen. We don't understand why people
do what they do. But if I were a betting dybbuk, I would bet
that it *might* have had something to do with your parents not
wanting you to grow up in a country full of Nazis."

"And," Berg added, "England is the only country that
would take you."

Max knew all this. His parents had applied for visas
everywhere—Australia, Chile, Argentina, the United States . . .

and every place claimed they had too many Jews already. Even the countries that didn't have any.

"They shouldn't have sent me here . . ." Max said. "I could *help* them."

"Max, *bubbeleh*, you're a *child*," Stein replied.

"It is a parent's job to help their child, not the other way around," Berg told Max.

But Max had never felt that way. His papa was such a kind, gentle man. He was a watchmaker, with a repair shop on the first floor of their apartment building. He spent all day bent over the black-velvet-covered table, wearing a magnifying glass—a loupe, it's called—over one eye and moving tiny watch pieces around with tweezers. In the evenings, Papa was always exhausted, his neck aching and his eyes too bleary to see. Mama spent her days walking all over the neighborhood, offering to do mending for anyone who could spare a pfennig to pay for it. She came home nearly as tired as Papa—but somehow she always managed to have a hot meal ready at dinnertime.

They were good, loving parents. But they needed Max. They said it all the time: "You're a miracle, *Liebchen*. What would we do without you?"

Max didn't know what they would do without him.

And he didn't know what he would do without them.

Max flicked the wireless back on. Joseph Goebbels had finished, happily. Unhappily, the Berlin Opera was performing

Wagner's *Das Rheingold*. Max hated Wagner. The syrupy harmonies felt like they were assaulting his brain.

But it reminded him of home.

So he turned it up.

The music was so loud that Max didn't hear the footsteps outside his door.

He didn't hear someone lean their head next to the hinges.

He had no clue that this person recognized the radio station that Max was listening to, recognized immediately that it was the Berlin broadcast, coming through loud and clear—as it couldn't just an hour before.

And Max certainly had no idea that the person listening through the door was a spy.

CHAPTER
Seven

It was Max's first day of school.

He'd only been in England a few weeks. His English had improved from mediocre to whatever is just slightly better than mediocre, and his accent was still quite thick.

David and Anthony Montagu attended St. West's School, which stood in the shadow of the Houses of Parliament, in ramshackle old buildings that still looked very much like they had when they had been built four hundred years ago. Max would be in David's class. David was *not* happy about it.

As Mr. Ken steered the long black Rolls-Royce through the streets of central London, David and Anthony tried to tell Max everything he needed to know. There were so many strange customs, and weird words for simple things, that Max couldn't possibly keep it all straight.

"For example," said David, "we'll have lunch at School."

Max said that yes, he figured as much, since school was far from their house and going back and forth would be a pain.

"No, the *hall* where we eat lunch is called School."

"We eat lunch in a hall?" Max asked.

"It looks like a church," Anthony added.

"And it's called School," said David.

Max didn't understand: "If 'School' is where we eat, then what do we call the place we're going to now?"

"St. West's," said David.

"Not 'School'?"

"It is a school, but we don't call it that."

"Why?"

"Because 'School' means 'hall,' which is where we eat!"

Max said, "So we eat in a hallway that looks like a church that we call a school?"

David screamed and Anthony laughed.

David let his head fall back against the seat: "Whatever you do, just don't mention that we're Jewish. I mean, they all *know*, but try not to bring it up."

Max nodded. "Don't worry. I am used to not bringing up that I am Jewish."

David stared at him for a moment, and then said, "Oh. Right. Sorry."

"Good morning," said Master Yarrow, standing before the class, an open black robe hanging from the shoulders of his suit jacket. Master Yarrow was aptly named. He was tall as a yarrow tree and thin as a yarrow branch and when he spoke his words stung like a yarrow switch on the back of your hands.

"We have a new boy joining us in second form. Mr. Bretzfeld, come up here, if you please."

Max slid out from behind his desk and walked to the front of the room. The boys were all staring at him with an expression of bored cruelty that is the special domain of both the very rich and the very stupid. Max knew that they were the former— and suspected that they also might be the latter.

David was the only one not staring. David appeared to be praying.

"Don't worry, Max," Stein was saying. "I'm sure you're gonna do *fine*."

Berg replied, "Do you think so? Given how his legs are shaking and the expressions on these other boys' faces, I think he is going to do *terribly*."

Stein said, "Yeah, Berg, I'd like to introduce you to my friend named *sarcasm*."

Max stood facing the class. In addition to all the things he felt awkward about—that his clothes didn't quite fit, that his English was just slightly better than mediocre, that these boys were staring at him like they were sleepy tigers at a zoo and he had just fallen into their cage—he felt perhaps most awkward about the fact that *he had two immortal creatures sitting on his shoulders*. True, no one could see them. But standing here at the front of the class, Berg and Stein made Max feel so self-conscious his brain was on the verge of exploding.

"Tell us about yourself, Mr. Bretzfeld," said Master Yarrow.

Something about the way he said *Bretzfeld* made Max feel uncomfortable.

He looked around at the faces of the boys, their dripping blond forelocks, their pouty pink lips. "I, uh, what should I say?" Max asked.

David, sitting near the back, put his face in the crook of his arm on the table.

Master Yarrow suggested, "Well, tell us about your father. What does he do?"

Max said, "My father is a watchmaker in Berlin."

"A *watchmaker*," said Master Yarrow, suddenly interested. He inclined toward Max like there was a breeze in the classroom. "He owns one of the German watch companies? Montblanc? Lange & Söhne? You wouldn't happen to be one of the titular *sons*, would you?"

"No," Max corrected Master Yarrow. "He owns a little shop in Berlin. Bretzfeld Watch Repair."

"*Oh,*" said Master Yarrow. It was the most withering single syllable Max had ever heard.

"Well, he did own it. But the Nazis closed the shop," Max added. The boys were staring open-mouthed, their perpetually bored eyes no longer ogling but rather verging on disgust.

"Well, Mr. Bretzfeld," said Master Yarrow, "or should we call you *Herr* Bretzfeld?" The boys guffawed loudly, making Max's neck turn bright red. *Herr*, of course, means "Mister" in

German. "Well, *Herr* Bretzfeld, it will be most . . . *interesting* . . . to have you at St. West's this term."

Max slunk back to his chair. The St. West's boys' hungry eyes tracked him.

Except for David's, which were being mashed into their sockets with the palms of his hands.

Master Yarrow launched into his welcome-back-to-school speech:

"I do hope you all had a fine Play, and are fully rested and ready for Play Term." Max didn't know what that meant. "Huh?" he said to Stein and Berg.

"No idea," said Stein.

Master Yarrow rolled on. "Max, you are, of course, a shadow. Your substance will be David, as that's only fair."

"Awww!" David Montagu groaned. All the other boys snickered. Max didn't know why David was groaning, or why the other boys were snickering, but he didn't have a chance to ask.

"Please remember, as Play has been interminable this year and war seems just around the corner, that as much as you all aspire to glory in battle, there is no ragging in yard, even during a tie, and any ragging will result in a very good tan. Max, that would be David getting your tan, as he is your substance, so *do* be careful. And, of course, Max, you being the lowest form of life in the second form, you shall be the sport come tea. Sport is, as usual, at three at the fields. Don't forget that station on

Thursday is trials for ruggers, and if you don't make the first team, you can always try for the second, and if you don't make the second team, you can always bear the colors."

All the boys laughed.

Suddenly, Master Yarrow looked at Max. "Did you follow, Herr Bretzfeld?"

Max had not.

Master Yarrow then lectured for two consecutive hours. Max understood almost nothing of what he said. It was slightly entertaining, though, because Berg crawled off his shoulder—which created a weird empty sensation and made Berg instantly disappear—and knocked Master Yarrow's book off his desk and onto the floor. Master Yarrow picked it up and put it back, then turned to continue his lecture—and it fell off again. The schoolmaster cursed floridly and picked the book up again. As soon as he resumed the lecture, Berg again knocked it to the floor. Yarrow screamed and turned and looked at the kids as if they'd done it. But no one appeared to have moved at all. When Berg reappeared on Max's shoulder, Stein flashed him a tiny grin.

Then Max said to Stein, "Why do you let Berg make all the mischief? Isn't that your job, too?"

"Me? No! I don't make mischief. I just sit here and make sure you feel terrible. How am I doing?"

"Great," Max answered truthfully.

Berg flashed Stein a tiny grin right back.

Around eleven the boys were let out into a wet courtyard with gray flagstones for a break. Ancient gray buildings rose up around them. The Houses of Parliament were visible over slanting, wet roofs. It seemed to Max that everything was wet and gray in England.

During recess in Berlin, the boys played violent games like soccer and Hit the Yid, where the non-Jewish boys would chase Max and his Jewish classmates around the yard trying to punch them. But here, instead of playing, the St. West's boys seemed to be *loitering*. Just hanging around, looking bored and mean. Even the younger ones. Max saw Anthony standing under a dripping tree like he was just waiting to be let back into class. What kind of recess was this?

Suddenly a tall boy with freckles and curly black hair loomed over Max. The boy was in his class. His name was Circuitt.

"*Sci*s are allowed in the yard now?" Circuitt said.

Max gazed up at the large, sneering boy. He didn't understand. So he asked: "What is a *sci*?"

Circuitt snorted. "He doesn't know!" he announced to a short boy standing at his side. The short boy was called Bonner and his forehead hung over his nose like a cliff about to fall into the sea. But Circuitt was kind enough to explain it to Max: "A *sci* is a boy who doesn't belong here. Not knowing the word *sci* proves you're a *sci*."

But Bonner disagreed. "No, Circuitt. He's not a *sci*. He's a *spy*."

"Is he?"

Other second formers saw that something was happening around Max, and they hurried over to join the fun.

"A *German* spy," Bonner went on. Suddenly, he reached out and pushed Max's shoulder. "A bloody *Nazi* spy."

The boys of the second form had made a ring around Max. Max could feel their body heat and tension on his skin. The circle slowly tightened as boys from other forms rushed over and pushed in from the back, trying to see.

"Say something!" Berg urged Max.

So Max said, "How could I be a Nazi? I am Jewish!"

Bonner and Circuitt hesitated for a moment. The army of boys appeared to waver. In the back, Max could see David covering his face with his hands. Anthony had come over, too. He was standing on his tiptoes, wanting to catch Max's eye.

And then Circuitt made his hand into a fist. He raised it . . .

And placed it on the end of his own nose. Next, with the index finger of his other hand, Circuitt stroked the top of his fist.

"*Groo,*" Circuitt said, rolling the *r.* "*Groo groo.*"

The other second form boys, except for David, all copied Circuitt at once. They put their fists to their noses, stroked the tops of their knuckles, and said, "*Groo groo.*"

"Uh . . . Max? What are they doing?" Berg asked.

Stein guessed, "Pretending to be elephants?"

"This is your big nose," said Bonner, indicating his closed fist. "And *groo* is you scheming to steal our money. It's what you Jews do, isn't it?"

Max had heard every foul thing anyone could say about his people. He'd grown up in Nazi Germany, after all. These idiot boys had nothing on Joseph Goebbels and Adolf Hitler.

So you'd think Max wouldn't feel hurt by something so immature, so stupid.

But for some reason that Max could not understand, it never hurt any less.

"*Groo groo*, Jew," Circuitt said. "*Groo groo.*"

CHAPTER
Eight

That afternoon, as Mr. Ken drove them home in the spacious Rolls-Royce, everyone was lost in their own thoughts: David stared out the window and thought about the rugby trials on Thursday. Anthony thought about whether a *Tyrannosaurus rex* could kill a blue whale. Berg thought about a very beautiful river spirit he'd met seven thousand years ago, who had complimented the shape of his nose, and he wondered if, had he returned the compliment, they would still be in love to this day. (He had instead asked her what the little fish he'd caught in his hand was . . . and when she'd come over to look, he'd squirted water in her face. Which was pretty funny and almost as good as falling in love forever.) Stein thought about the moment just after he'd been created and wondered again if God had given some sort of *instructions* or a *lecture* or some *guide* and how Stein could have missed it. And Max thought about his school.

Not St. West's. His school in Germany.

Max was sitting in the last row, as always. His teacher, Professor Goldenschaft, was writing something on the chalkboard.

Professor Goldenschaft stepped aside so the students could see what he had written.

On the dusty chalkboard, in large yellow letters, were the words JEWISH SCIENCE.

Max and the three other Jewish boys in the class sank down in their chairs in the back row. They did this whenever the subject was Jewish anything.

"Actually," Professor Goldenschaft said, "we should write: so-called *Jewish science, shouldn't we? Who can tell me why?"*

Pause. Max knew exactly what was coming.

He tried to slide a little lower in his chair.

"Max? Why should we write the words 'so-called,' before 'Jewish science'? Explain!"

There were rumors that Professor Goldenschaft had been a good teacher once. In fact, when he was not teaching from the Nazi curriculum, but instead teaching something neutral like grammar, he was still a good teacher. Not kind, but clear and precise and fair.

But when Professor Goldenschaft was teaching from the Nazi curriculum, he changed. He became . . . cruel.

"I don't know, Herr Professor. Why should we write the words 'so-called' before 'Jewish science,' sir?" Max did his best at these times to be as respectful and invisible as possible. If he could manage to repeat the exact words Professor Goldenschaft said, he was less likely to make a mistake. As long as he watched his tone. If he repeated Professor Goldenschaft's words with the wrong tone, he was liable to get slapped with a ruler on the ears. Or, worse, the

non-Jewish boys in class would chase him around at recess until they caught him and jumped on him and pummeled him.

Professor Goldenschaft glared at Max, as if measuring whether his tone was respectful enough. At last, he must have decided that it was. Barely. "Because the 'science' that the Jews pretend to do is ersatz science. Fake. Imaginary. Who is the most famous Jewish scientist?"

The rest of the boys in the class were tapping pencils on their desks, or staring out the window. Hans Himmerl, in the first row, was picking his nose with the lead of his pencil.

"Max?" said Professor Goldenschaft.

Max did not know why Professor Goldenschaft liked to pick on him more than on Felix or Benjamin or Walter, the other Jewish boys. But he did. Perhaps it was because he suspected that Max was smarter than he was.

"Albert Einstein is the most famous Jewish scientist," said Max.

"Correct! And what did Albert Einstein supposedly do?"

No one said anything.

"Max?"

Max tried not to sigh audibly. "He discovered the theories of general and special relativity."

"No! Wrong! He did not discover them! He invented them! He invented theories of imaginary physics! And the worldwide Jewish conspiracy praised these theories, as if they were works of genius, when in fact they cannot be tested! They are unprovable! Pure fantasy!"

Max was fairly certain that Einstein's theories had been tested, and proven, many times. But he didn't dare say so.

"And this is the man that they hold up as proof of Jewish contributions to science! Einstein's theories cannot do anything! They cannot make a boat float. They cannot help an airplane fly! They couldn't make something explode if you wrapped them in dynamite! They are nothing! Useless!"

Which was when Max raised his hand.

He didn't know what made him do that. He never raised his hand. Ever.

Felix and Benjamin and Walter saw this and all ducked their heads at once.

Professor Goldenschaft stared.

Some of the non-Jewish boys turned around and stared, too.

"Yes, Max?" Professor Goldenschaft said, very softly.

"The Aryan scientists are the ones who do real things," said Max.

Professor Goldenschaft hesitated. "Yes . . ."

"Such as Fritz Haber, who discovered how to use poison gas against enemy soldiers."

"Haber was a great German," Professor Goldenschaft agreed cautiously.

"Or Alfred Nobel, the Swedish scientist who discovered dynamite, which he said would end all wars."

Professor Goldenschaft was really not certain where this was going. "Indeed, Nobel was a genius."

"*And Richard Willstätter,*" Max went on, "*a good Aryan German, who invented the gas mask, thus saving millions of German lives when the cowardly French and English used poison gas against our heroic soldiers!*"

"*Of course!*" said Professor Goldenschaft, apparently not aware of the contradiction of praising the inventor of poison gas, Fritz Haber, and then calling the use of poison gas "cowardly" moments later.

"*Wait!*" said Hans Himmerl, who had finally taken his pencil out of his nose. "*I thought Willstätter was a Jew?*"

"*Nonsense!*" bellowed Professor Goldenschaft.

"*How dare you!*" Max bellowed at Hans.

Now all the boys were confused.

Max went on: "*How dare you say that the great German scientist who invented the gas mask was Jewish! Ridiculous! Insane! Professor Goldenschaft just told us that so-called Jewish science isn't science at all, but just make-believe! Are you calling Professor Goldenschaft a* liar?"

Hans was completely at a loss, the rest of the boys were mumbling to each other, and Professor Goldenschaft looked like he had no idea what was going on.

"*Yes! No! Are you?*" Goldenschaft demanded of Hans.

Hans said, "*No! Yes! Of course not! I just thought . . .*"

"*Thought* what? *That the inventor of the gas mask was a* Jew?" Professor Goldenschaft bellowed. "*You think Willstätter is a Jewish name?! IT'S NOT!*"

He yelled this part too loud. Which was not surprising.

Everyone knew that Professor Goldenschaft was so militant in the classroom about Jews because he was constantly asked if Goldenschaft was a Jewish name. Many Jews in Germany had names that started with "Gold." Goldman, Goldstein, just plain Gold. Professor Goldenschaft was quite plainly insecure about his name. The last thing he wanted was to be mistaken for a Jew. Not in Germany. Not these days.

"This is easily solved," Professor Goldenschaft snapped, and he turned to the set of encyclopedias behind his desk. He grabbed the volume labeled W *and started flipping the pages. Max slid so far down in his seat that he nearly disappeared behind his desk.*

"Here!" Professor Goldenschaft barked. "'Richard Willstätter. Discovered chlorophyl, the naturally occurring chemical that makes plants appear green and allows them to process sunlight as food.'" He looked up. "Did you know that? Write that down! Another Aryan discovery!"

The boys all opened their notebooks and began to scribble that Willstätter the German Aryan scientist had discovered chlorophyll. If only they could figure out how to spell chlorophyll.

"'Also created a model of gas mask that was widely used during the World War to protect German soldiers from chlorine and other nerve gases. Write that down, too! Born of a Jewi—'"

Professor Goldenschaft stopped reading.

The room was so silent they could all hear the air whistling in and out of Professor Goldenschaft's nostrils.

Professor Goldenschaft smacked Max on his ears over and over with a ruler as the boys watched.

Max had gone home that day with bloody streaks crisscrossing his head.

They were completely and totally worth it.

As the Rolls-Royce pulled up to 28 Kensington Court, Max was smiling.

CHAPTER
Nine

The next day Max stood in St. West's yard during break, warily eyeing Circuitt and Bonner. The other second form boys followed them like remora fish around sharks. David stood at the edge, trying to laugh at some joke that he clearly didn't think was funny.

"Why do people like bullies?" Max asked Stein and Berg.

"Because everyone is scared," Berg replied. "All you humans. All the time. You are scared of being beat up, or of being alone, or of your own thoughts. At least if you've got a bully on your side, you've got one less thing to be scared of."

"Huh," said Stein. "I never thought of it that way."

"You don't think very much, Stein," Berg replied. Stein didn't disagree.

Just then, Max saw the first formers walking across the yard in twos and threes, going back into a building for class. Anthony was there, laughing with another boy. Just as he drew even with the group of second formers, there was a shout.

"You!"

Anthony froze.

The scrum parted, and Circuitt emerged. Bonner was glued to his hip, as always.

Anthony's little friend scurried away.

"Are you the little Montagu?" Circuitt asked. Anthony nodded and looked for David—but David was melting into the back of the group of second form boys.

"Montagu isn't even his real family name," said Bonner. "Their grandfather changed it from Samuel. That's what I heard."

Bonner put his fist to his nose and stroked it. "Groo groo," he purred.

Circuitt said, "This place is lousy with Yids. And you're bringing more in, what with that Kraut Jew Herr Bretzfeld. Thanks a lot for that."

"I'm not a Yid!" Anthony said. "And neither is Max!"

Max was certain that Anthony did not know that *Yid* is a hateful word for a Jewish person. But clearly Anthony could tell that it was something unkind, because under the straight dark fringe of Anthony's hair, his forehead was turning red. Max could see it halfway across the yard.

Max lifted himself off the wall he'd been sitting on.

"You say you're not a Yid," Circuitt went on. "All right, then. So you won't mind saying, 'Jews are the scum of the earth, and long live Adolf Hitler.'"

That, little Anthony understood.

He stared up at Circuitt and Bonner. He tried again to see his brother, but David had now completely dissolved into the group.

"Go on," said Circuitt to Anthony. "Just say it. They're only words."

Anthony swallowed hard. His face and neck were crimson. He opened his little mouth. "Jews—"

"Excuse me," said Max, sliding his body between Anthony and Bonner and Circuitt.

Everyone was very surprised.

"Do you know," said Max to the two big boys, "what we 'Kraut Jews' do to bullies who pick on little children?"

Circuitt and Bonner were still too surprised to answer.

"We take a penknife and we *jab* it into the bully's kidney." Max made a quick, underhand stabbing motion with his fist. Circuitt and Bonner each took a swift step backward, their eyes bulging.

"That is not true," said Berg.

"I know," said Stein, "but it sounds *great* right now."

Max was saying to the boys, "I'll do it. What would happen to me? I'm just a child. Would they expel me? Fine with me. I would love to get out of this place. Send me back to Germany? I wish." He was gazing up into Circuitt's eyes and not blinking at all.

Circuitt and Bonner both took another step backward.

"Pick on *me* if you want to," Max concluded. "I don't mind. But if you ever *speak* to Anthony again, you won't even have time to regret it."

Max turned his back on the bullies. He knew that it was risky to turn your back on an enemy. Circuitt and Bonner could smash him over the head. But Max didn't look over his shoulder. He had learned long ago not to show fear. "Get to class now, Anthony," he said.

Anthony stared up at him. Max couldn't recall the English word for Anthony's expression.

And then he recalled it. The word was *awe*.

As the boys slid into their desks after break, Master Yarrow stood with his hands behind him at the front of the classroom, rolling from his toes to his heels and back again and smiling like he was looking forward to something.

Max found this sudden optimism highly disturbing, while Stein said, "He looks like he's just invented a new form of torture."

Stein wasn't far off.

"We're going to review geography this period," Master Yarrow announced, still rocking and smiling. "The history of Great Britain is recorded in the names of its counties, towns, and cathedrals . . . Bretzfeld!"

The sudden use of his name made Max feel like a bucket of water had just been dumped on his head. Also like a bucket of water had just been dumped on his head, everyone had swiftly swiveled around to stare at him.

"Yes, Master Yarrow?"

"Will you come up to the front of the class, please?"

"What would happen if you just ran out of here?" Berg asked. "Would they stop you?"

Max had been wondering the same thing. But he pushed himself up and out from behind his desk and made his way to the blackboard, where Master Yarrow continued to anticipate with pleasure whatever was about to happen.

"*Herr* Bretzfeld," Master Yarrow began, and all the boys gave a dutiful snicker. "Have you studied any English history in your Nazi schools back home?"

Sometimes, a question is asked that assumes so many things that it lands on you with the weight of an iron stove. How could Max even begin to answer this question? Max's school hadn't always been a Nazi school—though all schools were Nazi schools now. Yes, they had studied some English history—but mostly it was about how the English were trying to destroy Germany and turn it into a colony like Rhodesia or Jamaica. Max wasn't sure that was true and he certainly didn't want to go into it now.

Max shrugged. "Not much, sir."

"Not much," Master Yarrow mused. "Of course not. Too busy goose-stepping and saluting Hitler, I imagine."

"You think he *wanted* to salute Hitler, you jerk?" Stein shouted.

"Did you really learn to goose-step?" Berg asked, referring to the ridiculous form of marching that Nazi soldiers did in military parades, pointing their toes out with every step.

"*No,*" Max replied.

Master Yarrow was writing on the board now. "Let's start with the basics, then, shall we?"

In big white letters on the board he had written
WORCESTERSHIRE.

"Right," he said, turning back toward Max and wearing that
small, creepy smile again. "You've heard of this place, right?"

Max had not. He shook his head.

Master Yarrow frowned at him indulgently. "Please read it
out for the rest of the class."

Max squinted at the word. "*Wor-sess-ter-shire?*"

Suddenly there was an explosion of laughter from the room.

Max spun around. Everyone was laughing at him. Even
David. Had he pronounced it *that* badly? He looked in con-
fusion to Master Yarrow. Yarrow was grinning. "Try again,
Bretzfeld."

Do I have to? Max wondered. But he obeyed: "*Wor-kess-ter-
shire?*"

Another explosion of laughter, louder this time.

Max looked desperately at Master Yarrow.

His teacher said, "It's *Woostersher*, Max."

Max couldn't help himself. He pointed at WORCESTER-
SHIRE. "*That* is pronounced *Woostersher?*"

Yarrow failed to suppress a smile. "I'm afraid so, Max. Let's
try another one."

He wrote on the board: LEOMINSTER.

Max winced before offering, "*Leo-minster?*"

The boys slapped the tables as they guffawed. Stein grumbled, "It's really not that funny."

"That'll be *Lemster*, Max," Master Yarrow informed him.

"You know, in German," Berg said, "when we want you to say a sound, we spell it out. And if we don't want you to say a sound, we leave it out. Here, it appears to be the opposite."

"All right, one more," Master Yarrow was saying as he scratched long white letters onto the chalkboard. They read: GODMANCHESTER.

Max's face must have looked as pained as he felt, because Yarrow said, "C'mon Max. You're a clever boy, aren't you? Give it a try."

Max stared at the name like he was going to choke on it.

He sighed: "*God-man-chest-er?*"

Sudden howls of laughter erupted from all over the room. David was howling loudest of all.

Max threw up his hands. "How do you say it?"

Master Yarrow was now cackling, doubled over with his long thin hands on his knobby knees. He managed to collect himself long enough to say, "It's *Gumster*, Max."

And then he went back to laughing in the refugee boy's face.

Max just stared at GODMANCHESTER and wondered how on earth you could get *Gumster* from that combination of letters.

That afternoon, in Mr. Ken's car, Anthony said to Max, "What's a Yid?"

David cut in, "It's what they call Jews like us, Anthony."

Anthony thought for a moment. "So I *am* a Yid?"

David looked at Max, suddenly unsure.

Max had heard his people called too many awful things back in Berlin to even remember them all. And he had asked his parents the same question, a hundred different times in a hundred different ways.

So Max told Anthony what his papa always used to tell him, translating it into English as best he could: "We are Jews, Anthony," he said. "They call us names when they want us to feel weak. But we are not weak. We are tough. Tougher than they are."

Anthony nodded and turned to gaze out the window at the traffic. After a few moments, he turned back to Max. "*Why* do they want us to feel weak?"

David and Anthony waited for Max to say something. As if Max would have the answer to the question that both of these boys silently asked themselves every day at school.

But Max didn't know.

He only wished he did.

CHAPTER

Ten

Thursday afternoon was the first "station" of the new term: trials for the second form rugby team.

Max stood at the edge of a field in a leafy park near the center of London, a few minutes' walk from the rest of the school. Victor Square looked like any other park in London, except this one was private, owned and used exclusively by St. West's.

The boys stood in a line along the edge of the field. Max was next to the only boy who stuck out more than he did: Harold Wadia, who had light brown skin and black hair, and whose grandfather was apparently the Cotton King of Bombay. Max was secretly hoping that Harold would be his friend. It was not at all clear that Harold hoped the same thing.

In addition to being their teacher, Master Yarrow was also the second form rugby coach. He kicked at some pigeons that had congregated on the field. "Avaunt, ye filthy flying rats!" he snarled. Then he turned to the boys. "Now, who will do St. West's proud at the opening day ruggers match against the Harrow boys?"

Every hand went up. Except for Max's.

"No, not all of you," said Master Yarrow. "That's for certain."

Master Yarrow began to stroll down the line of boys. "Mr. Bonner! What happened yesterday?"

"War was declared, sir!"

A pit formed in Max's stomach. Germany had invaded Poland on Friday. By Sunday, Great Britain and France had declared war on Germany. Mr. Montagu had announced the news triumphantly at their Sunday luncheon. Ever since, Max had been trying his very best not to think about the fact that the country he was in and the country his parents were in were now at war.

"Indeed!" bellowed Master Yarrow. "War was declared! And who will win the war?"

"Britain, sir!"

"*Specifically*, Bonner, who will win this war?"

"Uh . . . we will, sir?"

"You will! Boys like you!" Master Yarrow barked. "Your elder brothers, your fathers, your uncles, and you! Who is the greatest race on earth?!"

"The English!" the boys shouted. Except for Harold, Max noticed.

"Who conquered America, China, Africa, *and* India?"

Harold winced.

"The English!"

"Who liberated the fields of France, when the vicious German polluted it with his poison gas?"

"The English!"

"And who shall put the filthy Krauts back in their place again?"

"The English!"

"It starts on the rugby field, boys. It ends in the streets of Berlin!"

"Huzzah!" the boys cheered.

Max did not cheer. He was imagining a battle in the streets of his hometown, his parents peeking out from their windows as tanks blew holes in the buildings across the way.

"Did he just call us *Krauts*?" Berg asked. "How offensive! I don't even *like* sauerkraut."

"Which is strange," said Stein, "because you smell like it."

Master Yarrow said, "So try your hardest! Best boys will make the first team, but effort will get even you gormless gits on the second! And failing that, there are always the colors!" Which elicited a chuckle, just as it had done on the first day of class.

Max leaned over to Harold. "What are 'the colors'?"

Harold whispered, *"The school flag. It's large and pink and you* don't *want to bear the colors."*

Max said, "Got it."

The trial began with Master Yarrow hurling a rugby ball out into the middle of the pitch, at which point two boys ran after it and pummeled each other until one of them got the ball and ran back to the sideline.

Harold began speaking to Max again, quietly and urgently.

"Now, listen to me. You have to fight back. If someone throws an elbow, you throw one, too. Do you understand me?"

Max nodded. His legs were shaking as he watched a large boy get pummeled in the face by a *really* large boy.

"What is that child doing to that other child?" Berg shouted.

"I think he's trying to kill him," Stein suggested.

"And don't cry," Harold added. "That'll just make it worse."

"What if I cry now?" Max asked as blood began to run down the side of large boy's face.

Master Yarrow scribbled in a notebook. Then he blew his whistle. "Wadia! Bonner!"

Harold sprinted out into the field. Since Bonner was round and short, with short and round legs, Harold easily got to the ball first and scooped it up. But as he turned to run to the sideline, Bonner stuck out a foot and tripped him, and then jumped on Harold's back. Harold tried to wriggle out from under him, but Bonner put an elbow in Harold's neck, grabbed the ball, scrambled to his feet—placing a sharp cleat on Harold's spine—and then hustled back to the line.

"Very good!" Master Yarrow barked.

"If that's 'very good,' I'd hate to see what felony assault looks like," Stein muttered.

"I think it looks like that," said Berg.

Harold returned to Max's side, trying to rub the spot on his back where Bonner had cleated him, but it was just beyond the reach of his fingertips.

"Are you all right?" Max asked.

Harold nodded curtly and managed to say, "'Course. Fine."

The whistle blew. "Circuitt! Herr Bretzfeld!"

Max froze. The ball was flying into the field, and Circuitt was sprinting after it.

Max knew what this was. This was Circuitt's opportunity for revenge.

"Go!" Harold hissed.

Max forced himself to run out into the field. Circuitt had already collected the ball.

"Just let him have it!" Berg told Max.

"Yeah, who wants a dirty, sweat-covered pig's bladder anyway?" Stein asked. "It's all his!"

Max slowed down, happy to take Berg and Stein's advice.

But Circuitt was not running back to the line.

Max stopped.

"Come *on*, Bretzfeld!" Circuitt called in a singsong taunt. "I'm *waiting*!"

"Let him wait!" said Stein.

Max slowly walked toward Circuitt.

"HUSTLE!" Master Yarrow called. Max ignored him.

Circuitt grinned as Max approached.

Five yards away. Three yards. One.

Then, in a quick burst that surprised even Berg and Stein, Max lunged and grabbed the ball before Circuitt knew what was happening.

Max turned and sprinted for the sideline, the ball cradled under his arm.

Suddenly Max had the impression that a small bus had fallen on top of him. He could not breathe. He was gasping. He panicked. No air.

And then he felt something hot by his ear.

It was Circuitt's mouth.

Max heard, "You should have stayed in Germany, Yid. Hitler knows what to do with your type. He's not *all* wrong, is he?"

And then Circuitt was up, with the ball, and sprinting back to the line. The whistle blew. Master Yarrow was writing in his notebook.

Max came back to his place.

"Don't cry," said Harold.

Max's shoulders were going up and down.

"Just remember, *you've* got it lucky," Harold went on.

Max turned to him in disbelief.

"Don't give me that look," said Harold. "If you can just keep your mouth shut, you look rather English, don't you? Eventually, they'll forget about you."

Max's expression changed. Harold was still speaking, but mostly to himself now:

"They can't forget what I am. And they won't let *me* forget." Then he seemed to remember that Max was there. "Just keep quiet and they'll let you alone eventually."

Max, trying to control his ragged breath, said, "I am kind of sick of keeping quiet."

Harold raised an eyebrow. But Max didn't notice, because he was gazing across Victor Square—at a pack of pigeons, pecking at the wet slate sidewalk beyond the wrought iron fence.

The tryouts had ended, and the boys were heading off the field. But Max hung back.

"Excuse me," he said to Master Yarrow.

Master Yarrow was studying his notebook. Without looking up, he said, "You won't be making the team, Herr Bretzfeld. First or second."

"Of course," Max replied. "But I was thinking that, to show how much I want to support St. West's, I could try to bear the colors?"

Stein said, "What?"

"He wants to wave the flag during the games?" Berg said. "I think that's what that means."

"I know what it means," said Stein. "I don't understand why he would want to *do* that."

"Me neither," Berg agreed.

Master Yarrow seemed to be having the same thought. He'd lowered his notebook and was gazing down at Max. "You *want* to be color-bearer?"

"Yes sir."

"You *do* realize that might bring you in for a bit more . . . ah . . . *attention* . . . than you're already getting, don't you? Just trying to look out for you, Bretzfeld. It is rather a large pink flag."

Max straightened up. "I want to show everyone that I am here for the school! I am proud of the pink!"

Master Yarrow failed to hide a sudden smile at Max's terrible English and misplaced enthusiasm. "All right, then. The colors are yours. They're in the shed at the end of the fields." Master Yarrow pointed.

"And I can practice, yes?" Max asked. "Perhaps early mornings, before first period?"

"*Practice?* Carrying the school flag?"

"I don't want to make a fool of myself."

Master Yarrow looked down at Max pityingly. "Good luck. And sure, Max. Feel free to *practice*."

Max smiled, nodded, and hurried after the other boys.

CHAPTER
Eleven

That night, around the dinner table, Mr. Montagu was beaming. "My boy, my eldest son, making the St. West's rugby team!"

"It's the second squad, Dad," David reminded him. "Let's not make a big deal out of it."

Mrs. Montagu laughed. "Oh, I'm sure we *will* be making a big deal out of it!"

Mr. Montagu wasn't listening, as usual. "*I* was on the second squad at St. West's! Nothing to be ashamed of! Very respectable! Wait till I tell Uncle Ewen!"

"He was on first squad, wasn't he, Dad?"

"Sure he was! So what? He'll be thrilled! We'll all come to the big opener against Harrow, won't we? A family affair!"

"Did Uncle Ivor make the team?" Anthony wanted to know.

"Ivor?" Mr. Montagu laughed. "No, no, table tennis is his sport. If you can call it a sport."

Max got up his courage. "I didn't make the team either," he said.

Mr. Montagu made a sad face that couldn't have been less

believable if it was painted on. "Quite a disappointment for you, Max, I'm sure. But there's always next year!"

"You'd never even heard of rugby until a few weeks ago, isn't that right?" Mrs. Montagu added kindly. "You'll learn, Max. Not to worry."

"I am not worried," said Max. "I volunteered to be the color-bearer!"

Mr. Montagu dropped his fork onto his plate. The clatter was so loud, and the room was so suddenly silent after it, that Mrs. Henshaw the housekeeper stuck her head through the swinging door from the kitchen to see if everything was all right. She caught one glimpse of the adults' faces and disappeared instantly.

"You *volunteered*?" David exclaimed. "To be *color-bearer*?" He let his head fall so far it nearly landed in his asparagus. "This is going to be *awful*."

"I think it's a *lovely* idea!" Mrs. Montagu replied, rallying. "That's the way to show school spirit!"

"Good on you, Max," Mr. Montagu agreed, trying to follow her lead. "We can't all be sport stars, can we? Best to find a *place* for yourself and *excel* in that."

Max nodded energetically. "That is why I was thinking, if it was all right with you and Mrs. Montagu, I could go to Victor Square early each morning to practice?"

Mr. and Mrs. Montagu looked as confused as Master Yarrow had.

"You want to *practice* waving a flag?" Mr. Montagu said.

"I want to *excel!*" Max replied.

Mr. Montagu looked at Mrs. Montagu. Almost imperceptibly, they both shrugged.

David's forehead was now in the asparagus.

"We can have Mr. Ken run you by the fields an hour before school starts," Mrs. Montagu said. "That will give him plenty of time to drop you and come back for David and Anthony."

"*I* want to practice waving the colors, *too!*" Anthony said.

"You *really* don't," David muttered.

"No, Anthony," Mrs. Montagu agreed. "This is Max's special project."

And Max, to Stein and Berg, said, "They have no idea."

Berg replied, "Neither do I. Stein, do you have any idea what Max is up to?"

"Not a clue, Berg. Not a clue."

The next morning, Max woke, dressed, and ate an hour earlier than David and Anthony. He rode silently in the back of the Montagu car all the way to Victor Square.

Once Mr. Ken had let him out and pulled away, Max gazed down the narrow streets surrounding the square. There, down a small side street called Waterloo Place, he spotted the shop he'd noticed yesterday.

He stepped into the street—and a car *slammed* on its brakes and blew its horn loudly. Max waved in apology and darted across to the sidewalk on the other side of the lane. He had grown up looking left, then right, when crossing the road; in England, where they drove on the left, that could get you killed. It very nearly had.

Stein said, "If I had a heart, I woulda just had a heart attack."

Max walked down Waterloo Place until he came to Potters' Pots. Plants hung in the windows. Max could see an older woman arranging the displays inside.

He ignored the CLOSED sign that hung on the door and went in.

"Oh, hello, dear!" the woman said, smoothing her apron and then her wild strands of hair. "Are you lost?"

"Good morning," said Max, trying as best he could to hide his German accent so as not to arouse suspicion, now that England and Germany were at war. "I would like to buy a very large bag of birdseed."

The woman looked over her spectacles at him.

"Okay," said Berg. "I *feel* as confused as she *looks*."

"Talk to us, Max, honey. Tell us—what are you doing?" Stein asked.

But Max ignored them.

"You would like to buy a very large bag of birdseed?" the woman repeated, certain she had somehow misunderstood this small boy in the St. West's uniform.

"Yes, please," Max replied. "Do you have forty-pound bags?"

"Do you think you could *carry* a forty-pound bag?"

"Yes, I believe I could."

"Dear, *why* do you need a forty-pound bag of birdseed? I'm afraid we're not even open—"

"My mother has asked me to get it." Max revealed a shilling in his hand. The Montagus had given him spending money. Five shillings every Sunday.

The woman continued to gaze over her tiny glasses.

"And now he's lying to strangers," Stein moaned. "Berg, what has happened to our sweet little Max?"

Berg just shook his ugly face in confusion.

A few minutes later, Max was lugging a forty-pound burlap bag of birdseed across the street. Cars roared past him, honking their horns angrily at the tiny boy who was staggering through traffic with a giant birdseed bag on his shoulder. (Berg sat on top of the bag. Luckily, Berg didn't weigh anything at all.)

Max entered Victor Square and tossed the bag onto the grass. Then he went to the shed. It was unlocked. He pulled open the door and located in the musty darkness a polished wooden flagpole with a rolled-up pink flag on it. He withdrew it and unfurled the flag. It was very, very pink, with the St. West's crest on it. He waved it around a few times.

"Good, you practiced," said Stein. "Can we leave now?"

Max went over to the bag of birdseed. He tore a small hole in the burlap, then hefted it onto his shoulder again. On the other shoulder, he had the flagpole, with the bright pink flag trailing behind him.

Max started to walk the length of the field, letting birdseed trickle onto the ground.

Up and back and across he walked, covering every yard of the field and then doubling back and covering most of the yards again. Finally, the bag of birdseed was empty. Max walked to the shed and rolled up the flag and replaced it in the musty gloom.

He shoved the empty burlap bag into a trash can on his way to school.

The next morning, Max walked into Potter's Pots again.

"Well, hello!" the woman with the spectacles cooed. "Back already?"

"We have very hungry birds," Max said.

She laughed. "You certainly do."

He gave her more of his spending money, and lugged the forty-pound bag of birdseed across the busy street, disturbing a large flock of pigeons that was searching for breakfast on the sidewalk.

When he unfurled the colors, a few pigeons spread their oil-slick-gray wings and flew onto the field.

CHAPTER
Twelve

The day of the opening match had finally arrived.

All the second form families came to Victor Square. Not just the parents, but also aunts and uncles and grandparents.

Max couldn't quite understand how, just a month after the outbreak of war, Uncle Ewen could take half a day away from his job with the British government—which seemed to have something to do with the war, but which Ewen never said much about—to watch a bunch of eleven- and twelve-year-olds playing rugby.

Either Uncle Ewen's job wasn't very important, or this match *was*.

Max was less surprised that Uncle Ivor was available. Uncle Ivor's main occupation seemed to be playing table tennis and publishing England's only table tennis magazine. Also, he made films that he was always talking about but never showed to anyone.

Uncle Ewen and Uncle Ivor sat beside Mr. and Mrs. Montagu in the spectator stands that ran along the edge of the field.

The day was cool, and yellow leaves plastered the wet

pavement and dangled from the plane trees that surrounded the square. Max looked out over the wide green pitch. The St. West's boys warmed up in front of their side's bleachers, while, across the field, the Harrow boys did jumping jacks. David straightened up from a toe touch to wave nervously to his family in the stands.

"Today's the day," Stein said. "The day you've been preparing for."

Max nodded. The colors were leaning on his shoulder, still tightly furled around the wooden flagpole.

"All of your practice running up and down this field with a pink sheet trailing behind you will finally pay off," Berg added.

A pigeon fluttered up from the sidewalk outside the wrought iron fence of Victor Square and glided gracefully over the stands of parents.

Max smiled.

Master Yarrow walked into the middle of the pitch and blew loudly on his whistle. Then the Headmaster of St. West's joined him. The Headmaster bellowed a few words to the parents about the great tradition of rugby at St. West's, and how these boys were honoring not just their school, but all the Old Wets (which is what alumni were called). In the stands, Mr. Montagu clapped and hallooed loudly. The Headmaster explained that the second teams of each school would play first, and then the first teams would play. Max saw David shift nervously from one cleated foot to the other. "And now," the Headmaster bawled, "let the match begin!"

This was Max's cue. As David and the rest of the second team ran onto the pitch, Max went sprinting down the sideline along the west side of the field. The colors unfurled behind him. A great rectangle of pink, flapping in the wind. Max expected some of the boys to jeer at him as he ran past with the pink flag—maybe the Harrow boys, maybe Bonner and Circuitt. But everyone was too focused on the upcoming match to worry about the colors now.

As Max passed by the stands of St. West's families, the flag flapping behind, the adults rose to their feet and roared with approval. It was a good effect. His practice had paid off. Max was sure he saw Mrs. Montagu nudge Mr. Montagu and say something, to which Mr. Montagu nodded happily. Uncle Ivor was grinning. Uncle Ewen smiled his crooked, knowing smile.

And then, there was a beating of wings.

Dozens of wings.

Hundreds of wings.

Thousands of wings.

And every pigeon who had ever happened to pay a visit to central London in the last month—and discovered that the unfurling of a pink flag over Victor Square heralded the distribution of forty pounds of birdseed—rose over the high wrought iron fence and descended on St. West's rugby pitch.

They literally blotted out the sky.

Parents and children began shouting. Circuitt covered his head and screamed like he was in some sort of horrible nightmare. Bonner flailed his short arms furiously at the birds. But pigeons are brave creatures, and they weren't afraid of a short troll like Bonner.

The birds settled on the rugby pitch like a seething black-and-gray blanket.

"Wow," said Stein.

Max kept running, tracing a neat rectangle around the edge of the field, just as he had for the last month, though it was much easier without a forty-pound burlap sack on his shoulder.

The Headmaster and Master Yarrow were trying to wade through the sea of pigeons. The Headmaster was tiptoeing, trying not to step on one, while Master Yarrow was kicking at them and then shrieking whenever he unexpectedly made contact.

The pigeons pecked at the ground, trying to find the breakfast that they'd come to expect. When they discovered that there was no seed today, they were disappointed. But they weren't about to leave. They figured it would be served soon. And no one, not a shrieking man with flailing legs, nor a tiptoeing man in a black gown, nor many crying boys, would make these pigeons leave. They were city birds. They expected a meal. They'd stay until they got it.

Eventually, the matches had to be canceled. Everyone was furious. The second form rugby match with Harrow hadn't been canceled in four hundred years. Parents shouted at the Headmaster for not somehow bird-proofing Victor Square, as the Headmaster apologized and asked them how, exactly, one bird-proofed a great empty field in the middle of London.

Mr. Montagu led the Montagu clan to the sidewalk—but Mr. Ken wasn't supposed to return for them for another two hours, and Mr. Montagu refused to call from a public telephone box. So they all had to tramp angrily across London, Mr. Montagu insisting that they not stop until they arrived at 28 Kensington Court an hour later.

All the way home, David walked with his eyes open and staring, like he couldn't get the nightmare of ten thousand filthy birds out of his head. Uncle Ivor muttered to himself about how such a thing could happen. Mrs. Montagu held Anthony's hand and told him over and over, "No, that *isn't* supposed to happen. Yes, darling, I'm *glad* you liked it, but think of poor David. He didn't get to play his match." Uncle Ewen was the only one who didn't seem unhappy. He kept bursting out in unexpected fits of chuckling until Mr. Montagu fixed him with a furious stare, and he'd fall quiet again.

As they walked, Berg said: "Max, I must tell you something. I have never learned a prank from a human before. I will remember this day for the rest of my interminable life. I tip my cap to you." Max glowed. Stein seemed to be feeling proud, too—until he saw Max notice and he quickly went back to his customary scowl.

Mrs. Henshaw prepared a cold luncheon for them when they got home, and they all sat down around the long dining room table. The room was cloaked in a nervous silence. Max had never felt anything like it in this house. Cold chicken salad was put out, and Mr. Montagu attacked it with his fork as if the chicken salad had ruined his day. And then, with his mouth full of mayonnaise, he said, "What in *blazes* happened out there? What kind of strange act of God makes ten thousand pigeons descend on a rugby pitch all at once?"

Everyone stared at their plates. No one knew.

Except Max, of course.

And maybe one other person. Because Uncle Ewen said, "I daresay Max could tell us. Couldn't you, Max?"

Max's head jerked up. Uncle Ewen smiled crookedly at him.

Suddenly, everyone was staring at the little German refugee. Mr. Montagu's eyes looked like two volcanic craters.

But Max simply said, "I wasn't very fond of the way the rugby boys treated the rest of us. Especially everything they said about Jews." The adults glanced at one another, concerned. "So I may have stopped into the garden shop each morning, bought some birdseed, and taken to feeding the birds as I practiced running with the colors. It was *very* good exercise. And it made for *quite* a spectacle, didn't it?"

Max could see the insides of everyone's mouths now. Except for Uncle Ewen—he was still wearing that crooked smile.

And then there was an explosion of noise.

David shouted, "Mama, he *ruined* the ruggers match!"

Anthony cried, "What a good trick!"

Ivor threw his head back and roared with laughter.

Mrs. Montagu hissed, "Max! How could you *do* such a thing?"

And Mr. Montagu stood up so fast his chair went tumbling over and crashing to the floor as he bellowed, "OUT! OUT OF MY SIGHT! *NOW!*"

As Max scampered up the stairs, the cacophony continued. But above it all, Max could hear Uncle Ewen join Uncle Ivor in a fit of mad, uncontrolled laughter.

And then, amid the din, Max heard Uncle Ewen collect himself enough to say, "Sorry, Stuart, old boy. But that child is a *genius.*"

CHAPTER
Thirteen

"Okay, Maxy," said Stein. "Explain something to me."

"What?" Max asked. He could still hear the wild cacophony of crying, shouting, and laughter from downstairs, even through the closed bedroom door.

Stein asked, "How'd you get this way?"

Max flipped on the radio and tuned the dial until he heard the sweet sound of a trumpet—the Paris station was playing Louis Armstrong. Max jumped onto his bed. "What way?"

Stein said, "You came up with that pigeon prank what, a month ago? It was complex, it required deception and planning and . . . who are you, the next Napoleon?"

Max listened to the music and didn't answer for a full minute.

"What's happening?" Berg whispered to Stein. *"Is he thinking, or ignoring you?"*

"If he were smart, he'd ignore me. And we know he's pretty darn smart. So—"

But then, Max said, "It's just what you have to do."

The kobold and the dybbuk waited for an explanation.

"I guess it started when I was six, and I peed in my pants."

Stein said, "That's all it takes? Because I could do that . . ."

Max went on: "I peed in my pants and then I told my teacher, Professor Magdeburg. He called my mother and told her to bring me another pair of pants. But then, when she came, Professor Magdeburg accused her of never training me to use the toilet. He said it over and over, in front of the other children. 'You're a bad mother. Look at how your son has humiliated himself!'"

After a moment, Max added, "I was so angry. *So* angry."

"You had every right. He sounds like the worst teacher ever," said Stein.

"No, I wasn't mad at Professor Magdeburg," Max clarified.

"Huh?"

"I was mad at myself. *I should have known.* Had I just thought a little further ahead. Had I gone to the bathroom when I needed to. Or had I lied about the accident. Or had I hid it and kept my mouth shut. My mother wouldn't have been humiliated. I could have *protected* her."

"Max, you were *six*."

"I never made that mistake again," Max said quietly. The kobold and the dybbuk were squinting at him. "You always have to know what the bully is going to do before they do it. You have to think through all the possibilities—three, four moves out. *If he does this, I will do that, which will make him do this, and then I can do that . . .*" Max glanced between Stein and Berg.

"Nazi Germany is all bullies, everywhere you look. I learned to think four moves ahead. Otherwise I wouldn't have survived."

Unfortunately, Max's mother and father didn't think the way he did. Even when they tried to be four moves ahead, they never were. They were too emotional. Too reactive. His father was too sensitive. His mother was too proud. Max was always the one strategizing for the whole family. It had been like that ever since that day in Professor Magdeburg's class.

And now he wasn't there to strategize for them.

He wondered how they were surviving.

Stein and Berg gazed at Max, lost in his thoughts. "Poor kid," Stein muttered.

"Since when do *you* feel bad for anyone?" said Berg.

"Yeah," Stein sighed. "It seems to be a new development. I hate it."

CHAPTER
Fourteen

Nearly a year later, not much had changed, except that Hitler had conquered France, as well as Poland and Czechoslovakia and Denmark and Norway and Belgium and Holland. And now the Germans had turned their sights on England.

Since the rugby match, Max had:

- Turned twelve. Mrs. Henshaw had made an enormous buttercream cake. It was delicious and Max had eaten too much and gotten a terrible stomachache.

- Improved immensely at speaking English and gotten rid of his German accent. Thankfully, because anti-German sentiment was getting more intense by the day.

- Started his second year at St. West's. He still hated it, but at least all the boys were now afraid of him, and so they mostly left him alone.

- Received exactly zero letters from his parents.

The Montagus had assured him that the mail was just very unreliable between two nations at war. Max tried his hardest to believe them, and to trust that his parents were all right, and that somehow, somewhere, he would see them soon. Perhaps Goebbels and Hitler would "solve" their "Jewish problem" by forcing all the Jews to leave, and his parents would be able to come to England. Or the war would end and Max could go back home to them. He told himself some version of this story every single night before he fell asleep. He tried his hardest to believe it. But the effort was fraying his nerves like old wires in a radio. And, like a radio with frayed wires, his emotions were crackling with static.

One Sunday in September 1940, Mrs. Montagu rapped on Max's door. "Come downstairs, Max, dear. It's almost time for luncheon."

Max was listening to his radio, as usual. But, not as usual, he wasn't listening to the Berlin station. He had tuned the Murphy to the frequency that the Germans beamed to Britain from a huge transmitter they'd put up on the north German coast. Max hated this station—except at 9:00 p.m. on weekdays and 11:00 a.m. on weekends, when it broadcast a show called *Jazz Cracks* that played American-style jazz, with only short interludes of pro-Nazi propaganda. The propaganda made Max sick, but the jazz was actually pretty good.

Mrs. Montagu knocked again and spoke through the door: "Uncle Ewen is here, having his coffee in the parlor. And Uncle

Ivor's locking his bicycle up outside." Then she added, under her breath, "Like some common laborer."

Max jumped out of bed and switched off the radio. Ever since what the Montagus now referred to as "the Pigeon Incident," Ewen and Max had been getting along pretty well. And Ivor was the closest thing Max had to a friend here in England. Max hurried downstairs.

In the luxurious parlor of 28 Kensington Court sat Mr. Montagu and Uncle Ewen. Ewen had one long, trousered leg folded comfortably over the other, and in his hands he held a teacup on a saucer, which he was bringing to his mouth to sip—until he saw Max.

He lowered the cup, cocked one corner of his mouth, and raised a single eyebrow.

"Hullo, Max," he said.

Uncle Ewen always looked at Max as if there were some joke they shared, that they wouldn't say aloud just now, but that they both knew and found very funny. Max had *no idea* what the joke was. But he didn't want Ewen to know he didn't know. So he always tried to raise one corner of his mouth and smile knowingly back at Uncle Ewen. Which always made Uncle Ewen raise that corner of his mouth a little more.

"*What* is going on between those two?" Stein said as Max and Uncle Ewen smiled more and more cryptically at each other.

Mr. Montagu, who was also holding a cup of tea, hadn't

forgiven Max for ruining the second form match with Harrow. Coldly, he said, "Good mo—"

BANG!

Suddenly, the whole house shook—the chandelier in the dining room tinkled and a small oil painting on the wall above Mr. Montagu's head went slightly crooked.

Mr. Montagu instinctively ducked. Uncle Ewen instinctively sprang to his feet.

"Huuuuuullo-o-o!" came a voice from the foyer.

Mr. Montagu and Uncle Ewen both exhaled with relief. And annoyance.

"Uncle Ivor!" Max shouted, running back into the foyer.

"Max!" Uncle Ivor shouted, his arms extended, a pink scarf around his neck, his round face beaming like the moon, his curly black hair as messy as ever.

Uncle Ivor's arms were stretched in a way that appeared to be inviting a hug, but Max knew better. The English hugged even less than the Germans. Max extended his own arms and Ivor took his hands and shook them both at once, which was their little tradition.

Max grinned and Uncle Ivor grinned back as Mr. Montagu and Uncle Ewen came into the foyer.

"Good morning, brothers dear!" Ivor cried. Then to Max he said, "So . . . shall I demolish you in table tennis? Or should I let you win for *most* of the match, before roaring back and ut-terly *humiliating* you in the last moments?"

Max replied, "You should do your very best, Uncle Ivor. Old men like you need to try to keep fit however they can."

"Oh, you scoundrel!" Uncle Ivor bellowed.

And he chased Max down to the basement, where the tennis table was, leaving Uncle Ewen and Mr. Montagu shaking their heads—one smiling, one not.

Ivor was not really an old man, of course. They had realized, in fact, that Uncle Ivor had been bar mitzvahed the week Max was born. And Ivor was *very* good at table tennis.

Max, on the other hand, was *terrible* at table tennis. He played by holding the paddle straight up in his fist and pushing the ball over the net to Uncle Ivor, as Ivor restrained himself from smashing every pathetic offering back into Max's face.

Well, he didn't *always* restrain himself.

SMASH! Max froze as the ball went whizzing past his cheek.

"He was trying to kill you! That was attempted murder!" Berg shouted.

Uncle Ivor straightened up. "Right! Sorry about that! You offer me so many tempting sacrifices . . ." Ivor took on the voice and wild look of a monster from a horror film. "The evil god within me just can't resist . . . *My dark master must be sated!*"

Max laughed.

Max was entranced by Ivor. In addition to being hilarious, and a world-class table tennis player, he was a vivacious intellectual. He was a voracious reader, he made experimental films that no one had ever seen, and—to Max's great shock—he was an ardent defender of Communism.

This shocked Max so much because the only thing that the Nazis and the English seemed to agree on was that Communism was evil.

But Uncle Ivor was passionate about the *promise* of Communism. He gave poetic speeches about a future in which all humans were truly equal: equal in wealth, equal in status, equal in political power. Whenever he did this, Uncle Ewen liked to point out that, while that *sounded* nice, the world's leading Communist country was the Soviet Union, run by Joseph Stalin, who seemed intent on making all of his "comrades" equal by making them equally poor, equally oppressed, or equally dead. Uncle Ewen also always made sure to mention that Stalin and Hitler were currently allies, or close to it. When Hitler invaded Poland, so did Stalin, and they divided it up neatly between them. Now the people of Poland were being forced out of their homes, their land was being stolen, and they were starving to death in work camps. On both Hitler's side *and* on Stalin's side.

None of this seemed to make Uncle Ivor love the idea of Communism any less. He loved the world and everyone in it, and he wanted everyone to share everything so they could all have as good a life as he did.

The idea of taking everyone's hard-earned money and handing it out equally to everyone else enraged Mr. Montagu so much that it made him want to throw his pipe against a wall. Which he had done on many occasions during conversations with Ivor.

After Ivor delivered a particularly brutal smash that grazed Max's chin, they heard footsteps on the stairs. Uncle Ewen appeared.

"Ewen!" barked Uncle Ivor. "I am sorry that I had to devour this child! He was just too sweet and tempting!"

Uncle Ewen shrugged as if to say *Do what you have to do.* Then he winked at Max.

"Well?" asked Ivor of his older brother. "Are you here to submit yourself to my superior table tennis skills?"

"Ivor, as I recall *I* beat *you* last time we played," Uncle Ewen replied.

"That match is under protest!"

"Oh, is it? Why?"

"Because I never lose! And therefore you must have cheated!"

Max laughed and returned his adoring gaze to Ivor. When Max was with Uncle Ivor and Uncle Ewen, he always felt a strange tug in his heart. As if his loyalties were divided between the two. To favor one was to neglect the other. He wasn't sure why he felt that way.

Uncle Ewen was saying, "No, Ivor, I am not here to defeat you in table tennis again. I am here to inform you that the film projector is in the parlor."

"Splendid!" cried Ivor. "I've got the film in my pannier—which is . . . still on my cycle outside! Bloody hell!" He threw his paddle onto the table. "Urgent rescue mission, Max! Excuse me! Thanks for bringing it, Ew!" As Uncle Ivor hurried past his older brother, he asked, "Did you have to get Winston Churchill's express permission to take the projector from your office?"

Uncle Ewen chuckled. "No," he replied. "Just Admiral Godfrey's."

Ivor stopped with a foot on the steps. "No, really?"

Ewen nodded ruefully.

"Well," said Ivor, "I'm glad the man running Naval Intelligence against the Nazis is spending time dispensing projectors for my experimental films." And he bounded up the stairs, nearly knocking over Mary, the kitchen maid, who threw herself against a railing and hugged a bucket of ice to her chest. "Sorry, Mary!" Uncle Ivor cried over his shoulder. "Just need to prevent history's next great moving picture from being nicked from my pannier!"

There was always a moment of silence after Ivor left a room, just so everyone could catch their breath.

"What's Naval Intelligence?" Max asked Stein and Berg as Uncle Ewen gallantly helped Mary the rest of the way down the stairs.

"Well, *naval* means 'boats,'" said Berg. "So my theory is . . . *Naval Intelligence* means figuring out how smart boats are?"

"That's the dumbest theory I ever heard," Stein replied. "Dumber than a boat."

"Do *you* know what it is?" Berg retorted.

"No, but I don't go around making up idiotic—"

Max wasn't listening to them anymore. He had decided to simply ask Ewen: "Uncle Ewen, what's Naval Intelligence?"

Ewen raised an eyebrow at Max. "Don't you know?"

Max shook his head.

"It's spying, Max. Spying on the Germans, and stopping them from spying on us."

Max fell very still. He suddenly saw Uncle Ewen in a *totally* different light. "You're a . . . *spy?*"

Ewen put a finger to his thin lips. Then he left Max in the basement, tossing in a tempest of thoughts.

CHAPTER
Fifteen

Ivor spent all of lunchtime setting up the projector in the parlor. He arranged all the chairs to face the fireplace, and made a blank white space on the wall over the mantel by taking down a portrait of his grandfather Samuel Montagu, born Montagu Samuel, First Baron of Swaythling.

Max sat in the front row, eager to see Ivor's masterpiece, which was the very first film Ivor had agreed to show the family. Uncle Ivor was the only artist Max had ever met, and he was very clearly a genius.

"Do you think it will be a romance?" Berg said, jiggling his leg in anticipation. "I love a good romance."

Stein was less optimistic. "Let's not get our hopes up. It's probably going to be a two-hour documentary on the history of table tennis."

Meanwhile, Mr. Montagu had leaned over to Uncle Ewen and was saying, "If this is a moving-picture version of *The Communist Manifesto*, I'm leaving. Are you with me?"

Uncle Ewen grinned. "Not at all, brother. I'm absolutely

knackered from a long week, and will take any opportunity to catch up on sleep."

Mr. Montagu nodded. "Very good. I'll go smoke a pipe in the garden by myself, then."

"I can hear you both!" Ivor said as he fiddled with the film.

"I'm sure we're going to just *adore* the picture," said Mrs. Montagu. "You've worked on it for *so* long. What is it, two years now?"

"Nearly three!" Ivor replied, his head turned totally upside down as he tried to see how he'd messed up loading the film into the projector.

"Is it a comedy?" asked little Anthony. "I like comedies the best. Is it like the Marx Brothers?"

"Probably a different Marx brother, Anthony," Mr. Montagu muttered.

"It's both a comedy and a tragedy," said Uncle Ivor.

"I don't want to see a tragedy!" David complained.

Max piped up, "I think it's going to be *splendid*, Uncle Ivor."

Ivor stood up and beamed at Max, which made Max's chest swell.

"There!" Ivor exclaimed. "Ready! Mrs. Henshaw, would you dim the lights, if you please?"

Mrs. Henshaw flipped a switch, the antique chandelier above their heads was extinguished, and the room went dark.

Ivor started the projector. It whirred. A white square appeared on the wall above the mantel.

Torn film flipped by. Max locked his fingers and squeezed his knuckles.

And then, in black and white, there appeared a discarded sheet of newspaper, lying on the grass near a path in what looked like Hyde Park.

The only word of the paper's headline that was legible read ETERNITY.

A pair of feet walked by. Then another pair, in another direction.

A dog passed, though only its belly and its four thin legs were visible. Then the feet, presumably, of its owner.

Torn film flipped by again.

A white square, over the mantel.

"Lights!" Ivor cried.

The lights went on, and Max squinted.

"What happened to the movie?" Anthony asked.

Ivor was standing at the front of the room now, his hands on his hips in a directorial pose.

"Are you going to fix the film, Ivor?" Mrs. Montagu asked. "It was . . . *intriguing* . . . so far, anyway."

"Actually, I had *already* nodded off," said Uncle Ewen.

Mr. Montagu chortled.

Max glared at both of them.

Uncle Ivor smiled serenely, artistically, at the assembled family. "You misunderstand, my dears! That's it! That's the film!"

There was a moment of very deep silence.

"*That's* the film you've been working on since 1937?" Mr. Montagu asked.

Ivor nodded. "So what did you think?"

"I think you're missing the rest of the picture!"

"And a plot," Ewen added, trying not to laugh.

"It *was* a good beginning!" Mrs. Montagu ventured bravely.

Another moment of very awkward silence.

And then there was an eruption of laughter.

Mr. Montagu threw his head back and guffawed. Mrs. Montagu tried to cover her mouth. "I'm sorry, sport!" Ewen said, "I know it means an awful lot to you." But he couldn't help himself.

"I want to see a movie," Anthony whined, not understanding what was so funny.

Ivor did not see the joke either. "You don't get it! That was art! You bourgeois pigs!" he shouted, his face turning red. "You utter cretins!"

Max had the sudden urge to rush up to Uncle Ivor and give him a hug. Except that the English never hugged. And besides, Ivor was already storming out of the parlor, crossing the foyer to the front door, grabbing the handle—

BANG!

This time the bang was much louder than before.

The antique chandelier swung so hard that it hit the ceiling. The projector fell off the small card table and crashed to the floor. Anthony fell out of his chair.

"What in *blazes* was that?" Mr. Montagu asked.

Stein suggested, "Ivor needs to learn how to open a door?"

Uncle Ewen was already out of his seat, out of the ballroom, and into the foyer.

"Ivor!" he shouted.

Max was up and after Uncle Ewen in an instant.

The door was open, but Ivor was lying on the carpet on his back.

Max fell to his knees beside Uncle Ivor and grabbed his hand.

"Are you okay?" Max asked him.

Uncle Ivor said, "Yes, I think so. Thank you, Max." Max kept holding his hand.

The rest of the family, and the household help, too, had gathered around Uncle Ewen, who was staring out the front door.

"God be merciful . . ." Ewen muttered. And then, very loudly, he barked, "Everyone to the basement! Now! NOW!"

"Are we going to play table tennis?" asked Anthony.

Uncle Ivor pushed himself to his feet, Mr. Montagu scooped up Anthony and threw him over his shoulder, and everyone in the household, family and help alike, scrambled to the basement steps.

Everyone except Max. He went to stand beside Uncle Ewen, who had not moved. They stood in the doorway, side by side, gazing up at the iron-gray sky.

Under the low clouds, impossibly close, were hundreds and

hundreds of airplanes—some fat, others small and sharp. They buzzed like a swarm of furious hornets. It made your ears tickle.

"What are those?" Max asked.

And Uncle Ewen said, "Those *appear* to be German bombers. With an escort of German fighter planes."

"In London?" Max asked. A new terror opened in his stomach.

"It would seem so."

Max saw a bomber, very nearby, drop a cluster of what looked like bowling pins—black against the steely clouds. The pins tumbled through the air, right toward Kensington Palace. Then they disappeared from view.

BOOM!

Max was knocked back a step. Smoke slowly billowed up over the buildings. The angry buzzing would not stop. The low gray clouds were lit from below by sudden fires.

"Excuse me, Max," said a voice from his right shoulder. "We, being ancient and immortal creatures, cannot die."

Max stared out the door at the new world.

"You, being a twelve-year-old boy, are made of very delicate flesh and bones that snap like dry grass when they are hit by a bomb, or shrapnel, or flying bricks."

Buzzing, burning, bursting—framed by an ornate mahogany doorway.

"What my good friend Berg is trying to say," Stein added, "is *close the door, you granite-headed dope!*"

Uncle Ewen seemed to have come to the same conclusion. He slammed the door and said, "Come on, old chap. It's the basement for all of us."

"What is happening?" Max wanted to know.

"The Germans are bombing London, my boy. And not our military installations, either." In disbelief, he said, "They're bombing our people."

CHAPTER
Sixteen

The Montagu family spent three hours in the basement of 28 Kensington Court on 7 September 1940, the first day that Hitler used his fearsome Luftwaffe to pummel London's homes, shops, bridges, schools, and hospitals.

For the first fifteen minutes, no one moved and no one spoke. They were in the large finished basement room, with a thick wool rug, many chairs, and the tennis table. Anthony sat on Mrs. Montagu's lap, his arms around her neck. Mr. Montagu and Ewen lit pipes and stood, puffing on them and listening to the explosions from the street above. David sat on the floor, his legs crossed, his cheeks in his hands. Ivor took a pack of cigarettes out of his jacket pocket, until he saw Mrs. Montagu shake her head sharply. There was no cigarette smoking at 28 Kensington Court.

Mr. Margrave, the butler, poked his head into the room and inquired about the health and well-being of the family. When he was informed that everyone was fine, he reported that the staff were all fine, too, and they had congregated in the kitchen—which was also in the basement—and had begun playing cards.

"Well, that's the spirit!" Ivor exclaimed as Mr. Margrave retreated. "Let's not sit around moping! Who's up for a game of table tennis?"

"I must say," replied Uncle Ewen, "that earlier today I watched with horror as you *brutalized* poor Max here, no better than a German bomber yourself. What do you say if His Majesty's Royal Air Force takes a shot at you?"

"I thought you were Navy, Ewen." Ivor grinned.

"Temporary transfer," Ewen replied, handing his pipe to Mr. Montagu, who considered Ewen's pipe for a moment and then put it in his mouth next to his own. Even Max had to smile at that.

The game started calmly. But by the time the score was 10–10, the whole family was watching the Olympic-quality table tennis match that raged between Ivor and Ewen. They lunged, slammed, slid across the tile floor (no rug under the tennis table, of course). Cheering sections formed. The adults all egged on Ewen—but the children were for Uncle Ivor. And no one cheered louder than Max.

Occasionally, a bomb shook the house. But when one did, and if it caused Ewen to duff a shot, or Ivor to whiff altogether, there were no do-overs. No complaints. No appeals to the judge (the judge being Mr. Montagu, gripping the two pipes solemnly, puffing one and then the other).

This was the new reality—what would be called "the Blitz."

The Germans dropping the largest explosive devices yet invented on the homes of London.

So it was. Everyone would live with it. The less said about it, the better.

"I can't believe what I'm seeing," said Stein.

"Me neither," agreed Berg. "I have been alive for all of history. I have seen a lot of people go through a lot of misery. But playing table tennis while enormous planes set your city on fire?"

"I know," Stein said. "These people are nuts."

Max thought so, too.

Nuts in the most admirable way imaginable.

It was that night, thirteen months after his arrival, that Max finally fell in love with the Montagu family.

After three hours of bombs falling and the Montagus cheering and booing and laughing, it dawned on Max that, through it all, he had not thought of his parents once. He felt, for the first time in over a year, like he was home.

As soon as he realized that, he said to Berg and Stein:

"I have to get back to Berlin."

CHAPTER
Seventeen

The assault ended about an hour before sunset. The Luftwaffe bombers and fighters banked and headed back to the airfields of Germany. The house stopped shaking. But Ivor and Ewen were knotted at fourteen points a side, in the sixth game of their tournament. When Ewen won that game, it brought the set to three games each, and everyone agreed that, no matter what was happening at street level, a tiebreaker was *required*.

So they played one more game, and Ivor won. They were both wearing their white shirtsleeves, and great gray wet patches had developed under their arms. After Ivor had raised his fists to celebrate his victory, they shook hands. Then Ivor passed his fingers through his soaking black hair, and Max cheered and clapped for his hero Ivor, as Ewen got a firm handshake of condolence from Mr. Montagu. And his pipe back.

"Well," Ewen said, "shall we survey the battlefield?"

And so the family marched upstairs, followed by the staff. A quick inspection revealed that the house was unscathed. They threw open the front door.

For an instant, their British resolve left them. Ewen stood

in the doorway, with Mr. Montagu and Max right behind him, staring at Kensington Court.

There was half a building. *Half* a building. It was just three doors down and across the street. Half a building, intact from the street level to the middle of the first-floor windows. And then, above that, lead pipes stuck up at strange angles, as if searching for the sinks and tubs they used to feed, and forlornly failing to find them.

Bricks were scattered in the street, the top two and a half floors of the home now a garbage heap. Mrs. Montagu, peering over her husband's shoulder, exclaimed, "The Harrises!" She pushed past the frozen men and hurried down the steps toward the destroyed house.

The Harrises were standing out front. They were bloodied and bruised, but they were not dead. They looked, mostly, perplexed. Hands on their hips. Staring at what was once their beautiful, stately home. Now disassembled in the middle of the road.

The Montagu family began a slow walk through dusky London. Some leafy streets of Kensington were as pristine as they had been that morning. And then there were lanes that looked like mouths after a boxing match, random teeth shattered.

"Dropping bombs on homes," Uncle Ewen marveled. "I don't understand it."

"What's to understand?" Mr. Montagu retorted, his pipe still in his teeth. "Hitler's a madman. You can't understand a madman. You can just hope to knock his block off."

"Hitler may be a madman," said Ewen as they passed a schoolhouse where all the windows had been blown out by a bomb that had fallen through the roof, "but what about everyone else? What about the lads in the sky who dropped the bombs? What about their commanders? What about their wives and children? What will the bomber pilots tell their wives when they come home tonight? *Guten Abend, Liebchen, I dropped bombs on schools and hospitals today.* And what will she say? *Oh, good for you! I hope lots of children died!* Is that what they're saying over their *Wiener schnitzel* this evening?"

"Ewen, please!" Mrs. Montagu murmured, covering Anthony's ears.

"Sorry, Iris," said Uncle Ewen. "But how in God's name does Hitler get them all to go along with it?" He dropped his voice but kept speaking, as if to himself. "*Damn it all!* We should have known this was coming! Where are our *bloody* eyes and ears?"

Uncle Ewen started walking back to 28 Kensington Court, ahead of them and alone. He kicked at the puddles of fire-hose water, which were reflecting the flames that were consuming London.

"Oh," said Max as he watched Uncle Ewen wrestle with his thoughts.

"Oh what?" asked Berg.

"I think . . . I think I just figured out how to get home."

CHAPTER
Eighteen

Max was perched on a grassy bluff overlooking a gray river.

From a portable wireless set that Max had assembled arose the fourth movement of Beethoven's Ninth Symphony, with cellos groaning and French horns declaiming, played live by the Berlin Philharmonic and broadcast from the Haus des Rundfunks, in Berlin. The chorus sang: *Freude, schöner Götterfunken . . .*

Invisible waves traveled from a tower in Germany, through the air, through clouds, through trees, through brick walls, through Max himself—and when they collided with a small crystal inside this little box Max had nailed together, they were transformed into the world's most beautiful music.

If only Max could ride these invisible radio waves back home.

Well, in a way he could.

At least that was the plan.

He'd been developing it for weeks now. Weeks of bombs falling on London, all day and all night. Weeks of Max lying in his bed wondering whether one of those spinning bowling pins would fall on 28 Kensington Court. Weeks of wondering whether his parents would even know if Max died. Weeks of conversations over the dinner table about when Max and David and Anthony would be sent away to the countryside.

Away from London.

Away from Uncle Ewen.

Which meant, if Max was going to ride these waves back to Berlin, time was running out.

And then, strangely, Uncle Ewen had invited the whole family—except for Ivor—to join a Sunday-afternoon fishing excursion with him and his boss, Admiral John Godfrey.

For the entire fifty-four-minute car ride into the countryside, Ewen had lectured David and Anthony and Max:

When Admiral Godfrey and I are fishing, keep your distance. Only Stuart—your father, Mr. Montagu—will fish with us. Don't listen to anything we say. Above all, do not *interrupt the meeting.*

Ewen had repeated these rules over and over again. Apparently Mr. Montagu had a way of helping the work that Ewen and Admiral Godfrey were doing, something about his bank and government accounts and things, and it was *crucial* that this meeting happen—and that it look like an innocent Sunday-afternoon fishing outing.

At one point, Mr. Montagu had asked Uncle Ewen, "And will you be bringing up our *special concern?*" Ewen had nodded curtly and demanded of the children again: "Do *not* interrupt us. Do you understand?"

And they had responded: "Yes, Uncle Ewen, we understand."

Now Max leaned over the edge of the bluff, as the tall grass bent in the cool wind and the Berlin Philharmonic's chorus sang:

Deine Zauber binden wieder,
Was die Mode streng geteilt . . .

He didn't want to miss his cue.

Admiral Godfrey, Uncle Ewen, and Mr. Montagu were standing in the wide, shallow river below, wearing brown rubber waders and holding fly rods, talking quietly from the sides of their mouths.

Though, at the moment, Admiral John Godfrey was *not* talking out of the side of his mouth. He was staring up at the German boy on the bluff who was treating them to Beethoven's Ninth Symphony.

Admiral Godfrey's face was red and puffy and wrinkled, like a wilting rosebush, while his posture was like a rosebush that had been strapped to a fence post. "Been sitting there nearly an hour," Admiral Godfrey announced sourly. Max could just hear him over Beethoven's Ninth and the burbling of water over rocks.

"Give him a radio and he tends to do that," drawled Mr. Montagu.

"How strange," Admiral Godfrey said.

From Max's left shoulder, Stein shouted back, "You think *he's* strange? You're standing in a river wearing rubber pants!"

"Ewen, is that boy secure?" Admiral Godfrey grunted. "Do we have a bloody German national with a bloody *radio* listening to a top-secret conversation? Just checking, mind you."

Uncle Ewen gave Admiral Godfrey that crooked half smile of his. "He's twelve years old, John. Also, he's not a German national, he's a *Jew*. Hitler has made it *very* clear that we Jews don't count as German nationals, no matter where we were born."

"Well, yes, I suppose. Still, highly bloody irregular," Admiral Godfrey grumbled.

"Speaking of bloody irregular," said Uncle Ewen, stealing a sidelong glance at Mr. Montagu, who nodded urgently and then stopped when Admiral Godfrey noticed him. Ewen went on, "We've learned more about these so-called *concentration camps*. They're quite horrific. And, it seems, getting worse."

"Oh?" murmured Admiral Godfrey. He didn't seem very interested.

"We've received reports that they're *starving* the prisoners and working them to *death*."

"Mm-hmm," said the admiral. But he might have been commenting on the way his fishing fly was sitting on the water.

"We've *got* to let the prime minister know, Admiral. And President Roosevelt, too. If we're not careful, these concentration camps are going to turn into *death camps*."

Admiral Godfrey's puffy face looked like it was going to drop its wilted blossoms. "*Death camps?* Ewen, please, where do you even get terms like that? These are prison camps. We have them, too. The prisoners—*political* prisoners, and not all Jews, mind you—are *working*. Making guns and whatnot for Hitler's bloody war. We know this. So *why on earth* would the Germans work them to *death*? It makes no sense!" Uncle Ewen tried to cut in, but Admiral Godfrey wasn't the sort of man who allowed himself to be interrupted. "You'll get no argument from me that the Nazis are nasty, brutal beasts. But we still have rules of war, you know, and murdering political prisoners is *not done*. Even by the Germans. If I've told you once, I've told you a *thousand* times. Focus on *winning the war*. That's the way to help your beleaguered Jewish tribe in Germany. Not these fantasies about mass murder. It's just *not happening*."

Ewen glanced quickly at Mr. Montagu, who was frowning down his fishing rod.

"Besides," Admiral Godfrey concluded, "you work for Great Britain. We are fighting to protect *ourselves*. Not Jews in Europe. Focus on what *matters*."

Ewen inhaled slowly and tried to maintain his composure. "Admiral, I believe we need more men on the ground, to help us understand what is happening inside Germany. We have agents, but not enough! And not in the right places! We need eyes! We need ears! We need—"

"MAX!" Mr. Montagu bellowed.

Uncle Ewen's and Admiral Godfrey's heads snapped around.

Max was standing in the river, water up to his thighs.

"Max, your trousers will be ruined!" Mr. Montagu exclaimed.

"And you're scaring off the fish!" Admiral Godfrey added.

"And now you look as weird as they do," Stein put in.

"Weirder," said Berg. "Because at least they're wearing rubber pants. You're just wet."

Uncle Ewen's long face was bright red, like a battleship that had been hit with with a torpedo and was erupting with flames up and down the deck. But his eyes . . . instead of the knowing look that was meant only for Max . . . Ewen's eyes were *hurt*. "*Max . . .*" he said, and the way he said it was so wounded, so disappointed, that Max wanted to walk back up onto the bluff and curl into a ball with shame.

But he couldn't, because he hadn't said what he'd walked into the river to say.

"I want to be sent to Germany. As a spy."

There. Now he'd said it.

The river burbled and whorled around Max's cold, wet legs. The three men's mouths all flopped open like trouts'.

Max said, "I know Berlin intimately. I speak perfect German, of course. Give me a false name and forged papers, and I could blend in totally. I could find out whatever you want to know."

The men's mouths were gaping so wide that Max could have inserted a fishhook into them.

Which was, in fact, exactly what he was trying to do.

Finally, Admiral John Godfrey cleared his throat.

"*Young man,*" he said. "I am sorry to inform you that we do not take *volunteers* in the British secret service. Especially not German nationals. Who are in *primary* school."

Max stood staring at Admiral Godfrey.

There was more coming.

He was going to say something else.

He was going to say *But in this case . . .* Or *For you, though, we will make an exception . . .*

Max waited for it.

And waited.

After what felt like an eternity of icy water swirling around his legs, Max heard a low growl.

"Out, Max," snarled Mr. Montagu. "*Now.*"

Max looked at Admiral Godfrey once more. The wrinkled bloom of his face had gone from magenta to crimson.

Max turned to Uncle Ewen. Ewen merely shook his head like he had been betrayed.

CHAPTER
Nineteen

Max climbed up the bank from the river, his clothes freezing and sopping wet.

"That went well!" Berg announced.

Max picked up his portable radio and walked past Mrs. Montagu, sitting on the picnic blanket. "May I go into the car and change?" he asked her.

She looked away from her boys playing tag and saw Max's pants. "What happened?!" she exclaimed. Then, without waiting for an answer, "Do you even *have* a change of clothes with you?"

"I brought one."

"You did? Why?"

"I knew I would get wet."

She squinted at him curiously as he climbed into the back of the Montagus' automobile. He stripped down, reached into a soft leather satchel he'd stowed under his seat, and brought out a small towel and a change of clothes.

Once he was dry, Max peeked out the car window. Mrs. Montagu was starting in on some needlepoint while shaking her head and muttering to herself, probably about Max. David was trying to hoist Anthony up into a stubby apple tree. The men were out of sight below the riverbank.

Max clambered into the front seat of the car. He was holding a screwdriver and some wires.

"What are you doing, Max?" Stein asked in a low, warning voice.

Max didn't answer.

Fifteen minutes later, he slipped out of the Rolls-Royce and opened the door of the red Aston Martin two-seater convertible that Admiral Godfrey had parked next to the Montagus' car. Max slid into the passenger side.

"Um, Max," Berg warned him. "This is the vehicle of the director of British Naval Intelligence. You should stop."

"For once, Berg is not wrong," Stein agreed. "What you're doing is one hundred percent illegal."

"Also," Berg interrupted, "why are you unscrewing Admiral Godfrey's radio?"

Indeed, Max was removing a screw from the car's dashboard. Then another. Then another—

"Hullo, Max."

Max froze.

He slowly turned his head.

Anthony was looking over the door of the Aston Martin.

Max did a quick survey of the players. Mrs. Montagu was

still at her needlework, and unless she stood up, she could not
see into Admiral Godfrey's car. The men were still in the river.
David was trying to haul himself into the upper branches of the
apple tree.

"What are you doing?" Anthony asked.

Max hesitated. Then he said, "I'm going back to Germany."

"What?" said the little boy with the straight fringe of
brown hair.

"You are?" said Berg.

"You mean, *we* are?" said Stein.

Max grinned at Anthony. "Just kidding. I'm playing a prank.
You'll see soon enough. Just . . . *shhh*. Don't tell, until the fish
is caught. Okay?"

Anthony gazed at Max with wondering eyes. Then he straightened his back, clicked his little heels together, and saluted.

"Now go climb a tree," Max said. Anthony ran off.

Max exhaled and went to work on the fourth screw.

Berg looked at Stein. "Do *you* know what our little mischief-
maker is up to?"

Stein just shook his head and gazed at Max's small deft
hands.

An hour later, Uncle Ewen had four trout in his hamper—
enough for Mrs. Henshaw to panfry a feast for dinner that evening. And yet he didn't look happy about it.

Admiral Godfrey had caught two fish, which was perfect for him and the missus, he said with satisfaction.

Mr. Montagu had caught exactly no fish, so between the lack of fish and Max's astonishing breach of protocol, Max expected Mr. Montagu to be in a very sour mood indeed.

But he wasn't. He shook hands vigorously with Admiral Godfrey while saying, "Glad to be of service, Admiral!" and then he called, "Brood! Into the Phantom!" Which meant *Family! Get into the car!*

Admiral Godfrey kissed Mrs. Montagu's hand, and shook both Anthony's and David's hands at the same time, which made Anthony giggle. He said to Uncle Ewen, "See you Monday. And *try* not to get distracted with all these rumors about the Jews. Win the war. That's how you'll help them."

Uncle Ewen's long face reddened as he replied, "Yes sir."

Finally, Admiral Godfrey's rheumy gaze fell on Max, who was standing silently, looking at his feet. "Boy," Admiral Godfrey said. Max raised his eyes. "I appreciate the offer of service. But for now keep your nose clean, lest I clap you in irons and throw you in the Old Bailey."

That meant prison.

"Yes sir," Max replied.

"And watch out for those bowling pins that keep falling from the sky!" Admiral Godfrey called as he climbed into his convertible and slammed the door shut.

And on that cheerful note, the Aston Martin's engine roared to life.

The Montagu family piled into their car—Mr. Montagu driving, Uncle Ewen at the passenger-side window, Mrs. Montagu sitting between them on the wide white-cushioned bench seat in the front, and the three children in the back.

"How did the meeting go?" Mrs. Montagu asked.

"We don't talk about it," said Uncle Ewen quietly.

"The admiral is a hoot, though, I must say." Mr. Montagu chuckled. "Curses like the sailor he once was, doesn't he? *Bloody* is every third word."

"Stuart!" Mrs. Montagu chided him. "Language!"

Ewen smiled. "You know, I call him Uncle John. Because he's *so kind.*"

Mr. Montagu threw his head back and laughed.

"Whose uncle is he?" Anthony asked.

"Whoever it is, I feel sorry for them," Ewen replied.

Admiral Godfrey pulled his red sports car out from the grassy area by the river onto the single lane road. Seeing no one ahead of him, he shifted quickly from first gear to second to third, accelerating like a race-car driver. The wind blew his thin white hair back. He turned the radio on high. Fiddled with the knob to fight the static. Then he heard:

We don't talk about it.

The admiral is a hoot, though, I must say. Curses like the sailor he once was, doesn't he?

Admiral Godfrey looked at the radio. What program was this? He didn't recognize the actors. In fact, they didn't sound terribly professional.

Bloody *is every third word.*

Stuart! Language!

You know, I call him Uncle John. Because he's so kind.

The blood drained from Admiral John Godfrey's face.

Suddenly, his car was turning hard, skidding across the narrow lane, leaving deep tire trenches in the dirt. Laughter was vibrating through the convertible's dashboard.

Whose uncle is he?

Whoever it is, I feel sorry for them.

The voices on the radio were *very* familiar to Admiral John Godfrey.

When we're in the office, I have *heard him use words other than curses, but they're mostly conjunctions to string the curses together.* More laughter.

The black Rolls-Royce Phantom was driving slowly down the lane toward Admiral Godfrey's speeding Aston Martin. The reception on the radio was getting better.

Godfrey blasted his horn. The Phantom stopped. The admiral slammed on his brakes just as he pulled even with the Phantom's driver's side. Mr. Montagu cranked down his window.

"Admiral?" Ewen asked, leaning over Mrs. and Mr. Montagu. "Everything all right?"

Uncle Ewen's voice echoed tinnily through Admiral Godfrey's radio.

Admiral? Everything all right?

Admiral Godfrey spoke to Uncle Ewen—but he was gazing over Mr. Montagu's shoulder.

At Max.

"Better bring the boy in first thing tomorrow morning," said Admiral Godfrey. "Camp 020, if you please." Then he switched off his radio, threw his car into first gear, and roared away.

The entire family turned and stared at Max.

Max tried his very hardest not to grin.

Flick of the wrist. Cast of the fly. Hooked.

CHAPTER
Twenty

Max stood on the steps of 28 Kensington Court with a sick, twisty feeling in his stomach. It was *very* early in the morning. The sky was still closer to night than day. The air was wet and cold and smelled like *something is about to happen.*

Mr. Ken was bringing around Ewen's car.

Uncle Ewen stood beside Max. He hadn't gone back to his own flat last night. In fact, Max wasn't sure Uncle Ewen had slept at all. Max had the feeling that he'd spent the whole night sitting in a wingback chair in the living room, angled so he could see straight up the stairs to Max's bedroom door. As if Max were under surveillance.

Also, Uncle Ewen had taken away Max's radios.

He had not said a word to Max since yesterday afternoon. Not *Good night.* Not *Good morning.* His face was buttoned up tight as his eyes scanned the wet, empty street.

"Excuse me, Uncle Ewen."

No reply.

"May I ask a question?"

Still no reply.

"What is *Camp Oh-too-oh?*"

As Mr. Ken pulled Ewen's blue Lagonda sports car up by the curb, Uncle Ewen's thin lips finally opened.

"Camp 020. It's a British Intelligence Service special outpost."

Max's face began, very slowly, to relax into a smile.

"Oh no," said Uncle Ewen, seeing his expression. "It's not a good thing, I'm afraid. It's not a good thing at all."

Mr. Ken climbed out of the Lagonda, and Uncle Ewen briskly descended the steps. Over his shoulder, he said, "Camp 020 is a prison."

After they'd been driving for twenty minutes, London gave way to the leafy suburbs and rolling parkland of Richmond. Ewen's car sped down a straight, narrow road between two lines of ancient trees whose branches met above their heads to form a ceiling of yellow leaves illuminated by the rising sun.

They were silent. Max saw his portable radio behind Uncle Ewen's seat. He wanted to grab it, to turn the dials, summon from the skies the invisible waves beamed from Berlin. Just for comfort. Instead he squeezed his hands in his lap.

Ten minutes more, and they were turning between two tall brick walls into a driveway.

In front of a small white guardhouse, a soldier with a rifle saluted Uncle Ewen before raising the gate.

They drove toward a ramshackle sprawling old building.

"Weird prison," said Stein.

"It looks like a hospital," said Berg. "A spooky, abandoned hospital. There might be banshees."

"True," Stein agreed. "We should be careful."

"Banshees are real?" Max asked.

"Of course."

"Are they dangerous?"

"To us? No. But once they start talking, they just will not shut up."

Ewen brought the car to a stop in front of the building's main entrance. They got out and Max peered up at the looming edifice. There was another soldier with a rifle at the door. His wide steel helmet looked like a plate balanced atop his head. He nodded at Uncle Ewen without taking his eyes off Max.

Uncle Ewen said, "Morning. Here for Tin Eye, if you don't mind."

"He's been waiting," the soldier said, eyes still locked on Max. He picked up a bulky telephone receiver. "Colonel Roberts's *guest* is here."

"I do *not* like the way he said *guest*, Max," Stein muttered.

"I think we make a run for it," Berg added.

"Are you kidding? They'd shoot him in the back!" Stein objected.

"Not him! *We* make a run for it. *He's* screwed."

The door swung open.

"Well, *good* morning," said a short man in a military

uniform unlike any Max had seen before. Also, he had one eye made of metal.

Well, it *looked* like it was made of metal. On closer inspection, Max could see that it was a monocle, jammed into the flesh around the man's right eye. The man was peering at Max, his square face jutting out so far his jaw was over the threshold of the old building, though the rest of his boxy body was still inside.

After a moment, he barked: "Right! Come in!"

He spun like a man drilled in military maneuvers and marched into darkness.

Max's chest was quivering.

"Step to," Uncle Ewen said. "Let's *not* keep Colonel Roberts waiting."

The man with the monocle—Colonel Roberts—led Max and Uncle Ewen down a long corridor of thick doors, each with a small window looking into an empty cell.

Max wondered which one would be his.

Max wondered how long it would be his for.

Max wondered if, when the war was over, they'd let his parents come visit him here.

Max wondered not for the first time, if, when the war was over, his parents would still be alive.

At the end of the hall, Colonel Roberts jerked open a door and gestured with his chin for Max to enter.

Two chairs faced a blank wall.

"Cozy," said Berg.

Max stopped in the doorway. His body suddenly wouldn't go any farther. "Are—are you . . . ?" Max stammered.

Colonel Roberts said, "I'm just going to ask you some questions, boy."

For some reason, the way he said it sounded even worse than if he'd said, *I'm going to beat you to death.*

Max's eyes found Uncle Ewen.

Uncle Ewen's expression gave him no comfort. His eyes were half-closed. "Over there, Max," he said, gesturing at the empty middle of the room.

"But what have I done?" Max pleaded. "I'm sorry I fiddled with Admiral Godfrey's radio!"

"Right here, boy," Colonel Roberts said, pointing at a spot on the floor between the two chairs and the wall.

Max forced his body to move over the threshold.

Uncle Ewen took one of the chairs. Colonel Roberts—Tin Eye—remained standing behind the other. He was so short that he was only slightly taller than Uncle Ewen was when seated.

Max examined Colonel Roberts's uniform most closely. It was dust brown, and had a half collar. Perhaps Colonel Roberts had been in the British Army in India. Max wondered if the British had different rules for what an officer could do to a prisoner there.

Colonel Roberts stretched his neck, rolling his head around.

"That's what they do before they beat the kreplach *out of you,"* Stein whispered.

"Uncle Ewen is here," Berg whispered back, even though there was no reason for them to whisper. *"He wouldn't let this man do that to Max."* And then, after a pause, he added, *"Would he?"*

They looked at Uncle Ewen's half-closed eyelids. Finally, Stein concluded, *"Unclear."*

"Now," said Tin Eye. He smacked a folder he was gripping in his left hand. "In this dossier I have your entire life history. I'd like to go over it with you, *if* you don't mind."

Max shook his head.

"What? Speak up!" Tin Eye barked, and Berg almost fell off Max's shoulder. Colonel Roberts shot words like bullets: "Don't shake your head like a weathervane in a typhoon! Speak!"

"I don't mind," Max said, glancing at Ewen.

"*Good.* Now," said Tin Eye, "this shouldn't take long. No more than two days."

Despite everything, Max half grinned.

"Why on *earth* are you smiling?" said Roberts, peering through his monocle at Max.

Max erased the smile. "Sorry," he said hastily. "I thought you were making a joke."

"I don't make jokes."

"You're going to ask me questions for *two days?*"

Tin Eye jutted his chin out again. "Longer if we have a bloody *conversation* every time I say something."

Max shut his mouth. He looked to Uncle Ewen for help. Or sympathy. Or *something*.

He got nothing. It was like Ewen didn't know Max at all.

"Right," said Tin Eye. "*Shall* we get started?"

CHAPTER
Twenty-One

Tin Eye had taken up a position behind Max, which made the hairs on Max's neck stand up. Max tried to look over his shoulder so he could see the short colonel with the huge jaw and the shining monocle, but whenever he did, Tin Eye barked, "Face forward, *if* you please!" And then Tin Eye would move just enough that Max still couldn't see him.

"Don't worry," Stein whispered. *"We'll keep an eye on him for you."*

"First report," announced Berg. "He looks like his mother was a bulldog and his father was a tree stump."

"Where were you born, Max?" said Colonel Roberts.

Max had the sudden fear that all of his memories—all his most private, personal memories—were going to be dragged out and examined. In that very moment, in the interrogation room at Camp 020, Max realized that since coming to England he had barely told anyone *anything* about his family.

Why was that? Why had he not told even Ivor about them? Why did he never reminisce about his parents aloud at the dinner table? Or at least at the tennis table?

Was it because he thought that he could, by not talking about them, *protect* them?

Or, maybe, protect the memory of how they were before he was sent away?

"Max!" Colonel Roberts blurted. "If *this* question is too hard for you, I'm afraid we're going to be here a *very* long time."

"Berlin." Max sighed. "I was born and raised in Berlin."

"*Thank* you. Year?"

"It was 1928."

"Which makes you how old?"

"Twelve."

"What name were you given at your birth?"

"Max Abraham Bretzfeld."

Uncle Ewen focused his gaze behind Max's head, reacting to something Tin Eye had done. Max tried to swivel to see what it was, but Tin Eye took a step to his right and remained firmly in Max's blind spot.

Tin Eye went on: "How many domiciles did you inhabit during your time in Berlin, *Max Abraham Bretzfeld*?" He pronounced the name like it disgusted him.

Max furrowed his brow. "Sorry?"

"Domiciles! Homes! How many homes did you live in between your birth and the time you came to England?"

"Just one, sir."

"Sir? I like that. Keep it up. Tell me about this one domicile, *Max Abraham Bretzfeld*."

Sweat was collecting all over Max's body. He had never been so stressed by such simple questions. He didn't know how Colonel Roberts was doing it.

"It was an apartment above my father's watch repair shop. It was in Kreuzberg. That's a neighborhood of Berlin."

"Were you the only one who lived in the building?"

"No. There were a handful of families. Directly above us was a Lutheran minister."

"Tell me about the Lutheran minister."

"Pastor Andreas Maas. Old, but not *very* old."

"Unlike *you*, you rotting tree stump!" Stein said to Tin Eye. Tin Eye, of course, did not hear him.

"Be precise, boy! How *old but not very old* was this Lutheran minister?"

"I don't know. In his forties, I think."

"And your parents. How old were they?"

Something about that question made Max's insides seize up. For a moment he was speechless.

"How old were your parents, Max?" Tin Eye asked again, iron creeping into his voice.

"I was just calculating," Max replied sullenly. "My father *is* forty-eight now. My mother *is* thirty-nine."

"I see," said Colonel Roberts. "Tell me about your father's work."

"He's a watchmaker. But mostly he fixes old watches. He

would like to make his own, but it is expensive and people like to buy their watches from the nicer shops in Leipziger Platz."

"And your mother did not work, I take it?"

"She took in people's mending."

"So they didn't earn a *lot* of money, then?"

"No."

Colonel Roberts said, "Tell me about school. Good at it?"

This was another painful subject. "I . . . I used to be," Max murmured.

"Used to be? What happened? Subjects got too difficult for you once they got beyond two plus two?"

Max had the sudden urge to turn around and kick Colonel Roberts between the legs.

"Do it," Stein whispered, guessing his thoughts.

"School got too stupid for me," Max said. "Our teacher turned cruel, and they replaced our regular schoolbooks with textbooks written by the Nazis."

Suddenly, Colonel Roberts's face appeared in Max's peripheral vision. Uncle Ewen raised his head slightly, too. "Did they?" Tin Eye asked. "Tell me about these new Nazi textbooks."

Max cast his mind back to some of the new "facts" from these books. "They say that Jews lost the War for Germany."

"You mean the Great War," Colonel Roberts clarified.

"We don't call it that in Germany, but yes. The textbooks

say that Jews stabbed Germany in the back during the War, and that's why Germany lost."

"Nonsense," said Tin Eye. "They lost because we English pounded their ugly faces into the mud of France."

"They lost," Uncle Ewen piped up, speaking for the first time, "because they ran out of ammunition."

"Nonsense!" Tin Eye exclaimed again. "It was jolly old England! Anyway, they told you the Jews stabbed Germany in the back. Yes, I've heard that one. That's a rather Jewish thing to do, but in this case it isn't what happened. Go on."

"What? What did he say?" Stein cried.

"Well, that was remarkably rude!" said Berg.

Max looked at Uncle Ewen, certain that he would not stand for that sort of anti-Jewish abuse. But to Max's disbelief, Uncle Ewen was gazing, apparently half-asleep, into his lap.

Max studied Tin Eye's squat face, which was hovering over his left shoulder. Stein was having to duck to avoid inhabiting the same physical space as Tin Eye's chin, which would have been metaphysically awkward.

So Tin Eye hated Jews, too?

Why?

Why do they all hate us? Max wondered.

"I said *go on!*" Colonel Roberts shouted.

Max went on: "Professor Goldenschaft told us that we were racially inferior. That the Germans were the greatest of all the races, that the Russians were awful, and that Jews were the worst."

"And what about the English, where did he put us?" Tin Eye wanted to know.

"He thought you were almost as good as the Germans."

"A damn sight better, I'll have you know. Germans are the scum of the earth. Even worse than Russians and Jews. And the French! Being worse than the French is *really* an accomplishment, mind you."

Uncle Ewen had looked up and was, at last, staring with mild disbelief at Colonel Roberts.

Max had heard many of these opinions expressed over the year he'd been in England—most often among the boys at St. West's, though occasionally from grown-ups. But never all at once, never quite like this.

Through gritted teeth, Max said, "You sound just like the Nazis, you know."

Colonel Roberts straightened like he'd been slapped.

Max continued bravely, "If you believe these things, why are you on *this* side, and not on theirs?"

Tin Eye slowly came around in front of Max. He brought his nose so close to Max's that Max was breathing in the air that Colonel Roberts was breathing out.

"Say. That. Again."

"Don't say it again," whispered Berg.

"No. *Shout* it," Stein said.

Max stared at the colonel with the glittering monocle. And then . . . he looked down.

"That's what I *expected*," Tin Eye gloated, grinning. "Quailed under pressure. Just like a Jew. No offense, Montagu," he added hastily.

"Of course not," Ewen muttered. Max looked up. Uncle Ewen caught his eye, just for a moment, for the first time.

Courage surged through Max.

He used that courage to remain silent.

"I am on *this* side, *Max Abraham Bretzfeld*," Colonel Roberts said, and this time the disgust at the Jewish-sounding name was completely unconcealed, "because I am a born-and-bred Englishman. Englishmen conquered the globe, from Hong Kong to Boston. We have subdued every race under the sun. The French. The Zulu. The Malay. The Red Indian. The Brown Indian. I fight for England—not Britain, mind you," he interrupted himself. "The Scots and Welsh can go hang. And the exchange rate between the Irish and the Jews is just about one to one. No, I fight for *England* because we are the greatest race on earth. And we will *not* be overcome by a bunch of scheming, filthy Germans."

Max thought that Tin Eye and Professor Goldenschaft might have been friends if they weren't on opposite sides of the war.

Suddenly, the monocle was flashing directly in Max's eyes.

He couldn't see. But he could feel the heat of Tin Eye's red skin, inches from his face. His breath smelled like cigarettes and tea.

"So tell me," Colonel Roberts said, "what made you decide to work for the Nazis?"

Max's knees weakened, and he desperately tried to steady himself.

"What did he say?" Berg cried.

"SAY THAT AGAIN!" Stein demanded. "I dare you, you short, ugly bigot! You might look like a stump, but you're only half as smart! And half as tall!"

Max glanced wildly at Uncle Ewen. Ewen appeared to be actually sleeping now.

Colonel Roberts said, "Your dear 'uncle' there can't help you, Max. So tell me. What on *earth* could inspire a Jew like you to work for the Nazis?"

Max was speechless.

"Or could it be," Tin Eye went on, "that you are *not* a Jew at all? That this is a cover identity, as we call it in spycraft?"

All Max could manage to say was "I *am* Jewish, and I am *not* working for the Nazis."

"Very good," Colonel Roberts said, though he didn't sound like he believed Max at all. "Let's move on."

"Max," Berg announced, "it appears that this stupid man thinks that you are a Nazi spy. This is bad. Do you know what they do to Nazi spies?"

"Tell him," said Stein. "That'll raise his morale."

"They hang them. Or shoot them. Or maybe both."

Max swore to himself he would stay four steps ahead of Colonel Roberts, just as he always did with bullies. Until Tin Eye said, "Let's talk more about your parents."

Then Max's legs buckled, and he nearly fell down.

CHAPTER
Twenty-Two

"So," Tin Eye began, glancing at a file folder that he had pulled out of an attaché case, "your father was Jacob David Bretzfeld, and your mother was Miriam Wohl Bretzfeld, and they lived at 182 Oranienstrasse, in—"

"Excuse me," Max interrupted.

Colonel Roberts looked up from his file very slowly and uttered a glacial *"Yes?"*

Max said, "It's Jacob *Daniel* Bretzfeld. Not David."

"My apologies," said Tin Eye. "I must have misread the file."

"No, you didn't," said Max, and Uncle Ewen and Tin Eye both appeared surprised by the force of Max's contradiction. "You're trying to rattle me. It's also why you're talking about my parents in the past tense, when we both know they're alive."

Tin Eye said, "Do we? How do we know that, Max?"

"I . . ." Max said, and his voice faltered.

"Have you *heard* from them, since you arrived in England?"

Max shook his head.

"Have your Nazi masters given you some *assurances* that your parents are still alive, then?"

"No. I don't have Nazi masters."

"Of course. I'm sorry, I forgot. Do you have siblings?"

"No."

"So your parents sent away their *only child*, to a foreign country, and they never even write to you?"

Max's heart felt like it was crumbling inside his chest.

"Now, Max, can you explain why on *earth* they would *do* that? An explanation other than the obvious one: which is that they *didn't*, and that you are, in fact, a Nazi spy?"

Max took a deep breath. Uncle Ewen was watching Max carefully now.

Max's mind traveled back to lines at the visa offices. To his parents reading and rereading the paper aloud every time a new anti-Jewish law was announced. But if he had to give *one* reason that his parents sent him away, if he was being really honest, it was:

"November 9, 1938."

Tin Eye looked confused. He turned to Uncle Ewen. Ewen murmured, *"Kristallnacht."*

"Yes," said Max. "The night of the broken glass."

Tin Eye said, "And why would a single night in November cause parents to abandon their child to the seas and a foreign nation?"

Max often wondered the same thing. And the wondering hurt him as if the broken glass was inside his chest.

"Max?"

"I had been sleeping," said Max, "when I heard shouting outside."

Tin Eye and Uncle Ewen both watched Max carefully.

"Then there was the sound of screaming. I ran to my window, threw open the shutters. A rabbi who lived near us, Rabbi Kolski, was being dragged through the streets by his *payot*. Those are the curls that fall down over your ears—Orthodox Jews wear them, my family doesn't. But Rabbi Kolski is from Poland, and he's very religious. So these Nazis in their uniforms were dragging him. It looked like it hurt *so* much. He was screaming and trying to get away. Rabbi Kolski's hat and yarmulke had fallen off. I ran out of my room. My father was trying to get down into the street to help, but my mother didn't let him go.

"Then one of the Nazis gestured at our storefront. He shouted, 'This store is owned by Jews!'

"My mother couldn't hold my father back any longer. He broke free and was out of the apartment and running down the stairs.

"The Nazis were looking for something to use to smash up our shop. Then they remembered Rabbi Kolski. They picked him up by his wrists and his ankles. They counted, '*Ein, zwei, drei!*' Like they were having fun. And they threw him through our window.

"Just then, my father arrived out front and started shouting. But they just laughed and grabbed my father and . . ."

Max stopped. Tin Eye looked uncomfortable. Uncle Ewen was riveted.

"They started punching him in the stomach. He's not a big man, my father, and not very strong.

"I tried to run downstairs to help him, as my mother screamed from the window for them to stop. But when I got to the doorway of our apartment building, Pastor Andreas was standing there.

"Pastor Andreas told me I couldn't go outside. I guess he had been watching from the window above ours.

"'I'll call for help!' my mother said. And she ran to the phone and asked the operator for the police."

Max spoke very slowly and very quietly now:

"I will never forget that phone call. Never in my whole life. When the police came on the line, my mother said, 'We're being attacked!' The police asked what her name was.

"She told them . . . and then I heard laughter. The policemen were laughing.

"Then they hung up."

After taking a few breaths, Max said, "Can you imagine living in a country where you're being attacked and the police just . . . *laugh*?"

Tin Eye looked at the floor.

"By the time I got back to the window, my father was gone. He was gone for three days. We did not sleep that whole time.

My mother and I curled up together in my parents' bed and at every sound in the night we ran to the door, praying that it was my father.

"He came back around breakfast time on the third day, and we cried with relief, but also with fear.

"His head was shaved and he had bruises all over his body. We asked him where he had been, what they had done to him, but all he said was 'Sachsenhausen. A camp.' And he refused to tell us any more."

Ewen took a small notebook out of his pocket and wrote something down. Max went on.

"Wooden boards were put over our shop's windows, and the word *Jude* was painted on them in bright red letters. Suddenly, we were making almost no money. A few friends would come by and quietly ask my father to fix their watches. Sometimes even when there was nothing wrong with them. They felt bad for him. Pity is awful. We all felt so ashamed. Ashamed for something *we* hadn't even done. We felt shame for something that had been done to us.

"A few months later Pastor Andreas came downstairs and told us about a group that was getting Jewish children out of Germany. Not the adults. The Nazis wanted the adults to leave, but nobody would take them. Not England, not the United States." Max looked from Tin Eye to Uncle Ewen accusingly. Ewen's eyelids had become heavy again, and he was rubbing the bridge of his thin nose. Tin Eye, on the other hand, looked unapologetic.

"England was accepting a few children. So it had to be me, alone." Max paused. He felt like his insides had turned to ashes. "I didn't want to leave my parents. But here I am."

CHAPTER
Twenty-Three

Uncle Ewen and Colonel Roberts were both gazing very intently at Max.

Colonel Roberts sighed heavily. He bit his fat lower lip and watched Max through his monocle. Finally, he said, "Max, I owe you an apology."

"You're darn right!" Stein shouted.

Colonel Roberts's voice was a low growl. "I can't even imagine what a difficult situation this is for you. And here I was, making it worse, saying terrible things about you, and about the Jewish people—most of which I don't even believe."

"MOST of which?" Stein cried.

Colonel Roberts put a thick, calloused hand on Max's arm.

"I cannot *fathom* how you're managing. Your parents held hostage by the Nazis, and you forced to spy for Hitler and his lunatics in exchange for keeping your parents safe. No need to deny it!" Colonel Roberts said quickly, to stop Max from objecting. "We know it's true. We have all the evidence. And we respect what you're doing. We want to *help* you, Max. And we think maybe *you* can help *us*, too. Come clean with us right now

and we can help you keep your parents safe. So tell me. Where
are they? And who is your case officer? Who is the man—or
woman—in Germany who's telling you what to do?"

A huge weight sat on Max's chest. It made it hard to
breathe. It made it almost impossible to speak. Colonel Roberts and Uncle Ewen were both leaning forward now. Ready for
Max's answer.

At last, Max said, "You're right."

Uncle Ewen sat back hard in his chair. Tin Eye did not move.

"It's *terrible*. I don't know *where* my parents are. I write to
them and write to them and they don't write back."

Colonel Roberts nodded as if Max's pain were his pain, too.

"And you're right: I absolutely *would* be spying for the
Nazis, if it would protect my parents."

Tin Eye frowned.

"I hate the Nazis more than you do, Colonel Roberts. Trust
me. But I would absolutely spy for them if it meant my parents
would be safe. Between what is right and my parents, I choose
my parents."

Colonel Roberts's gaze looked like it could burn a hole in
Max's face.

Max said, "I wish the Nazis had offered to let me spy for
them. But they didn't. They hate me even more than I hate
them. Even though I never broke *their* windows or stole *their*
father. I *wish* the Nazis had offered me that deal, Colonel

Roberts. I would have taken it. Maybe then I would be able to protect my mama and papa."

Max looked at Uncle Ewen. "Also, if I were actually spying for the Nazis, maybe it wouldn't hurt so much that my 'uncle' brought me to a prison to let a horrible Jew-hater like you interrogate me."

Max expected Uncle Ewen to look at the floor in shame.

But he didn't.

Instead, Ewen Montagu slowly turned his gaze away from Max, shifting all his attention to Colonel Roberts.

Tin Eye seemed to be chewing something. Literally, his jaws were working like he was chewing. And he was still boring a hole into Max's face with his eyes.

This went on for what felt like an hour, but was probably three full minutes.

At last, Uncle Ewen demanded, "Well?"

Tin Eye appeared to swallow whatever he was chewing on. It seemed very sour indeed. "Secure," he snapped.

"About time!" Uncle Ewen shouted, standing up. "And?"

Tin Eye snorted like he was in pain. "Secure *and* cleared."

"Righto!" Ewen shouted. "Come on, Max!" He reached out to the boy.

Max was completely lost. "What's happening now?"

Uncle Ewen gave him that crooked smile—for the first time since Max had walked into the river yesterday—and it felt like

the hot sun breaking through the clouds on a cold gray morning. "Surely, Max, you can figure *that* out, with that great big
brain of yours?"

"I can honestly say, Uncle Ewen, that I have no idea."

"Why, Max! You're *not* a spy!"

"I know!" said Max.

"Well, let's see if we can't change that, shall we?"

And a sound escaped Max that was halfway between a laugh
and a sob.

CHAPTER
Twenty-Four

The next week passed in a blur of trunks and valises, servants rushing through the halls and the shuttering (and shuddering) of the house as bombs crashed down upon London.

Everyone was leaving. St. West's school had closed their campus and opened a new site out in the country, far away from London. The Montagu family had managed to find a large home not far from the new school location, and they would be moving there for as long as the Germans had bombs left to drop. Max was packing up his things, too.

But he wasn't going with the Montagus.

"I just want to be clear," Berg said, crouching on Max's right shoulder, his tiny elbows on his tiny knees. "They are going to make *you* a *spy*, Max? This is the plan?"

"It seems to be the plan," Max replied as he checked the inventory of his portable wireless set. They weren't letting him take it with him to wherever he was going, and he didn't know whether he'd ever see it again, here at Kensington Court or anywhere else. But amid all this uncertainty, it made him feel a little better to know that at least when it came to his radios, everything was where it should be.

"I'm *sorry* to be a stick in the mud," Berg said, "but isn't being a spy *dangerous*? You are a *child*! Don't they have labor laws in this country?"

"Hopefully I won't *be* in this country. Hopefully I'll be in Germany. As an undercover agent."

"Maxy, that is not going to happen," said Stein. "The British might be lunatics, they might be willing to train you as some kind of spy, but they're not sending a Jewish child to Nazi Germany."

Max merely said, "We'll see."

Everything that week was a blur, except for one moment.

Uncle Ivor had thrown open the front door of 28 Kensington Court, causing the house to shake and the servants to cover their heads and Max to take two steps toward the basement to shelter from falling bombs—before hearing, "Who wants to lose at table tennis?" Which made him sprint for the foyer.

When Uncle Ivor had caught sight of Max, he grinned and spread his arms wide. And even though the English did not hug, Max ran straight into Ivor's arms. And while Ivor might have been surprised, and certainly let out an "Oof!" as Max made contact, he wrapped the boy in an embrace and patted his back.

"There, there, Max. I know," he murmured. "I know how

afraid you are that I am not going to let you score a *single* point. But fear not. I'll let you score . . . *one*."

Max, his face smushed into Ivor's black felt coat, said, "It's not that, Uncle Ivor. I'm just thinking of you in hospital, after you throw out your back trying to return my serve. That's all. I'm just thinking of you."

Uncle Ivor squeezed Max a little tighter. Then they separated, both grinning, and headed downstairs to play.

After polishing his circular glasses on his shirt—a shirt that probably had been white once, but was now yellow with age and ancient sweat stains—Uncle Ivor tossed a ball into the air and served directly at Max's head. Max ducked.

"Max! Courage! If you're going to be risking your life for Britain, you've got to be braver than that!" Ivor chided him.

"Am I going to be risking my life?" Max asked as he ran to collect the ball from the tile floor.

"I dunno," said Uncle Ivor. "Aren't you? Aren't you going to work with your uncle Ewen? A seven-year-old British intelligence agent?"

"I'm twelve and you know it!" Max objected, serving the ball to Uncle Ivor, who smashed it mercilessly back at Max's face. Max squealed and ducked again, laughing and diving for the ball as it bounced away from the table.

"Okay, I'll take it easy on you—as long as you give me some information. *What* is going on?" Uncle Ivor said. "I'm serious.

I don't know what happened to you. Apparently there was an outing to the river, I *wasn't* invited, and the next thing I know you're joining His Majesty's Secret Intelligence Service! What did I miss? Everything?"

"You weren't invited," Max said, serving the ball again, which Ivor lobbed back, "because you're a communist and Admiral Godfrey doesn't trust you. Uncle Ewen said so."

"*Admiral Godfrey* went *fishing* with the family?" Ivor exclaimed. "Am I being replaced?"

Max laughed and pushed the ball back over the net, using his elbow and no wrist, exactly as Ivor always told him *not* to do.

"And they didn't want *me* there because I believe all people should be equal?" Uncle Ivor complained. "That's decidedly unfair!"

"You don't like fishing!"

"No, of course not! It's a cruel sport! But I do like the river! And *we* might have had some fun."

Max smiled and completely whiffed on the ball.

"That was pathetic!" Ivor informed Max.

"He's right," Stein added.

Max laughed and collected the ball again.

"So I still don't understand," Uncle Ivor said. "You go fishing with Admiral Godfrey and now you're going to be a *spy*?"

So Max told Ivor about his trick with the car radios. Uncle Ivor had to stop playing and put his hands on his knees when

Max got to the part where their conversation was broadcast to Admiral Godfrey's radio, because Ivor was laughing so hard.

"I swear, boy, I don't know what they have in mind for you, but I am sure you're the right man for the job."

Which made Max feel like a thousand-watt light bulb.

"Will you be able to stay in touch?" Ivor asked as they started the rally again.

"I don't know."

"Do try." Uncle Ivor caught the ball in one hand and wiped his round, shining face with a sleeve. "I don't want to lose track of you, Max. Listen—and I'm only half joking when I say this, so *do* listen—these capitalists will exploit anyone and anything they get their hands on. It's not their fault. Ewen is a lovely man—you know I adore him. By far my favorite brother."

Max grinned. He knew that. Everyone did.

"But Ewen is a slave to the stories he tells himself. I suppose everyone is, really."

Max said, "Huh?"

Ivor tossed his paddle onto the table and plopped down on the rug, cross-legged. "Come here, Max," he said. Max sat next to his uncle Ivor. "You've got to understand the British if you're going to work for them. Okay?"

"Okay."

"We Brits tell ourselves stories like 'We are bringing Christian brotherhood to the world' while we enslave other human beings. We tell ourselves stories like 'We are bringing the masses freedom!'—and that *always and only* means 'freedom to make money'—while we get an entire continent addicted to opium. You know we Brits did that. In China. One of the worst crimes in history, if you ask me. Though no one *is* asking me."

Max asked, "Worst in history? Worse than the Nazis?"

"How do you compare crimes like that? I would hazard the Nazis are the worst, if you pressed me. The stories they tell are even more evil than British ones. Most of the time. But here's another thing we British do." Uncle Ivor pointed a soft, chubby finger and touched the middle of Max's chest with it. "We find a *resource* and *exploit* it. Coal, trees, opium, silver, human beings. We wring it dry, till it's all used up. Or dead." Uncle Ivor leveled his eyes through his moon glasses, and Max could smell his cigarette breath. Ivor touched the center of Max's chest with his forefinger again. "In this case, Max, *you* are the resource. Do you understand me?"

Max's body had become very tight. He sat beside Ivor on the floor of the basement of 28 Kensington Court, London. Thinking. About Uncle Ewen. And Admiral Godfrey. And Tin Eye Roberts.

"So *do* try to keep in touch," Ivor added as he stood up to resume their game. "Write to me. Tell me where you are, and what you're doing. Ewen and the other spies may not *want* you to, so you may have to mail letters secretly, or hide the important details amongst a lot of guff. But do let me know what they're doing with you. If it's somehow not *right*, I'll let Uncle Ewen know."

Max studied Uncle Ivor. His round cheeks, his round glasses, the round curls of his dark hair, his round red lips. A hundred thoughts drifted through Max's mind. About the stories we tell ourselves. And each other.

Another word for *stories*, Max thought, is *lies*.

CHAPTER
Twenty-Five

Ewen steered through the traffic in front of Kensington Palace and then took a left toward the northern suburbs of London.

"Where are we going?" Max asked. He was experiencing a jumble of emotions: sadness at leaving the Montagus, nervous anticipation about whatever Ewen was planning, an urgent hope that it would involve going back to Berlin, and a buried—but constant—terror for his parents. Though the terror was barely buried. It threatened to burst through and pour out of Max's eyes and down his cheeks at every moment.

Ewen kept his eyes on the road. "Where do you *want* to be going?"

Max caught his lower lip in his teeth. This seemed like a test. Like he was supposed to say *Wherever I can be of most service to the war effort*, or some other rubbish. But his brain was screaming the truth, and eventually Max gave in and let his mouth say "Berlin."

The kobold on Max's right shoulder and the dybbuk on his left shook their warty heads.

"Max," said Stein, "somehow I've become attached to you.

And not just in the metaphysical sense." He dropped his voice. "I kinda *like* you."

"Stein!" cried Berg.

"I know!" Stein cried back. "It's very wrong. What would the Boss say?"

"Who knows? I have not heard the Boss's voice since the Beginning. Have you?"

"No. It's very disconcerting. *Anyway*, Max, I've gotten to the completely unfamiliar state of affairs where I actively want bad things *not* to happen to you. And a Jewish *child* going back to Nazi Germany as a *spy* is a *great* way for every bad thing ever invented to happen to you in a very short period of time."

"I know," said Max. "But my parents are there."

To which Stein had no reply.

Ewen hadn't heard any of this. He was smiling ruefully. "We are *not* going to Germany," he said.

Something inside Max trembled. Like the structure that held up his emotional life was on the verge of crumbling. He stared at his knees and tried to keep himself from falling apart.

Then Ewen added, "Not now, anyway."

Stein and Berg both shouted, *"What?!"* and Max nearly jumped out of his seat.

Ewen saw Max's reaction. "Steady on. First, training. How well you do in training will determine what happens after."

Max tried to keep his voice even. "Meaning, if I'm good at training, I'll go to Germany?"

For a moment, Ewen didn't answer.

"Say no," said Stein.

"Say no," said Berg.

Ewen said, "No."

The immortal creatures sighed with relief.

Then Ewen said, "To go to Germany, you'll have to be *extraordinary.*"

Berg and Stein groaned.

Ewen went on. "We have precious few men in Germany. It's too dangerous. Too difficult. Practically every German is a Nazi informant. To be a British agent and survive for long is almost impossible. If we're to convince Admiral Godfrey to send you, not even a teenager yet . . . well, you'll have to be the best we've ever had."

Max silently swore to himself, to his mother, to his father, to God above, and the weird creatures on his shoulders, that he would be.

After another hour of driving, they were in a woodsy area of tall pines and narrow lanes. "So where *is* this training?" Max asked.

"Nearly there," Ewen replied. "It's at a place called Tring Park. The manor of the Rothschild family."

Max said, "What? Really?"

The Rothschilds were probably the richest family in the whole world. Richer even than the king of England, it was rumored. They were also Jewish. The Rothschilds were so rich and so famous that Max had even known about them growing up in Berlin. In fact, every time the Nazis talked about English bankers and rich Jews controlling Germany, they usually mentioned the Rothschilds by name. Max didn't think there really *was* an "international Jewish conspiracy," despite what Hitler and Goebbels insisted, but if there really was, the Rothschilds would be in charge of it.

And Max was going to train at their *house?*

Uncle Ewen said: "The Rothschild family has moved out, and the Mansion at Tring is being used by the Rothschild Bank for storage and other things. But there are some cottages in the park around the Mansion, that the Rothschilds have been kind enough to lend to us. You'll be staying in one of those."

So he *wouldn't* be staying at their house, just on their grounds. Okay, Max found that slightly less intimidating. "Will you be staying at Tring Park, too?" he asked.

"Yes. We've got a little team assembled for you, Max. We'll live in the cottages here. Your Mother will be just next door to you."

There was a sudden silence in the little blue sports car.

Very slowly, Max turned in his seat, until his whole body was looking at Uncle Ewen.

"What did you say?" Max asked.

"What? Your Mother will be staying in a cottage, not commuting back and—"

Max was staring at Ewen, uncomprehending.

"Oh!" Ewen cried, realizing his mistake. "Your Mother! Not really your mother, Max! Dreadfully sorry! 'Mother' is lingo. You'll have a woman looking after you. *Not* your mother, in any way."

Max sank back into his seat and waited until his heart stopped trying to beat its way out of his rib cage.

Ewen was still talking about Max's "Mother." "She's a young woman—nineteen or twenty, I think. But she's sharp as a whip, athletic, and she'll keep you on your toes." Ewen glanced quickly at Max, whose head was pressed back against the seat like he'd just been hit in the face with a telephone pole. "Anyway . . ." Ewen trailed off awkwardly.

A few minutes later, Max said, "Uncle Ewen."

"Yes?"

"I will be *extraordinary* in training. The best you've ever seen. I promise you."

Ewen glanced out the corner of his eye at Max.

His only reply was: "Look. Here we are."

CHAPTER
Twenty-Six

Uncle Ewen piloted the car off the narrow road and up to a small white-painted guard station with a lowered gate. An officer of the Military Police—you could tell because he wore a red beret—stepped out toward the car, and Ewen cranked down the window.

"Morning!" Uncle Ewen said. "Lieutenant Commander Ewen Montagu, Naval Intelligence."

"One moment, sir," the man said. He had a rich bass voice, beautiful deep brown skin, a thick black mustache, and an accent that Max could not place. In the small guard station, on a white wooden pedestal, sat a large book, which the military policeman walked to. He ran his finger down the page, and then came back out. "Welcome to Tring Park, sir. I'm Sergeant Toby Thompson, Head of Security."

"Nice to meet you, Sergeant! And *this* is Max Bretzfeld."

"Yessir. I saw him in the book. Welcome, young man!"

Sergeant Thompson opened the gate and waved them through.

As they pulled away from the guardhouse, Ewen said,

"Always make friends with security. You never know when Sergeant Toby Thompson might get you out of a jam."

"Yes, Uncle Ewen," said Max.

"And we'd better change that to 'Lieutenant Commander' now, I'm afraid."

"Yes, Lieutenant Commander," Max replied dutifully.

The winding dirt and pebble drive led into the middle of a number of squat brick houses, pleasantly matching, with white windowsills and steeply slanting slate roofs. Uncle Ewen stopped the car in front of a cottage marked *3* and pulled up on the parking brake.

"I think Jean should be waiting inside for us," said Uncle Ewen.

"Jean, Lieutenant Commander?" Max asked.

"Jean Leslie is your Mother."

Max swallowed. That term was going to be *very* hard to get used to.

Max's Mother wasn't inside waiting for them.

She'd burst out of the front door of cottage number 3 and was now waving a hand above her head in an exaggerated gesture.

Jean Leslie was tall and athletic, with brown hair that fell in waves to her shoulders, deep dimples, and the most frank and friendly smile that Max had ever seen. Also, her teeth were very yellow and fairly crooked.

Ewen and Max climbed out of the car, and Jean walked

straight up to Max and stuck out her hand. Her elbow bent just beyond a hundred and eighty degrees, which was somehow incomprehensibly charming. She was wearing a pale blue shirt, rolled up above the elbows, and olive trousers that looked like they would be suitable for both the office *and* a hike, and sensible shoes that you could walk in for days. Max shook her hand.

"Jean Leslie," she said.

"Max Bretzfeld," said Max. Something about the way Jean held herself made Max want to do what she did, exactly as she did it.

"She's very pretty," said Stein, nudging Max's ear.

"Except for her teeth," said Berg. "Those look like they were rearranged by a blind dentist."

Max snapped at them, "That's enough."

Stein and Berg were caught off guard. Berg crowed, "Maybe the boy is in love with her!"

But it wasn't love.

It was *recognition*.

Max recognized instantly that Jean was strong, clever, and confident enough to be kind.

Also, she was nineteen, and to a twelve-year-old, nineteen-year-olds are just inexplicably *cool*.

"I'm thrilled to have this assignment, Max," Jean told him. "Lieutenant Commander Montagu has told me a lot about you. Shall we go in and get you settled?"

Jean led Max and Ewen inside cottage number 3. They

entered a simple living area with a fireplace and a small writing desk in one corner. There was also a small kitchen.

"This is where you'll be lodging," Jean said, pointing out the various amenities—the icebox, the stove, the teapot, the wood stacked next to the fireplace.

"I'm staying here . . . *alone?*" said Max.

Jean turned and gave him an inquisitive smile. "Is that all right?"

"Oh! Yes! I just . . . I've never lived on my own before." And then, stupidly, Max said, "I can't quite believe it."

Stein shouted, "*That's* the part you can't believe? How about the fact that they're trying to train a *child* as a *spy* to be sent to his *death* in *Nazi Germany?*"

"Yah," said Berg, "but he has his *own kitchen.*"

"Oh, true. Right. Excuse me for missing the big picture here."

Jean continued the tour. "This is where you'll have breakfast. You'll make your own each morning. There's eggs and milk and butter in the icebox. All right, Max?"

Max nodded sharply, just as he'd seen Jean do.

Jean turned her head toward him. "All right, Max?" she repeated.

"Yes, uh, sir?" He turned very red very quickly. "No! I mean ma'am! Or, uh . . ." Max silently shouted at himself: *Max, you sound like an idiot!*

Jean said, "You can call me Jean."

"All right," said Max, trying to recover from his blushing fit.

"Good," said Jean. "I want to hear your voice. Make sure we're on the same page. Can you do that for me, Max?"

Stein said, "He would do anything for you, Jean."

Berg snickered.

Max told them to cut it out. Then he realized that Jean was waiting for him to use his voice again. So he said, "I can do that for you."

She said, "Let's head upstairs."

Once Jean had shown Max his bedroom and bathroom, Ewen announced that Jean would give Max a tour of Tring Park while Ewen got in touch with another member of Max's team. Jean led Max outside and he waited while she ducked into cottage number 2, next door.

Max tried to throw back his shoulders and stand in the relaxed, confident way Jean stood. But he felt unnatural and like he was going to give himself a crick in his neck. So he put his hands on his hips. He dropped them. Why was he so nervous?

"Breathe, baby," said Stein. "Just focus on what you're doing here: trying to get sent back to Germany and your imminent death. Thinking about your imminent death should focus your mind."

For once, Max took the dybbuk's advice and thought about his imminent death.

It *did* help a little.

Then Max's thoughts drifted to his parents, in their little

apartment, with the boarded-up shop below, and a thousand laws making their lives impossible, and the concentration camp—Sachsenhausen—waiting like a hungry beast for them to make one wrong move.

And he swore to himself again: *I will be extraordinary.*

CHAPTER
Twenty-Seven

Jean came back with a small khaki rucksack. "For you," she said. "It's got nibbles, in case you're hungry later."

"Aww!" said Stein. "She *is* a mother!" Max shot the dybbuk a dark look and Stein shut his mouth.

Jean led Max down the gravel road past the other brick cottages, with their neat white windowsills and empty flower boxes. "During your training we have the small cottages to ourselves—no one about but our team."

"Small cottages?" Max asked. "Are there large ones, then?"

"Just the one."

The road curved around a small copse of trees and then opened onto a clearing, revealing a beautiful home, made of the same brick as the cottages, with the same slanting slate roof. But this home was three stories high, with two chimneys, a cupola, and large, beautiful mullioned windows. On the upper stories, there was Tudor framing—big wooden beams encased in white plaster.

"Is this the Mansion?" Max asked.

Jean laughed. "No. This is the Large Cottage."

"This is a *cottage* . . . ?" Max murmured.

BOOM.

Suddenly, Max was lying on the ground.

It wasn't the *boom* that had knocked him down. It was Jean. With a quick, two-handed shove she had pushed him over. Now he was curled on his side in the fetal position with Jean crouched over him.

"What in the name of—?" exclaimed Berg.

Smoke was billowing out of one of the ground-floor windows.

Max stared in horror.

Jean leaped to her feet and ran toward the Large Cottage— but before she could reach it, the front door flew open and a man stumbled out. He was covered in soot and coughing violently.

Jean tried to help him, but he held up his hand as he coughed. She waited. Smoke followed the man out the front door, as if it were evacuating the building as well.

The man was no more than thirty, with a thick shock of curly hair that was standing on end, and he wore a suit that had probably been brown tweed a moment ago but would now have to be sold as "charcoal." He straightened, looked up at the sky, took one more deep heave, and exhaled like a truck starting.

Then he wiped some of the soot from his face and said, "Good morning!"

Max got to his feet.

"So sorry," the man said. "That must have given you a frightful scare."

"Probably less of a scare than *you* got, sir," Jean said.

"What? Me? Scared of a little ammonium nitrate? Not at all. Though it did blow a very fine desk of mine to bits. Pity. It was about two hundred years old. They don't make them like that anymore. Though they *do* make desks that are bombproof. Maybe I should invest in one of *those*."

"Sir," Jean said, "may I introduce Max Bretzfeld?"

"Oh! Of course! The boy wonder!" the man enthused, rubbing yet more soot from his eyes so he could appraise Max. "A pleasure to meet you! Welcome to Tring Park!"

"Max," said Jean with a new air of solemnity, "say hello to our expert in explosives, sabotage, and clandestine devices— and also our gracious host, Lord Rothschild."

And that was how Max met the richest man in the world.

Lord Rothschild assured Jean for the seventh time that he was all right, and that no, thank you, he could clean up his laboratory on his own, as there might be some unexploded material in there and he really should double-check that himself. He was now sitting on the front step of the Large Cottage, sucking on a pipe he'd fished out of his pocket and waiting for the smoke to clear. "Going for a walk up to the Mansion?" he asked.

"Yes sir!" Jean replied.

"Very good! Carry on! Be careful, though."

"More bombs?" Max asked.

Lord Rothschild threw his head back laughing. "No, my boy, I don't believe so." Then he suddenly became distracted and worried. "Unless I left that land mine in East Field . . ." He looked at Jean. "Do watch your step."

"Yes sir," said Jean. "Come on, Max. Look lively."

And off they went, leaving the shock-headed Lord Rothschild to puff distractedly on his pipe and wonder whether he had left a live land mine somewhere on his property.

"He's . . . not what I expected . . ." Max said as they tramped through the thick wall of trees and overgrowth that stood behind Lord Rothschild's cottage.

"No, Lord Rothschild is rather . . . unusual."

Max thought back to the Nazi newspaper cartoons of fat bankers with monocles and top hats and hooked noses, controlling the world with strings like puppet masters. Lord Rothschild wasn't fat at all, and though his nose had a bit of a bump on it, he wasn't even controlling the explosive materials in his own lab. He certainly didn't *appear* to be controlling the world.

They emerged from the woods into a hayfield.

"East Field?" Max asked, keeping his eyes on the ground.

"West Field," Jean reassured him. "Though I wouldn't worry too much. Lord Rothschild is much more responsible than he gives himself credit for."

"He nearly blew himself up just now!"

"He is always nearly blowing himself up. But he never does seem to," Jean said.

West Field was dotted with huge round bales of hay.

"Follow the leader!" said Jean, and she suddenly broke into a run. Max sprinted after her. They ran to one of the bales—it was just about as tall as Jean. She put both hands on it and fluidly pushed herself on top the bale. Then she stood up, thrust her arms in the air, and jumped off, landing on her feet.

"Your turn!" she chirped.

"No thanks," Max said, laughing.

But Jean didn't smile back. "You don't get to say that, Max. This is part of training. Anything I ask you to do is part of training. Got that?"

"Uh, yes! Sorry!" Max tried to scramble up onto the hay bale. It wasn't easy. His hands couldn't grip the hay without pulling out chunks of it, and his shoes slid off the side of the bale, which was surprisingly slick. Jean looked at her wristwatch as Max struggled to pull himself halfway up, hung in the air for a moment, and then fell down again.

He moved to take off his backpack. "Oh, no," said Jean. "If you were in hostile territory, that rucksack might contain documents that could sway the course of the war."

Max sighed, tightened the straps, and attacked the hay bale again. He heaved and pulled and slid down and jumped up and flailed and slid down again.

Every time he failed panic rose in his chest as his parents drifted before his eyes. *Be extraordinary!* he told himself.

Once, he caught a piece of twine that ran along the top of the bale in his fingers and tried to pull himself up that way. Until Berg walked to the end of his arm and started gnawing through the twine with his teeth.

"Hey!" Max shouted at him.

"No fair!" Stein cried.

Berg said, "I don't want to go back to Germany! Do you?" Stein shut up.

Max slid down the side of the hay again.

At last, Max jammed his foot into the hay, pushed himself up so he could get his elbows on top of the bale, and then kicked wildly until he got his whole stomach on top. From there, he wriggled the rest of himself up. He stood on top of the bale at last, panting like he'd just swum across the English Channel.

He looked down triumphantly at Jean. But she had already turned away and was striding off across the field.

Inside, Max wanted to cry a little.

But he just slid down the other side of the hay bale and hustled after Jean.

CHAPTER
Twenty-Eight

Max pulled even with Jean just as they left West Field and entered the woods again. Soon, Max began to catch glimpses of a building through the trees. It was made of red brick and had white windows, like the cottages. But it was "like the cottages" the way that Jupiter is like Mercury—both planets are the same shape, and in the same neighborhood. But you could fit Mercury into Jupiter twenty-four *thousand* times. That's how big Tring Park Mansion was.

And yet, the Mansion was not what Max was staring at as they emerged from the woods.

Max was staring across an impeccably green lawn . . . at a *zebra*. Actually, *many zebras*.

"I'm sorry," said Max. "Are those *zebras*?"

"What? Where?!" Berg shouted. "I have never seen a zebra! I've existed since the beginning of time and I've never seen a—HOLY BOSS! Look at those things!"

"What's the big deal?" Stein shrugged. "It looks like God painted some horses through a fence. I remember *dinosaurs*. Also *angels*."

Max told himself to ask Stein about both dinosaurs and angels later, but for the time being, he agreed with Berg—he had never seen a zebra either, and he couldn't believe he was seeing them now. "Why are there *zebras* in England?" Max asked.

"One of the Rothschilds brought them here from Africa a long time ago," Jean replied. "This is the second or third generation, I think."

"And what are *those*?" Max was pointing at birds bigger than he was, pecking at the lawn. They looked like brown ostriches.

Jean put a hand on her hip. "I can never tell. Those are either the emus or the rheas."

Max said, "This is unbelieva— *Aaahhhh!*" Suddenly, to his great horror, Max found himself emitting a high-pitched shriek.

Someone was pulling on his rucksack.

Not someone. Some*thing*.

A kangaroo.

A very large kangaroo. Which is why he was shrieking.

It was trying to yank the backpack away from him.

"WHAT IN CREATION IS THAT?" Berg shrieked.

Max tried to scramble away from the kangaroo, but it had the rucksack in its furry fists, and it would not let go. It had a long face, a black nose, and huge round eyes. And it was *very* strong.

"What should I do, Jean? What should I do?" Max asked frantically.

"Don't give her the rucksack, that's for sure!" Jean told him.

"How? How can I not give her the rucksack! She's way bigger than me!"

"Everything is training, Max," Jean said, backing away. "I can't help, I'm afraid."

"Forget the training!" Stein cried. "Max, run!"

Max *tried* to run, but the rucksack was still on both shoulders, and the kangaroo was hanging on tight. When he tried to pull himself away, the kangaroo jumped after him and quickly yanked the rucksack back.

"What should I do?" Max shouted at Berg and Stein.

"Give up and go home?" Berg suggested.

"Yeah, if being a spy means fighting kangaroos, I don't think you're gonna cut it."

Max continued to struggle with the kangaroo while Jean stood with her arms folded, leaning against a nearby tree. She seemed to be enjoying the show.

Which Max found both infuriating *and* humiliating.

The kangaroo managed to get the rucksack off Max's shoulders, so Max gripped one of the straps as tight as he could and pulled as hard as he could and stared right into the kangaroo's black eyes. "LET GO!" he shouted at it.

The kangaroo was not letting go.

"What does it *want*?" cried Max.

As soon as he asked, he knew the answer.

And he relaxed. But he did *not* let go of the rucksack.

Instead, Max looped one arm through the straps so the kangaroo couldn't abscond with the pack, and with his opposite hand he unlatched the flap that kept the pack closed. He reached in and found a sandwich wrapped in brown paper.

Instantly, the kangaroo dropped the rucksack and lunged for the sandwich.

Max dodged the kangaroo. He tore off the paper and held out the sandwich.

The kangaroo grabbed it and bounded a distance away and started to eat, very much the way a human would eat a sandwich.

Max spun on Jean. "What kind of sandwich was that?"

"*That's* the first question you ask after wrestling with a kangaroo?" Jean laughed.

Max said, "It looked like it was filled with tar. And smelled worse."

"Never had Marmite, have you, then?" Jean replied. "It's yeast jelly."

"It smells awful."

"Tastes worse. But the 'roos love it." Jean showed him both her dimples. "Come on, let's head back."

Jean led Max tramping through the underbrush. The sky overhead was bright blue through the half-bare branches and the ground smelled like decaying leaves. "So what did we learn from that little episode?"

"Don't bring Marmite anywhere near kangaroos?"

Jean gave Max a wry smile. "Sure. But I'd say there are three lessons we can take from your little wildlife wrestling match. First, no matter what someone is doing to you, no matter how strange or scary it is, stay calm. If you're calm, you can think. Right?"

"Right," said Max, and he found himself paying closer attention to a lesson than he ever had. He wasn't sure why. Perhaps it was Jean's confidence. Or maybe it had something to do with having just survived a kangaroo attack.

"Second," said Jean, "everyone has a motivation. The kangaroo's behavior seemed completely irrational. Why would she want a rucksack? But when you were calm enough to think it through, you realized that she had a very reasonable motivation indeed, didn't she?"

"She did," said Max. Max also thought about how the best lessons were completely obvious once you heard them, and yet you wouldn't have come to them on your own in a year of thinking.

Jean said, "Third, once you know someone's motivation, you can use it to control their behavior. You wanted that 'roo to get away from you. So you gave her the sandwich."

Max was nodding.

"That little encounter with the kangaroo is what being a spy is all about," said Jean.

Max cut in, "Wait, did you *plan* that?"

Jean was all dimples and charmingly crooked teeth when she replied, "All part of training, Max." Then she added: "Well done, by the way. First test, flying colors."

CHAPTER
Twenty-Nine

As Max and Jean returned to cottage number 3, someone was waiting for them outside the door who could easily have been mistaken for a young tree. He was enormously tall, so thin he seemed to bend in the breeze, and he had a ridiculous waxed mustache extending past the sides of his face. He also wore small glasses and was smoking a pipe.

"Chumley!" Jean called.

The tall bendy man waved.

"Max, this is your espionage instructor, Lieutenant Chumley," Jean said as they came within range.

"*This* is what spies look like?" Berg wondered out loud. "I thought spies were supposed to blend in."

"The only place this guy could blend in is a circus," Stein added.

"How do you do?" said Lieutenant Chumley. He and Max shook hands, and Chumley's fingers wrapped all the way around the back of Max's hand and enfolded it like an envelope. "Cheerio, Max. Cheerio!" His voice was deep, like a bassoon playing its lowest notes, and he had an accent so properly

English it sounded like he was imitating an Oxford professor. "Lots to show you, Max! Tricks, feints, fictions, the whole caboodle. Should be *rather* a good time, I'd think. Much to learn, though, and not much time to learn it. So shall we?"

Without waiting for an answer, Chumley began to walk. Max hurried after, then glanced quickly back at Jean. She waved by wiggling her fingers, which he was pretty sure meant *Good luck. You'll need it.*

Max almost had to run just to keep up with his espionage instructor's long stride. When he walked Lieutenant Chumley looked rather like one of the emus, Max thought. Or the rheas. Or whatever they were.

Chumley puffed on his pipe. "There are two overriding imperatives of clandestine work in enemy territory, Max."

Enemy territory? Max thought. *I think of Germany as* home.

"First thing: Don't get caught!" Chumley barked. "Second thing: you are *always* about to get caught! So *always* be able to get out!"

I won't get caught, Max promised himself. *But I won't "get out," either—unless my parents are getting out, too.*

"Max, are you listening?"

"Yes sir!"

Chumley gave him a skeptical sidelong stare and then announced: "Third imperative of clandestine work: Always pay attention! You never know when a piece of crucial information will be communicated, either intentionally or, more likely, unintentionally. And when it is, you will almost *never* have another chance at it. You never know when someone's *true motives* will be revealed. True motives, Max, are like gold doubloons to spies like us! Priceless currency! Do you know why, Max?"

"No sir."

"Very good! Excellent!"

"It's excellent that I don't know, sir?"

"On the contrary! It is excellent that you are being honest about your ignorance! The first step to curing ignorance is to acknowledge it!"

Max was getting the impression that Lieutenant Chumley saw everything in the world as a task that could be accomplished as long as it was broken into a series of steps. Which was, strangely, exactly the way Max's father saw the world.

The two men couldn't be more different, Max thought. Chumley, tall; his father, short. Chumley, a tweedy spymaster in England; Papa, a poor watchmaker in Nazi Berlin. Chumley, an active player in the war, Papa . . . well, who knew what Papa was doing? And yet, in this fundamental way, they had the same approach to life . . .

Suddenly, Max was back in his father's watch repair shop.

Papa was spreading out all the tiny cogs and springs of a Junghans pocket watch on the shop's black-velvet-covered table—back before Rabbi Kolski was thrown through their window and the shop had been shuttered forever.

"A lot of pieces, huh, Max?" his father said.

Max nodded.

"Overwhelming, isn't it? Where do you even begin? So much work to do! Makes you want to quit, no?"

Papa was staring at Max through glasses as thick as the bottom of a beer glass, kindly waiting. Papa did just about everything kindly. Max nodded again.

Papa raised a finger. "But actually, it's simple." He picked up a gold disc. "This goes first. Always." He laid it down on the black velvet. "That wasn't hard, was it?"

Max smiled. "No, not hard."

"Then this," Papa said, using long sharp tweezers to pick up a tiny pinion and laying it into a hole in the disc. "Was that hard?"

"No," said Max.

Then his father picked up another tiny pinion and laid it alongside the first, and then he slid a very small screw through them, so they were attached. "Was that very difficult?"

Max shook his head.

"When you look at the whole thing, Max," his father said, "it looks impossible. But each step is simple. The only difficult thing is focusing on each step." His father looked up from the watch pieces and through his thick spectacles at Max. "If you can focus on what you need to do right now, and not worry about what you have to do next, everything in life is easy. Easy as putting a Junghans back—"

"Max!"

Max was so startled he nearly lost his footing and went tumbling headfirst on the gravel path.

"Max! What is the third imperative of clandestine work?"

"Um . . . paying attention?"

"Righto! And were you, Max?"

How could Chumley tell? "No sir. I'm sorry. I was not."

Chumley stopped walking so abruptly that Max had to stop and turn around and come back to him. The lieutenant of Naval Intelligence waved a long finger in Max's face, looming menacingly over the German boy. "Max, I expect the very best from you."

"Yes sir."

"If you do not give me your very best at every moment, I will dismiss you from training on the spot, without conversation or chance for appeal. Is that clear?"

Max's chest began to quiver. "Yes sir."

"Very well, then!" Chumley said, and he was off to the races again, as Max desperately tried not to fall behind without breaking into a run. It was as if Chumley was delivering a lecture while participating in a speed-walking competition. They strode across West Field. Max stole a glance at the hay bales with wary respect, like you would a worthy adversary. He'd never felt that way about a hay bale before.

"Now, back to the second rule of clandestine work! Which was . . . ?"

"Uh . . ." said Max.

"Fourth rule of clandestine work!" Chumley bellowed. "Remember everything! You won't have a chance to write things down, and even if you *do*, writing things down is highly likely to get you *killed*! So you must remember what you hear! Do you hear?"

"I hear!"

"And will you *remember*?"

"I will!"

"Excellent!" Lieutenant Chumley barreled on as they took a sharp left at the end of West Field and instead of heading toward the Mansion, made for the brick wall that separated Tring Park from the road. Once they reached it, they took a left, walking along the wall back in the direction of the cottages. "The second rule of clandestine work is 'Always be able to . . .'?"

"Get out!" Max said.

"Very good! And in order to be able to get out of a hostile nation, it is highly beneficial to be in contact with our side. But how can you be in contact with our side without blowing your cover, eh? You can't just walk into the British embassy in enemy territory! First of all, there might not be one. Second of all, as soon as you do . . . ?"

"They'll know I'm working with the British," said Max.

"Exactly! Good boy! Sharp mind! So how *would* you communicate with our side without rousing enemy suspicions?"

"Radio?" Max asked hopefully. He had seen wireless sets equipped for Morse code in newsreels and films and he'd always wanted to get his hands on one.

"Afraid not. The Germans have a division called the Funkabwehr, which means, roughly, Radio Spies—they do have *rather* good names for things," Chumley admitted with some admiration. "Anyway, their Radio Spies drive around in unmarked trucks with antennas attached, looking for illegal radio transmissions. Too risky, I'm afraid. No, my boy, when in enemy territory, the safest way to communicate is to write a letter!"

"What?" That seemed like a stupid way to send something secretly.

"Indeed! And for this purpose, we have established a system of dead letter boxes!"

They were now standing in front of the brick wall at the edge of the property.

"What is a dead letter box, sir?" asked Max.

Chumley was gazing at the bricks in front of him like they interested him intensely. Slowly, he stuck out a thin finger and touched one of the bricks. He said, "That is." Chumley brandished his fingers as if he were a stage magician and then gripped the brick with his fingertips. Very gingerly, he pulled—the brick slid out from the wall, leaving a space.

Max said, "Whoa."

Berg said, " 'Whoa' what? He pulled a brick out from a wall."

But Stein said, "Look."

With his other spidery hand, Chumley reached into the space and removed a folded piece of paper. Then he replaced the brick. Looking at the wall, you would never know the brick was loose, much less that it was hiding something.

"That, Max," said Lieutenant Chumley, "is a dead letter box."

Max said, "Neat." And he meant it.

Chumley held out the slip of paper to Max. Max took it and began to open it—

"Not here, for heaven's sake!" Chumley hissed, scaring Max so badly he nearly dropped the note. "Look who's watching!"

Max glanced in the direction that Chumley was pointing. He was pointing at the guardhouse at the entrance to Tring Park, which they were now very near. Sergeant Toby Thompson was standing outside with his hands on his hips, looking at them.

Lieutenant Chumley waved his arm at Sergeant Thompson, beckoning him over. Sergeant Thompson checked the gate was down, locked his little guardhouse, and started toward them.

"Pocket that letter, Max," Chumley whispered as they watched the military policeman approach. "As nonchalantly as possible."

Max did, and Chumley said, "Cheerio, Sergeant!"

"Good morning, Lieutenant," Sergeant Thompson replied. "What can I do for you?" He glanced back at his guardhouse and the gate.

Chumley said, "You've met Max here, right?"

"Of course," said Sergeant Thompson, with a friendly nod at Max. "I know everyone who comes in and out of Tring Park."

"Righto. Naturally you do. Look, old fellow, we're training up young Max here for a mission. Potentially into enemy territory."

That snapped Sergeant Thompson's attention back to Max. "You're training this *boy* to go into enemy territory?" It looked like he wanted to say more but stopped himself.

"That's what he's hoping, anyway! And we are standing in front of a dead letter box." Lieutenant Chumley showed Sergeant Thompson what he meant by pulling the loose brick slightly out from the wall. "I would be very grateful if you would keep an eye on this box."

"Okay . . ." said Sergeant Thompson.

"Max's task is to post a response in this dead letter box. Do not let him! Do not let *anyone* let him. Spread the word to the military policemen under your command. If he gets a note into this box, with the correct message on that note, he will have succeeded in his training! We do not want that!"

Sergeant Thompson said what Max was thinking: "We don't?"

"No! If he succeeds, he will be sent on a mission into enemy territory, which, in my estimation, is highly likely to result in him being killed."

Sergeant Thompson smirked. "Well, we wouldn't want him to be killed, would we?"

"You talk as if I'm joking," Lieutenant Chumley replied. His voice suddenly became very quiet, and very cold. "I am not at all joking, Sergeant."

The smile evaporated from the military policeman's face. He looked at Max again, as if seeing him for the first time. "You're really training this boy for a mission into enemy territory?"

Chumley chewed on the stem of his pipe and studied Max.

Max, on the other hand, was studying the loose brick.

All he had to do was place a response in the dead letter box?

Perhaps this training would be easier than he'd expected.

"We'll be here at Tring for four weeks at the very most"— Chumley looked down through the round spectacles on the end of his nose like he was appraising Max—"if Max isn't dismissed before that."

Max felt the shudder in his chest again. He said, "And after four weeks? What happens if I haven't gotten the response into the dead letter box by then?"

"Then time's up, I'm afraid," Chumley said.

Lieutenant Chumley and Sergeant Thompson were gazing down at Max.

"Sounds like you've got a timer, Maxy," said Stein. "And it's running."

CHAPTER
Thirty

Max was famished when he returned to cottage number 3 that evening. He opened the refrigerator and was greeted with loaves of bread and jars of Marmite. He turned away in disgust. Then, next to half a dozen eggs and a small block of margarine, he spied a jar labeled BEEF STEW. Max emptied that into a small pot on the stove. He didn't even wait for it to be warmed through before ravenously devouring it.

Once Max finished, he started to explore his new lodgings. The cottage was small and plain compared to 28 Kensington Court. In fact, from the dull plaid curtains to the off-white kitchenette, it reminded him some of his apartment in Berlin. Which made Max smile.

Though, sadly, there was no radio.

There *was* a small writing desk in the corner of the living room. Max went over to it. It was stocked with cream-colored stationery. A fountain pen lay in a shallow well next to a leather writing surface.

Max stood above the paper, considering it. Then he sat down and wrote *Dear Uncle Ivor . . .*

And Max proceeded to pour the insane cacophony of his day's experiences onto the page. He told Ivor about Tring Park, about Jean Leslie, and Lord Rothschild, and the kangaroo, and—

There was a knock on the door. For some reason that Max could not explain even to himself, he quickly folded up the sheets of paper he'd been writing on—there were three already—and shoved them into a pocket of his trousers. Then he stood up and called, "Who is it?"

Uncle Ewen opened the door of the cottage. "Hullo, Max. Mind if we have a little debriefing from your first day?"

Max had stood up and moved away from the writing desk already. "Of course, Unc— I mean Lieutenant Commander."

Berg said, "Why did Max just hide that letter?"

"I'm not sure . . ." said Stein. He put his little head against Max's neck. "Also, I can hear his heart hammering like a church bell. Maxy, what is going on?"

Max honestly didn't know.

As Ewen and Max sat together in the living room of cottage number 3, the sky outside the small front windows faded from royal blue to ashen.

"So how was it?" Ewen asked. He wore his cryptic smile. But Max noticed that his eyes were not smiling along with his mouth. Max wondered what was wrong.

"It was great, Uncle Ewen," said Max, as earnestly as he could.

"Was it?"

"It was. Way more interesting than school. A million miles more interesting."

Uncle Ewen's smile filtered up his face until it almost reached his eyes. Almost. "Well, that's good to hear." He was chewing on the end of his unlit pipe and studying Max.

"Is everything all right, Lieutenant Commander?"

Ewen sighed and let his smile fall off. "I suppose so. I'm just wondering whether we're all blithering idiots for letting you even attempt this."

"You are!" Berg shouted. "Unless you *want* to get the boy killed! In which case, keep it up!"

Max watched Uncle Ewen, waiting.

Ewen worried the stem of his pipe with his teeth some more. Then he said, "There is an erroneous belief, Max, that to be a spy, you must be a *liar*."

At the word *liar* Max's attention suddenly went to the letter in his pocket.

Was he *lying* by hiding this letter from Uncle Ewen? And Berg had asked a very reasonable question: Why *was* he hiding it?

Ewen went on, apparently unaware of Max's interior monologue. "But being a spy is *not* about lying, Max. It is about the *creation of fictions*. To enter enemy territory under a false name, with a false background, one must invent a whole *history*. It's like writing a novel." Ewen chuckled. "We've got quite a few novelists in our department, actually. A young man named Ian Fleming. And Admiral Godfrey writes spy novels, did you know that?"

Max, forcing himself to forget about the letter, joked, "Are they just strings of curse words?"

Ewen laughed. "They're actually not half bad. But the writing of a fiction—a fake background—isn't the hardest part of spycraft, though you have to do a *frightfully* good job lining up all the pieces, making sure your cover identity is airtight. Much harder by far, though, is *living* the fiction."

Max was quickly becoming very aware how hard it was to live a fiction, given that he was trying not to mention the letter in his pocket and was consequently sweating through his shirt.

Ewen was saying, "You have to have a strange relationship with truth to live a fiction, Max. You have to *believe* the fiction you're living, and your mind needs to be totally and utterly free from the truth. *Except.*" Ewen stopped and emphasized the word. "*Except.* You cannot *lose* the truth. You must keep it buried, in a box under the stairs in the cellar of your brain. You might even struggle to find it some days. But if it's tossed out, if it's lost . . . then so are you."

Ewen sighed and said, "Sometimes I think that the whole of Germany is like that. Hitler invented a fiction for them, and they're all living it . . . and they've totally lost the truth." He got very quiet. "But why? How? How does a whole country bury the truth and forget where they buried it?"

Max didn't know. Nor could he give the question much

consideration, because all he could think about was the lie in his pocket.

A few minutes later, Max watched Ewen walk back to his cottage—number 4—through one of his small front windows. Then Max went upstairs to his washroom, took the letter to Ivor out of his pocket, tore it into tiny bits, and flushed it down the toilet.

As he did, he turned over in his head what Ivor had said to him:

Write to me. Tell me where you are, and what you're doing. Ewen and the other spies may not want you to, so you may have to mail letters secretly, or hide the important details amongst a lot of guff. But do let me know what they're doing with you. If it's somehow not right, I'll let Uncle Ewen know.

"Max, why did you write a letter and then flush it down the toilet?" Stein asked.

Max didn't answer because Max wasn't sure. All he felt sure of was that when Ewen had talked about living a fiction, the letter in his pocket had burned his leg like it was a hot coal.

Max lay in bed that night turning his day over in his head. He took each moment out and examined it like a piece of a watch. The letter to Ivor. Fictions and lies. Marmite sandwiches. The dead letter box.

The dead letter box!

Max threw the covers off his bed and dove at his trousers,

which were lying crumpled on the floor. He desperately searched his pockets for the note.

With a rising sense of panic, he realized that he didn't have it. Had it been in the same pocket with the letter to Ivor? Had he torn it up without realizing and flushed it down the toilet?

Without looking at it?

Max fell to his knees.

His instructions were probably in pieces, floating through sewage, already beyond the bounds of Tring Park.

He couldn't complete the mission.

He'd have to beg Chumley to give him a second chance. And Max had a feeling there were no second chances for spies. He could imagine the lecture now: *Rule number five: There are no second chances for spies! If you need a second chance, it means you are dead!*

Max felt exactly like he had when he was six years old and Professor Magdeburg was yelling at his mother. He had done something unforgivably stupid. And yet again the people who would be punished for his stupidity were his parents. Because he wouldn't be able to get to them.

Max started to cry.

He buried his face in his hands and his back shook.

"Why is he crying?" Berg asked Stein.

"No clue," said Stein. "Hey Max! Maxy! What's going on?"

But Max was unreachable. He saw his parents as war raged around them and the Nazis made their lives progressively more impossible. And he couldn't get to them. He couldn't get to them.

Stein sighed heavily. "C'mon Max. This is really bumming me out. I realize I'm supposed to make your life miserable, but this is too much. What is it, *bubbeleh*?"

Max snorted snot back into his nose and said, "I lost the note from the dead letter box. I can't complete my training. It's my first day, and I've already failed."

Stein glanced at Berg. "Lost the note?" he murmured quizzically. Then the dybbuk rolled his eyes. "Do you want to tell him?"

"No!" said Berg. "No, and neither should you! It is against the rules to help the humans we are haunting! I am sure of it! I mean, it must be, right? Besides, I don't want to go back!"

Max cried, "What? Tell me WHAT?"

Stein sighed even more dramatically than before. "Berg, you're right. I'm sure you're right. We shouldn't help. We've gotten too friendly with this human already." He gazed at Max. "I'm gonna tell him anyway."

"Stein, if you do this . . ." Berg warned him.

"TELL ME WHAT?" Max's shout was as loud as a silent shout can be.

"Check your—"

Berg leaped across Max's neck and tried to smother Stein's mouth with his tiny hands. Max was horrified. He'd never had two metaphysical incorporeal creatures fighting on his shoulders before and it was completely freaking him out.

Finally, Stein wrestled free of Berg and cried, "You put it in your fifth pocket, you dummy!" before Berg grabbed him by the throat and started choking him. Which, since Stein didn't technically need to *breathe*, wasn't that big a deal.

Max furrowed his brow. His *fifth* pocket?

His fifth pocket!

He reached into the small pocket nestled within the larger front pocket on the right side of his trousers. The one just large enough for a key. Or a small slip of paper.

Which was right there.

Max nearly started crying all over again.

He unfolded the piece of paper that Chumley had left for him in the dead letter box and walked to the bedroom window, to read by the light of the moon. Berg shook a tiny fist in Stein's face and then crawled angrily back to Max's right shoulder.

"What does it say?" Stein demanded.

"It says," Max read, " 'How do you spell my name?' "

"What?" Stein grunted.

"Huh?" Berg huffed.

Stein was incredulous: "*That's* how you pass training? Figuring out how to spell Chumley's name? I don't get it."

Neither did Max. The spelling of Chumley's name seemed pretty obvious—though now that he thought about it, he'd never seen it written out.

But at least training wasn't over yet.

CHAPTER
Thirty-One

Jean was waiting as Max came out of cottage number 3 into the gray dawn light. Fall fog was lying across the ground. Jean touched her toes, bounced up, touched her toes again.

"Morning!" Jean chirruped. "Join me?"

Max tried to mimic what she was doing.

He managed to touch the middle of his shins.

"Oh, you can do better than that!" Jean teased him.

Stein, standing upside down on Max's shoulder, looked into Max's red, straining face. "Nope," Stein announced. "He definitely can't."

As Max vainly tried to reach his toes, he said, "Do you happen to know how to spell Lieutenant Chumley's name?"

"I should think so," Jean replied, now bending over backward, looking up at the overcast sky while her hands touched the dirt behind her.

"How?"

"How do *you* think you spell it?"

Max, still folded over himself, said, "C-H-U-M-L-E-Y."

Jean came up out of her stretch and started to put her hair into a ponytail. "Sounds good to me!"

And Max thought, *Well, that was easy.*

"Now, here's the plan," Jean said. "We'll have a quick race to the Mansion each morning after breakfast, climbing the hay bale as we pass through West Field. If I beat you to the wall of the Mansion, I'll take out my pocket watch. Every second I stand there waiting for you is another push-up you have to do."

"What?! But I could be doing hundreds of push-ups!" Max objected.

"I would guess thousands," said Berg.

"Then I recommend you hurry up!" Jean shouted, and she took off at a sprint down the gravel road. Max ran after her.

Jean was *really* fast. She sprinted around a curve that bent past cottages number 7 and 8 and disappeared from sight. When Max rounded the bend, he glimpsed her bouncing ponytail just as she vanished behind the Large Cottage.

Stein put his fingers in his ears.

"What are you doing?" Berg asked.

"In case Lord Not-Careful-with-Nitrogen is doing another experiment."

When Max reached West Field, he saw Jean standing on top of a hay bale, hands on her hips, like a statue of a Greek goddess.

"She's waiting for you!" Stein said.

"How humiliating," added Berg.

But Jean didn't wait long, because as soon as she saw Max run into the field, she hopped down and sprinted ahead.

Max ran to the hay bale, grabbed the top of it, and tried to hoist his way up. But Berg crawled onto Max's face and started sticking his tiny hands in Max's nose. Max couldn't feel it, because Berg was incorporeal, but it was *incredibly* distracting.

Max lost his grip and fell flat on his back on the ground.

"Berg!" Stein cried.

"Stein!" Berg retorted. "You wanna go live with the Nazis again?"

Max got back up, managed to wriggle to the top of the hay bale, and looked around for Jean. But she was long gone. He slid down the other side and started running again.

By the time he reached the edge of the Mansion, Jean was standing there looking at her pocket watch.

"Three hundred and forty-four," she said.

Max thought he might cry.

"Start with thirty," Jean offered. "You can pay me in installments throughout the day, if you like."

Max did three push-ups and Jean stopped him.

"Not like that! Straight back! Arms under your shoulders!"

Max did his best. Which was awful.

After their morning run, Max went back to work on his mission for Lieutenant Chumley.

Avoiding a herd of grazing rheas—or were they emus?—Max

made his way to Tring Park's perimeter wall. He followed it until he was in sight of the little white guardhouse. He stopped. He knelt. He could feel his heartbeat in his throat.

Max watched as a car turned into the Tring Park driveway and stopped at the guardhouse. Sergeant Toby Thompson emerged, leaned down, and spoke with the driver for a moment, and then went back into the guardhouse—Max figured to check that the driver's name was in the ledger book.

Then Sergeant Thompson came back out, lifted the gate, and waved the car through.

Max waited.

As soon as another car slowed on the main street and began its turn into Tring, Max was off.

He sprinted, trying to stay as close to the wall as he could. He stopped in front of where the loose brick was, slid the brick out of the wall, placed a piece of paper in the hole, and then replaced the brick.

As Max hurried away, he glanced over his shoulder and saw that Sergeant Thompson had waved the car through—and was now squinting at the brick wall, as if he suspected he'd just missed something.

You have, Max thought. *You just missed me successfully completing my training.*

CHAPTER
Thirty-Two

When Max returned to cottage number 3, beaming from the quick and relatively simple success of his mission, he discovered Chumley and Jean both waiting for him.

Max nearly blurted out, *I did it!* But before he could, Lieutenant Chumley announced: "Max, this way, please! Lord Rothschild is waiting for us." So Max held on to the news of his triumph. He'd wait for a better moment. Maybe when Ewen was there, too, so Max could see his face when he heard.

Max, Chumley, and Jean tramped over to the Large Cottage, where Lord Rothschild was waiting for them on the stoop. His wiry hair was combed down against his head, his clothes were soot-free, and a mischievous smile played on his lips.

"Oho! The child spy!" cried Lord Rothschild. "Have I got something for you!"

"Oh really?" said Max nervously, hoping it wasn't something that might explode.

Lord Rothschild invited them inside with a sweep of his arm. The interior of the Large Cottage was luxurious and cozy all at once—though there was a thin sheen of black dust on the wallpaper, presumably from yesterday's explosion. But every-thing else seemed to have been cleaned up. Lord Rothschild al-ready had a new desk. Not bombproof, sadly, he explained, but a lovely antique that some of the boys had brought over from the Mansion for him. He *did* hope he wouldn't blow this one up, as it was rather rare and rather old and rather expensive.

Lord Rothschild led them through the house, into a large kitchen, and out the back door, saying, "One of my speciali-ties, Max, in addition to explosives research, is *inventing*. And I have built something that I think you'll like—and I daresay our friend Jean here will *love*. At least, I hope." And he glanced at them nervously. Did the richest man in the world really care what they thought about his invention, whatever it was? It seemed so.

They were in a small walled garden. Standing there was a stuffed dummy. The strangest dummy Max had ever seen.

It was made of stitched leather filled with straw—you could see bits of it sticking out from the seams—and at the bottom of each leg instead of feet there were thick springs that had been soldered to a large iron disk.

But the strangest thing about this dummy, by *far*, was that it was covered in *swastikas*.

"Well, that's *disturbing*," murmured Chumley, surveying the Nazi symbols.

The swastikas were drawn in seemingly random places.

For example, the dummy's arms stuck out straight to the sides, and under each arm, in the armpit, was a black swastika. There was another in the center of the chest, just below where the ribs would meet. There was a small one at the base of the neck, and another in the center of the throat. There was one on each hand, midway between the thumb and forefinger. There was also a swastika on the outside and inside of each knee.

And then there was the weirdest one of all: a red swastika, right where the dummy's private parts should have been.

"I have given it some thought," said Berg. "And have concluded that these people are all bonkers."

"Lieutenant Chumley," Lord Rothschild was saying, "I'm sure you could explain to our young friend the significance of the placement of these odious marks? This one, for instance?" He pointed at the swastika in the middle of the dummy's chest.

Chumley said, "Solar plexus. A sufficiently forceful punch, and your adversary will be on his knees in an instant."

Rothschild pointed to the swastika on the dummy's hand.

"Press there, Max," Chumley said, "with your sharp little thumb, and you will make a grown man scream in pain. Though watch out for his other hand, which is likely to come flailing wildly at your head."

Rothschild turned to Jean. "Miss Leslie, perhaps you can show Max what to do with the spot on the side of the knee?"

Jean walked around the side of the dummy, and then, with a sudden movement, landed a sharp kick on the swastika there.

"With enough force, such a strike would cause a man's leg to snap in half," Chumley narrated.

"But that wasn't quite enough force!" Lord Rothschild announced.

Jean put her hands on her hips, displeased.

"I am certain that you could remedy that, though," Lord Rothschild said to Jean, "by aiming right about . . . *there.*" And he pointed to the red swastika.

Jean set her jaw and came around to the front of the dummy. She took a step back and then launched her foot with shocking force and speed between the dummy's legs.

BANG!

Everyone jumped, Jean fell over, and Max threw himself on the ground and covered his head, certain that another bomb had exploded.

But when he cautiously looked up, all he saw were pink and green streamers floating down gently through the air.

"That's the ticket!" Lord Rothschild crowed, clapping his hands like a little boy. "You've made him blow his top! Oh, marvelous!"

Jean raised herself on one arm from the ground. "What on earth . . . ?" she muttered.

"I've outfitted this dummy with an internal hydraulic pressure system! Apply enough force to any of these spots, and *pop goes the weasel!* I will have to get another streamer-filled balloon before it works again, though."

Stein said, "*This* is what the richest man in the world spends his time doing?"

Berg replied, "Like I said: bonkers!"

Jean pushed herself to her feet and then helped Max up. "Well, Max," she said. "I guess you have a new best friend." And she patted the dummy on his shoulder.

"Though I don't imagine he'll like *you* very much," Chumley added.

Jean pointed to the dummy. "Tell you what, Max—each swift kick to this Nazi's groin will replace one of the push-ups you owe me. How does that sound?"

Max turned on the dummy and set to pulverizing his private parts.

That evening, they all dined with Lord Rothschild. Max could barely lift his fork, he was so exhausted.

"Well?" Lord Rothschild asked as enormous slices of roast beef drenched in horseradish sauce were laid down in front of them by a white-vested server. "How was your first full day of training, Max?"

"I'm rather tired, Lord Rothschild," Max answered.

"Good! Jolly good! Can't make life too easy for you. The mission won't be, will it, Montagu?"

Max's gaze jumped to Uncle Ewen. Ewen was studying Max,

just as he had the night before. His eyes were still not smiling. Ewen said, "Indeed, Lord Rothschild. I must admit, I'm having second thoughts."

Max became suddenly cold, and Lord Rothschild's knife and fork clattered to his plate.

"What? Why? He did well enough today, didn't he?" Rothschild demanded.

Uncle Ewen nodded ruefully. "It's not a question of Max's ability."

Max exhaled.

"It's a question of his safety."

"THANK YOU!" Berg shouted.

"But . . . but I passed my test!" Max objected. "Not in a *month*! In a *day*!" This was the moment Max had been waiting for. "Didn't I, Lieutenant Chumley? Did you check the dead letter box? Tell them what you found!"

Uncle Ewen looked at Lieutenant Chumley in shock.

Chumley smiled ruefully. "Max did indeed—"

"Then I can go!" Max cried.

"*Excuse* me. I was saying that you did *indeed* manage to slip a note into the dead letter box undetected. Well done. But you did *not* spell my name correctly." The tall lieutenant looked displeased. "Rule number five of clandestine work is to always be certain of your information. Bad information may get you *killed*. Worse, it could cause the deaths of others. Hundreds or even thousands of others."

Max pinched his lips together. He looked at Jean and felt betrayed—she'd said C-H-U-M-L-E-Y sounded right to her. She had lied.

Jean shrugged and her dimple said it all: *All part of training.*

"You *do* want to go on this mission, don't you?" asked Lieutenant Chumley (however you spelled his name).

"I do!" Max insisted.

"Then I *suggest* that you avoid another mistake."

Jean, Chumley, Rothschild, and Uncle Ewen all stared at the boy who sat with them at the table in the Large Cottage at Tring Park. Max looked down at his roast beef.

A slab of meat, waiting for the end.

He knew how it felt.

CHAPTER
Thirty-Three

Sergeant Toby Thompson was sitting on a tall stool in the little white guardhouse, studying the big ledger, when Max walked up. Sergeant Thompson stood and came outside, closing the door behind him. "Good afternoon young man! How can I help you?"

Max was a little sheepish when he asked, "You keep track of everyone who comes in and out of Tring Park, right?"

Sergeant Thompson said, "Sure do."

Max looked at his feet. "Any chance you can tell me how to spell Lieutenant Chumley's name?"

Sergeant Thompson grinned. "Sorry, little brother. I don't think I can help you there."

Max sighed. "I didn't think so."

He was about to turn away when Sergeant Thompson said, "You know, come fall in England, the sun barely even gets over those trees." He was squinting up at the treetops, where the sun was nestled. "I stand here and watch it rise through the sky, and then just kiss those treetops and dip right back down. It's depressing."

Max smiled. "I get sad in fall, too. Winter is even worse."

Sergeant Thompson said, "Yeah? You gotta visit Trinidad. It's never like that there, not even in the dead of winter."

"Is that where you grew up?"

"Yessir!" Sergeant Thompson smiled. "Trinidad is the *best.* Best food, best weather, best people . . ."

"I feel pretty far away from home, too," Max said.

"Is that right? Where are you from, then?"

Max was pleased Sergeant Thompson couldn't tell. "Germany."

Sergeant Thompson's eyes got wider. "Really?" He whistled. "I wouldn't want to be there right now."

"I do."

"That's crazy! Why you wanna go to Germany? You *like* those Nazis?"

"That's what I keep saying!" Berg cried.

Max got quiet. "My parents are there."

Stein raised his eyebrows at Berg. Berg scowled at the dybbuk.

Sergeant Thompson said, "All right. Well, if it's *love* that makes you wanna go there . . . *that* I can understand."

And it sounded like he really did. So Max said, "Yeah?"

"Yeah." Sergeant Thompson chuckled. "You think I want to live here on this cold island? Rather than being back in Trinidad?"

"Did your parents make you move here? When you were a kid?" Max guessed.

"Ah, no, little brother. Not my parents." Sergeant Thompson looked at Max. "You want to know why I came to England?"

Max nodded.

"Okay, then." He looked around. No cars were coming in, and there were no other people in sight. "I'm gonna tell you something. Can you keep it to yourself?"

"Yes," said Max quickly. He didn't know whether he would keep it to himself or not, but *yes* definitely seemed like the reply a spy would give. As Jean said: "Everything is training."

Sergeant Thompson whispered, *"Man, I used to* hate *the British."*

Now Max's eyes were the ones that grew wide.

"Oh yeah. First, they killed the Carib king and enslaved his people. You ever heard of the Caribs?"

"No," said Max.

"Why do you think it's called the Caribbean? But the British killed many and enslaved the rest. They're still around, but it used to be their island." Sergeant Thompson pursed his lips and his black mustache glistened. "Then the British kidnapped and enslaved my African forefathers and brought them to Trinidad to work their plantations."

"But the British freed the slaves," said Max. "Before the Americans did!"

Sergeant Thompson laughed bitterly. "The British only freed the slaves when they realized it was more expensive to feed them than it was to pay free men starvation wages. That's how they do it wherever they go," Sergeant Thompson continued. "The English show up and say they own the place, and anyone—especially we people with the brown skin—had better get out the way. Because when the English come there are only three things that can happen: you starve, you get enslaved, or you get shot."

Max couldn't believe Sergeant Thompson was talking this way. "Do you still feel like that?" Max asked.

"Of course!"

"Then why are you in the British Army?"

Sergeant Thompson said, "That's the story I'm telling you! Don't rush me."

Max closed his eyes, mad at himself. He made a mental note not to rush Sergeant Thompson—or anyone he was trying to get information from.

Sergeant Thompson went on: "So when I was younger, I was this big radical. Running around Trinidad going to meetings about the British, reading all sorts of books. But then I had to get a job, and I did what most boys do—I went down to the south side of the island and started working in the oil fields. Brother, do they work you down there. And brother, do they not pay you much. So me and some other young people—we started speaking up. Saying this wasn't right. Speaking out. Fighting back."

Max was surprised. And impressed.

"One of my friends was called Uriah Butler—a great man,

Uriah Butler. He became the leader of our movement. He read all about the labor strikes in the U.S. and Britain. The sit-ins. Civil disobedience. And he taught us how to do just what they did—but better. We took over those oil plants, sat down on the floor, locked arms. And then when they sent in the soldiers, we shouted: 'We want bread, not bullets! We want bread, not bullets!' " Sergeant Thompson tilted his head back, remembering.

Max couldn't see how any of this would have convinced Sergeant Thompson to join the British Army. It seemed more likely to have got him thrown in jail.

"Then Uriah took me and some other protestors to meet with the governor of Trinidad, to negotiate. You should have seen Uriah. The governor couldn't get the oil company to pay us more money—but Uriah made him promise to give us the right to vote."

"You didn't have the right to vote?" Max asked, surprised.

"Don't you know what a colony is?" Sergeant Thompson shot back. "No, we did *not* have the right to vote. But we will now. Real soon. And that was the *second* best thing that happened in those negotiations."

"What was the best?"

Sergeant Thompson got a sly smile on his face. "The governor's secretary was a woman from Jamaica. And believe me when I tell you she was a fine woman. Smart. Thoughtful. Beautiful. And wouldn't you know, I fell in love with her."

A car turned into the drive and approached the guard-house. Max stepped back as Sergeant Thompson looked through the window, raised the gate, and waved the person through. The car continued down the gravel road in the direction of the Mansion.

"Anyway, I'm talking too much," said Sergeant Thompson. "I'm sure you've got to get back to your training."

"No!" said Max. "Please, finish the story."

The military policeman smiled down at the German boy. "I'll make it real short. Don't want to get you in trouble. After promising us the right to vote, that governor got recalled to England. And he took his Jamaican secretary with him. This woman and me were separated by an ocean."

"Oh," said Max. "That's sad."

Sergeant Thompson nodded slowly. "You know, I was about to say, 'You have no idea.' But maybe you do."

Yes, Max thought. Maybe he did.

"Well, I wasn't just going to let her go. I had to get to England. But how? They don't give visas to black boys from Trinidad like me, you know. Even though our currency has the same king on it as they do here."

"So what'd you do?"

"I walked into a recruiting office for the British Army and I signed up for the Military Police. Requested to be transferred to England. And here I am."

Something bothered Max about Sergeant Thompson's story. "But what about making people starve, or slaves, or shot? If you feel like that, how could you work for the British military?"

Sergeant Thompson smiled ruefully down at Max. "You know what? There are some things that are so important, we will do *anything* for them. Leave our homes. Ignore what we believe. Betray our friends. *Anything.*"

Max was silent for a while. Then he said, "So what happened to that beautiful Jamaican secretary?"

"*Easy* now," said Sergeant Thompson. "Nobody calls my wife beautiful but me, thank you very much!"

Then he grinned, and he and Max broke out laughing.

Max promised himself that he would do *anything* to pass training—except betray Sergeant Toby Thompson.

CHAPTER
Thirty-Four

In the next week, Max felt like he did a month's worth of training.

Max waited for Jean outside the front door of cottage number 3, hugging his arms as the cool mist rose from the ground. The sun was not yet up.

When she bounced into view, Max did not smile at her. He took off running.

She still beat him to the Mansion by nearly four minutes.

After seventy kicks to the dummy's groin, Max panted, "I think . . . Lord Rothschild's . . . invention . . . is malfunctioning . . . The balloon . . . should have burst . . . by now . . ."

Jean stepped in, squared her shoulders, and unleashed a vicious upward kick between the dummy's legs.

BANG!

"Looks like it works fine," said Jean as streamers floated down, celebrating the obliteration of the dummy's reproductive organs.

Max felt almost as terrible as the dummy.

"I'll get a new balloon," Jean sang merrily. "In the meantime, keep kicking!"

Lieutenant Chumley showed Max how to follow someone without being noticed, and then they switched positions and Chumley showed him how to notice when you were being followed. Max walked around the grounds, and Chumley lurked a distance behind, ducking into doorways or pretending to read a paper.

"I'll tell you how you can notice him," Stein said. "He's eight feet tall and has a mustache like airplane wings."

Berg pulled a large clay pot off a wall as Max passed. The *crash* brought Chumley running: "Max for *heaven's* sake! You're hopeless!"

Berg said to a scowling Stein, "Just doing my job! What, may I ask, are *you* doing?"

For once, Stein seemed to be at a loss for words.

Max had no idea how to figure out the spelling of Chumley's name. He used the writing desk in his cottage to try out different possible spellings:

Chummly

Chummley

Chumely

Chummeley

But how would he know which was right? Lieutenant Chumley (Max still pictured the name that way) had made it clear that another wrong answer would result in failure and dismissal.

I have to be *extraordinary*, Max told himself. *Extraordinary.*

He tore up the list of names into a million little bits, but it didn't make him feel any better.

He started a new list.

Chumlee

Tchumly

Chomley

Ewen and Max sat in the chairs in the small living room of cottage number 3 again. The man with the battleship-shaped face stared at Max pensively, not even managing a cryptic smile.

At last, he spoke. "Max, what does the word *propaganda* mean?"

Max tensed. Was this a test? He said, "Uh, it's what the government tells us, right?"

Ewen said, "That's true, as far as it goes. But let's go a little further, shall we?" He sat forward in his chair. "What's the name of the ministry that Joseph Goebbels is in charge of?"

Max said, "Das Reichsministerium für Volksaufklärung und Propaganda."

"Translated?" Ewen asked.

"The Ministry for Public Enlightenment and Propaganda."

Ewen said, "Right. Public Enlightenment. How *charitable* of Dr. Goebbels. Here in England we have the Ministry of Information. What's the difference, Max, between propaganda and information?"

Max wasn't sure.

"There are two chairs and a sofa in this room," Ewen said. "*That's* information. It's a fact. Nothing more, nothing less."

"Okay," said Max.

"But *your* chair, Max." He pointed at the painted wicker chair Max sat on. "Oh, what a chair that is! Made for a bottom just like yours!"

Max smiled.

"And this chair that I'm sitting in," Ewen said, slapping the armrest of his large wingback leather seat, "well, that is occupied by the bottom of a lieutenant commander! And really only lieutenant commanders should sit in chairs like this! So be a good boy, and when I leave, don't sit in this chair. Keep it clean and save it for my bottom and my bottom alone!"

Max stopped smiling. "Truly?"

"No, Max!" Ewen laughed. "No! *That* is propaganda!"

Max thought about it. "Because you're trying to convince me to let you keep the nice chair?"

"Because I'm trying to convince you of something, yes! Nazi propaganda is designed to convince the people of Germany that we Jews are scum, that we English are trying to enslave all Germans, and that the common German man and woman and child should sacrifice *everything* to the Nazi war machine!"

"Do the English use propaganda?" Max wanted to know.

"We do," Ewen admitted. "We use it against the enemy, and we use it to rally our people, I admit. But it's to rally our people so we're not overrun by Nazi bombers and tanks! Not quite the same thing!"

But Max's mind was drifting back to his last, troubling conversation with Ivor, about the stories the British told while they enslaved Africans or imported opium to China.

Ewen went on. "So while the British might use it occasionally, the Nazis have made propaganda into an art and a science. Goebbels's Ministry for Public Enlightenment and Propaganda—you call it the ProMi, don't you? The ProMi is a machine designed to convince the Germans to do horrible things—like the Blitz, Max. And the ProMi's secret, their ace in the hole, is that they have no qualms about *lying*."

Max said to Stein and Berg, "Is *Ewen* lying? About the way the English use propaganda?"

Stein replied, "In my experience, which spans all of human existence, you humans lie to everyone, all the time. Even yourselves."

Ewen continued. "In fact, Adolf Hitler himself wrote that the most effective kind of lie is the *Big Lie*. He said that people won't believe small lies, because they themselves tell small lies every day, and so they recognize them. But the average person can't imagine someone would have the gall to tell an *enormous* lie, a *huge* fiction, a *total* falsehood, because it's something they couldn't get away with in their own lives. And so *those* are the lies that they believe. That's Hitler, mind you, not me. He goes on to say that it's the *Jews* who tell these Big Lies, whereas he will *always* tell the truth." Ewen's voice dripped with sarcasm when he said that. "But one thing to keep in mind, Max, is that a liar will always accuse his enemies of doing exactly what *he himself is doing.*"

And Max thought, *You mean like a British officer telling me that only the Nazis tell Big Lies?*

And he remembered one more thing Ivor had said: *We find a* resource *and* exploit *it . . . We wring it dry, till it's all used up. Or dead . . . In this case, Max, you* are *the resource.*

"Do you understand, Max?" Ewen asked.

Max sat there in silence. He was worried that he did.

CHAPTER
Thirty-Five

Another month's worth of training in a week.

Jean and Max raced to the Mansion. She beat him. By a lot.
But also by a lot less than she used to.

Max kicked the dummy in the groin and then punched him in
the nose and then delivered a stinging uppercut to his armpit.

"Yes, Max!" Jean cried. And Lord Rothschild, who was in
the garden, too, tending his plants, dropped his watering can
and broke out in applause.

Lieutenant Chumley (*Cholmely? Chemlee?*) had called Ewen,
Jean, and Lord Rothschild to his cottage. He'd pushed the living room furniture out of the way to make space for a circular
card table brought over from the Mansion. It was surrounded
by five chairs.

"From the reign of Napoleon III," Lord Rothschild said as
they all settled into them.

"Not the *most* comfortable," Jean murmured.

"No, they're not," agreed Rothschild. "I hate them."

Chumley was shuffling a deck of playing cards, his willow-wand hands manipulating them into bridges and inverted bridges and rainbows and all sorts of other shapes Max had no name for.

Ewen was passing out coins. Farthings, ha'pennies, pennies, three-pennies, six-pennies, shillings, and half crowns. It was rather a lot of money when you added it all up. Ewen made sure they all got a decent stack in front of them. "You'll have to return this when we finish," he told them. "Belongs to the Treasury."

"Then what's the point of playing?" Jean asked, grinning mischievously.

"The point for you is it's your job," Ewen replied, returning the grin. "The point for Max is he's got to win one of these games before the month of training is up."

Max blurted out: "Since *when?*"

"Since now, Max. And don't complain that I'm changing the terms . . . the terms of a mission change when you least expect it."

Max frowned at the table. It would be impossible to pass training if Ewen kept moving the goal line.

"I'll go rearrange the cards in the deck," Berg whispered.

"To help me win?" Max asked.

"No, to make sure you lose!"

But Berg stayed where he was for the moment.

"Righto," announced Chumley. "It's poker, but the purest form of poker there is. The deal is one card." He passed a single card, facedown, to everyone. "Take a look. Lieutenant Commander Montagu, would you start the betting?"

Ewen looked at his single card and suddenly his face was an utter blank, totally emotionless. He tossed a three-penny coin into the pot.

"Ooh, like your hand, do you?" Jean said.

Max looked at his card. "I don't understand."

"It's rather simple!" Chumley replied. "High card wins!"

"Then why are we betting? If someone has the ace, they should just show it and take the money!"

Lord Rothschild tutted. "Don't you see, Max? If I have a nine, and you have a ten, but I have more courage than you— and a better poker face—you might fold your hand, and *I'd* take the pot. Despite having a lower card!"

Max squinted. Jean "saw" Ewen's bet by throwing in a three-penny coin as well. Chumley threw his card down. "Fold," he announced. Rothschild folded, too.

"What do I do?" Max asked helplessly.

"If you think you have a good card," said Ewen, "you should see my bet by throwing in a three-penny. If you have a great card, you should *raise* my bet by putting in more than that. And if you have a bad card, you should fold like Lieutenant Chumley and Lord Rothschild have."

Max looked at his card again. It was a three. He said, "I'll fold, then."

"All right." Jean turned to Ewen. "Let's see what you have, Lieutenant Commander."

Ewen turned over his card. A queen. Jean threw her card, facedown, into the middle of the table.

"What did you have?" Max asked.

"I don't think I'll tell you that," Jean replied.

"But did you win?"

"If I'd won," Jean answered, "I'd have shown my card. I promise."

Ewen took the money from the middle and Chumley reshuffled and dealt again.

Lord Rothschild opened the betting with a penny. Chumley saw his bet and raised him another penny. They all looked to Max.

Max studied his card. It was a four. Nearly as bad as a three. "I fold," he said. "I have a four."

The table erupted:

"Don't tell us!"

"Keep that to yourself!"

"Bad play!"

Chumley quieted everyone. "Max, *never* give away information if you don't have to. As a card player *and* as a spy."

Max frowned. He should have known that. *Come on*, he chastised himself. *Be extraordinary.*

Ewen folded. Jean put two pennies in to match the bets before hers, and then added two half crowns.

The table erupted again:

"Well, that's moxie for you!"

"Slow down, Jean! We've got all afternoon!"

But Jean just sat there and smirked. Lord Rothschild tossed his card away, facedown. "Too rich for my blood." Which got a good guffaw from the assembled.

Chumley, on the other hand, studied the situation. He did not, Max noticed, study his own card. He studied Jean's face.

"Why is he looking at her like that?" Max asked Berg and Stein.

"Haven't you ever seen a card game?" Stein replied. "He's trying to figure out if she's bluffing or not."

Max had never seen a card game like this and was about to ask what bluffing was . . . when Chumley said, "Look, Jean. I'll fold if you promise to tell me what you have."

Jean replied serenely, "Under no circumstances, Lieutenant. Didn't you *just* teach Max here about not giving away information when you don't have to?"

Chumley sighed. He threw two half crowns into the center.

Jean frowned.

"Call," Chumley said.

Jean continued to frown.

"She's bluffing!" Ewen cried, clapping. "Look at her face! Oh, he's caught her!"

Chumley's mustache folded upward above his curling lips. "Have I, Jean?"

Jean turned over her card. It was a six.

"Ha ha!" Chumley hooted, and flipped over a jack. Lord Rothschild shook his head. Ewen clapped some more.

Max was confused. "Why did you bet so much with such a bad card, Jean?"

Jean looked at him like he was a little bit stupid. "I was *bluffing*, Max."

He said, "You mean *lying*."

Suddenly, everyone's eyes were on Max.

Jean considered. "I suppose you could say that. I *was* lying . . . about how good my card was."

Max made eye contact with Ewen. Ewen nodded ever so slightly.

Oh, Max thought. *I know how to play now.*

The next hand, Max bet two half crowns. Jean laughed and shook her head. "Trying your hand at bluffing the *moment* you learn of its existence?"

Max replied, "Why is that a bad idea?"

Ewen chuckled ruefully.

"It is if you admit it," Jean retorted. Everyone threw in two half crowns.

Max turned over a king.

The whole table started shouting at once:

"What in the world?!"

"But he *just* said . . . !"

Jean's voice cut through the din. "Max! That's not a bluff!"

Max looked at her coolly. "I didn't say it was. You did." And he collected the money.

And Max started to win. Not every hand. Sometimes he had bad cards, and he didn't bet at all. But just about every time he bet, he won. The pile of money started to grow in front of him.

"Are you sure you've never played poker before?" Lord Rothschild asked Max, as the stack of coins in front of the world's richest man dwindled to nearly nothing.

"It isn't difficult," said Max.

Ewen, who had nearly as little money as Lord Rothschild, demanded to know what Max meant.

"Well," said Max. "All I have to do is hide what I feel about my cards, and know what you feel about yours."

"And that's easy for you, Max?" Ewen said. "That's easy to do with a table full of trained clandestine agents?" Lord Rothschild cleared his throat. "And Lord Rothschild," Ewen added.

Max shrugged and looked at his card. He said, "One penny."

"Not very confident, are you?" Jean asked. She saw and raised him.

Chumley sized her up from the corner of his eye . . . and raised again.

Ewen and Lord Rothschild called.

It was back to Max. He said, "I want to bet everything."

A murmur ran around the table. Jean raised her eyebrows.

Chumley frowned at his card. Lord Rothschild cursed. Ewen chuckled.

Jean said, "You started with a penny bet, Max. You don't have a good card under there. Are you *sure* you want to risk your whole stack on whatever that measly card is? Because I am going to call you, I promise. I'll give you a chance to change your mind right now."

And Max . . . hesitated. His eyes quickly scanned the adults around the table. Sweat had beaded on his lip, so he rubbed it away with his sleeve. And then, at last, he said it again: "I'll bet it all." He was trying to sound confident.

"You don't sound the least bit confident," said Jean. She pushed all her money to the center of the table.

Chumley twisted his mustache. Then he put everything in as well.

Lord Rothschild said, "Oh, what the hell, it's nearly dinnertime," and pushed his money in, too.

Ewen was frowning at Max. He didn't look confused. He looked disappointed. "Max, you almost pulled it off."

"Huh?" said Max.

"It was a magical run," Ewen continued. "A great string of beginner's luck. But you gave yourself away just now."

Max said, "I did?"

"You did. Your upper lip started to sweat. And you wiped that sweat away. That means you're nervous. Either you're bluffing, or you've got a card you're not sure is good enough."

Max swallowed hard.

"There!" Ewen pointed. "Your Adam's apple! Just moved like you were gulping down a pint of lager. Another 'tell,' as they're called. Because they 'tell' everyone what you're thinking." Ewen pushed all his coins to the middle. "Call. You've got to show your card, Max."

Everyone looked. And Max suddenly felt like he was going to cry.

He turned his card over.

It was an ace of spades.

Max felt like he was going to cry . . . tears of joy.

"Blast it all!" Chumley shouted, standing up. Lord Rothschild threw his head back and guffawed. Jean pushed herself away from the table like there was something revolting on it.

Ewen just stared at the ace. "I . . . I don't understand. How . . . how did that happen? You were *sweating* for God's sake!"

Very quietly, Max said, "I told you. The game is about hiding how I feel and knowing how you do."

"Yes?" replied Ewen, not understanding.

"As a Jew living in Nazi Germany," Max explained, "that was my whole life."

All the grown-ups stared at the twelve-year-old boy sitting behind the enormous stack of money. After a long silent moment, Ewen said, "All right, I think we really don't need to play poker anymore."

CHAPTER
Thirty-Six

After the poker game, Lord Rothschild announced that he and Max would be dining together. Alone.

At the beginning, Max felt awkward sitting across from Lord Rothschild at the long polished table. But once Lord Rothschild said the Shabbat prayers, Max felt *even more* awkward.

He was having Shabbat dinner with the richest man in the world. He thought back to Germany, his life above the watch repair shop, saying the prayers with his parents, holding hands, as the schmaltzy chicken soup his mother always made on a cold Friday afternoon steamed between him and the candles. And now he was *here*?

He wished he wasn't.

And he wondered when he'd taste that soup again.

Tonight, they were having salmon. Max didn't usually like fish all that much, but his training at Tring Park was so exhausting that he voraciously ate everything on any plate put before him. Lord Rothschild, on the other hand, ate his salmon slowly, as if he were mulling something.

At last, he stopped mulling and spoke. "Sometimes I think,

Max, that we Jews spend our lives tiptoeing on a borderline. Do you know what I mean?"

After a brief pause, Max said, "Um . . . not really, sir."

"Ha! Very good! I appreciate your honesty!" Lord Rothschild smoothed his wiry, slightly wild hair. "Tiptoeing on the borderline . . . what exactly *do* I mean by that? I suppose it's this: On the one hand, you and I look like any good Englishmen. Am I right?"

Max instantly recalled what Harold Wadia had said that day on the rugby field at St. West's: *If you can just keep your mouth shut, you look rather English, don't you? Eventually, they'll forget about you . . . They can't forget what I am. And they won't let* me *forget.*

Max nodded.

"We can blend right in," said Lord Rothschild. "Move along through English society and no one needs know whether we're Jewish or not. And yet, when we're at home, we can light candles on Friday evening and sing songs in an ancient language from a faraway land! That's why I think of it as tiptoeing on a borderline. We can jump back and forth between Jewish and English—an Englishman at the office and a Jew at home, if I want, and no one is the wiser! How convenient! How excellent!"

"It's kinda like dybbuks," Stein put in. "Except we tiptoe on the shoulder-line. And collarbone-line."

"*The collarbone-line's connected to the shoulder-bone line . . .*" Berg started to sing. "*The shoulder-bone line's connected to the . . .*"

Lord Rothschild barreled on. "BUT! There is danger to tiptoeing on a borderline. Because while we can hop back and forth between our two identities—we can also be *pushed*. Anyone can push you one way or the other, in *or* out. So I'm a lord, I sit in the upper house of Parliament, I am probably the richest man in England, at the very peak of power and influence! And so anyone can say, 'Oh, the Jews rule England!' And they *do* say that. Doesn't Hitler say it all the time?"

Max nodded. Hitler, Joseph Goebbels, and all the other Nazis were always declaring that the Jews ruled England. Specifically Jewish bankers. And *specifically* specifically Lord Rothschild.

Max said this. And then he added: "I suppose I'm sitting in the lair of the greatest and most powerful villain in the world right now."

Lord Rothschild threw his head back and laughed—but not in a villainous way. In a sad way. "Right! Just exactly right! How ludicrous! I am indeed as rich as any man alive . . . and yet my role in the war effort is middle management in the British Intelligence Service! I make Nazi dummies for child spies and test explosives in my personal laboratory! And yet they believe I run the country!"

"But if I may ask, sir, what about influence? Couldn't you call Prime Minister Churchill at any time?"

Lord Rothschild nodded vigorously. "Indeed I could! I could visit him and give him a piece of my mind! And do you know what he would do? He would nod sagely and pat me on the head—an eccentric young Jew with delusions about knowing the right thing to do—and send me on my way! I am certain of this because we have gone through this ritual on more than one occasion already!"

"Hm," said Max.

"'Hm,' he says!" Lord Rothschild cried, pointing at Max. "'Hm'! You believed what the Nazis taught you about me?"

Max realized, with some horror, that perhaps he had.

"So it's said I rule England," Lord Rothschild went on, coming to the climax of his argument, "and yet—and here's the proof that we are indeed living our lives balanced on the borders of things—any London plumber walking down the street can point right in my face and say, 'He's not a real Englishman! He's a Jew!' And they do, Max. You know very well that they do."

Max did indeed know very well. He'd seen it every day in how David and Anthony were treated at St. West's.

"So I am the most powerful of all Englishmen one minute, and not *at all* English the next! Look at poor old Léon Blum. He used to be prime minister of France. Lovely man. He created the forty-hour workweek! Taxed the rich and gave the proceeds to the poor. Right he was, too! A kind and brilliant man. And Jewish. A Jewish prime minister. Can you imagine that, Max?"

Max, having grown up under Hitler, certainly could not.

"And do you know what they say in France now, Max? They say, 'Better Hitler than Blum.' Not just the Nazis. The *French* say it. Many do, anyway. Even those who hate the Nazis—many of them hate Jews more."

Lord Rothschild shook his head, and asked Max, "So what is a Jew? The tip of the top? Or beneath the heel of the boot?"

The eccentric lord grew silent and looked owlishly across the empty plates and guttering candles at Max.

"I think he wants you to answer!" Stein whispered.

"Oh!" said Max. "I really don't know."

But Lord Rothschild seemed far away now. "Tiptoeing on the borderline, Max. Or maybe it's perched on the sword's edge. Enjoy the good food while we can, take care of our children and the poor, and try to encourage the nation down a path of enlightenment. Because we Jews know far too well what happens when the darkness falls. *You*, Max, know far too well."

The flickering light of the Shabbat candles threw dancing shadows across Max's face.

He did indeed.

As did his parents, who were living in the darkness. Without him.

CHAPTER
Thirty-Seven

One week left in Max's training.

Max did not wait for Jean to greet him. As soon as the door to cottage number 2 opened and the sleeve of Jean's red jumper winked through the fog, Max was off like a shot for West Field and then the Mansion beyond.

He ran hard, his bent arms like two pistons—left up, right down, right up, left down—just the way Jean did it. Max was still ahead, miraculously, when they made it to the field. As he felt Jean pulling even, he threw every ounce of energy he had into his sprint, and they reached the hay bale at the very same instant.

Jean sprang to the top of it in one fluid motion, and Max could not help but admire, amid his fury and determination, how perfectly she moved, how *extraordinary* Jean was at everything.

Berg tried to make Max lose his grip but he was ready for the little kobold, and he used his right elbow rather than the hand Berg yanked on to get purchase on the hay. He reached the top of the bale a moment after Jean. Then they were down the other side.

As they ran the rest of the way across the field, Jean was just a step ahead. But try as he might, Max couldn't catch her. And as the Mansion came into view, the distance between them increased. She touched the brick wall of the grand house and turned to look at her watch.

Just ten seconds later, Max touched the wall, too.

"Well done, Max!" Jean crowed.

But Max spun away from her and gave the gravel at his feet a vicious kick, spraying tiny white pebbles everywhere.

Max held the dummy's hand and dug his sharp thumbnail into the space between the dummy's thumb and forefinger.

"Good," Jean called. "He'd be bending toward you now trying to grab you by the neck! Strike!"

Max raised his elbow and connected with the center of the dummy's throat.

"Good! End it!"

Max brought his opposite knee up between the dummy's legs and shouted, "HYAH!"

He looked up. The dummy's head remained disconcertingly intact.

Max cursed and punched the dummy in the solar plexus—and his fist bent back at an awkward angle.

As Max sat with an ice pack wrapped around his left wrist, Jean said, "You can't be so hard on yourself, kiddo. You're getting much better."

Max said to Stein and Berg, "Better is *a million miles* from *extraordinary*."

Stein said, "You'll get there."

But Berg tapped his wrist as if he were wearing an invisible watch. "Tick, tick, tick . . ."

Max's back was plastered to the redbrick wall of a walled garden on the east side of the Mansion.

Chumley was somewhere nearby, looking for him. Max had to stay hidden for only three more minutes, and then he'd have won this round of hide-and-seek.

Max had never thought of hide-and-seek as a spy game before, but the way Chumley played it, it was. Chumley stood in a stationary position and watched Max sprint away from him. Max had five minutes to go anywhere on the Tring Park grounds to hide. Once the five minutes of waiting had elapsed, Chumley had another ten minutes to track Max down.

Max hadn't won yet, but he was getting closer.

Max, hidden inside the walled garden, glanced at a wristwatch Chumley had loaned him. Two more minutes. Max took a deep breath. *Wait. Be patient.*

Trying to alert Chumley to their location, Berg grabbed at a ceramic vase that stood in a large niche—but Stein tackled him and pinned him down.

One more minute. As the immortal creatures grappled, Max slowly leaned forward to peer through the garden gate . . .

"MAX!"

Max ducked his head back as quickly as he could.

Too late.

Chumley was upon him in a moment, upbraiding him and wagging one of his preposterously long fingers in Max's face. "You *had* it, boy! Stay still and you'd have won! For God's sake, how many times do I have to tell you—the third rule of losing a tail: you *don't* have to *know* every damn thing! It doesn't *matter* where I am as long as I don't know where *you* are!"

As Berg got free from Stein, he said, "I didn't mess that up. *Max* did."

Max hung his head and tried not to let the tears of frustration leak through his eyelashes.

The writing desk, the floor, the living room sofa—they were all blanketed with sheets of paper with an infinity of permutations of Chumley's name. Max had exhausted every single possibility. The answer *had* to be here on one of these creamy leaves of stationery.

But which one?

Choose wrong, and the training was over.

Of course, the training would be over in a few days now, anyway. Pretty soon, he'd just have to submit a final guess.

Given the number of pieces of paper, and the number of spellings on each one, his chances of guessing right were just about one in infinity.

Max stood with his hands in his pockets. Sergeant Thompson leaned against the guardhouse.

This wasn't part of training. Max simply liked Sergeant Thompson.

Maybe that's *why* Max liked Sergeant Thompson. Because he was the only one who wasn't testing Max and watching him fail.

They were contemplating the sun as it fought through the tops of the trees before it started its early afternoon descent.

"Even when it's sunny, it's not sunny," Sergeant Thompson said.

Max shook his head. "Do you ever regret coming to England?"

Sergeant Thompson didn't hesitate. "Nah. I hate it here. But I told you, Max. When it comes to the people you love most in the world, you will do *anything*. And you'll be right to do it."

Max kept his eyes on Sergeant Thompson as he thought, *I would do anything. If only I knew what to do.*

CHAPTER
Thirty-Eight

Max couldn't sleep. Every time he tried to close his eyes, another version of Chumley's name occurred to him, and he would run downstairs and add it to a list—only to see it already there.

On his fourth time down the stairs, he decided to write another letter.

Dear Uncle Ivor,

I will never send this letter. I will destroy it as soon as it is written. Still, I cannot sleep, so I will write it.

I have good news and bad news. The good news is, I will likely see you very soon. I have missed our table tennis matches. I hope your advanced age has not stolen from you your last strength, and that you will at least try to score a couple of points the next time we play.

The bad news is I will likely see you very soon because I am a rubbish spy, I am slower than a tortoise, I also kick like a tortoise (which is to say not at all), and I have no idea how to spell English surnames.

Max lifted the pencil from the page. He caught his lips between his teeth. Then he wrote:

My mother and father gave me life. They worked so hard to raise me, to feed me, to keep me safe from the bullies and the tyrants and the Jew-haters. They took food from their own plates—when I could see how hungry they were—and put it onto mine. If I can't help them now—if I can't even be with them now, in case there's something I could do to help them—what kind of worthless son am I?

How worthless am I?
How worthless am I?
How worthless am I?

Utterly worthless.

He went back upstairs and lay in bed and his thoughts pummeled him like he was a dummy with swastikas all over his body.

When morning came, Max didn't get out of bed.

He had two days until the deadline.

Why even bother getting up?

He could lose a race to Jean. He could break his hands and feet and every joint in his body trying to make a dummy's head explode. He could play a child's game with Chumley / Tchumley / Chomlee / however you spelled his stupid name—and get beaten even though Max was the child and Chumley was a walking, talking umbrella.

But what was the point?

The only thing he had figured out over the last month was that he was worthless.

The door opened downstairs. "Max?" It was Jean. "Max, are you all right?"

He heard her walking around the living room and kitchen.

She's looking at my avalanche of failures, he thought. *The leaves of paper that represent the Fall of the Child Genius.*

Then she began climbing the stairs. "Max! Max, are you all right? Are you there?"

She came into the bedroom. Max had pulled the covers up over his head.

When Jean saw this, she let out a single sad guffaw. Then she sat down on the edge of his bed.

"May I?" she asked.

"Leave me alone," Max mumbled from under the covers.

He heard the rustling of paper. "Did you write this last night?"

Max didn't have to look to know what she was referring to. Nor did he need to reply for her to know the answer.

It was the letter. He had forgotten to destroy it.

"Max," said Jean. "I could tell you that you're not worthless, but you wouldn't believe me."

Nope, Max thought.

"Me neither!" Berg added, also under the covers.

Jean said, "I could remind you that we have *never* trained a child before, in the entire history of the British secret service. We are only training *you* because you are the *least* worthless boy we have ever come across. But that won't change your mind either."

And Max thought, *If I was worth something, I wouldn't be failing my training.*

I wouldn't be failing my parents.

"So instead of telling you those things," Jean said, "can I tell you why I joined Naval Intelligence?"

Still under the blankets, Max rolled his eyes. Here it came. A pep talk. How predictable. He groaned audibly.

Jean laughed and told him anyway. "On my application, I wrote that I wanted to join up because I love my country and I want to win the war. But if I'm really being honest, that's not why."

Max waited. He was listening. He was skeptical, but he was listening.

"The real reason I joined up, Max, is that life can be so *deadly dull.* There is so much sitting in small boxes—also known as *rooms*—and staring out holes in those boxes—also known as *windows*—wishing you were climbing *through* those holes and *out* of those small boxes."

Despite himself, Max knew what she meant.

"There is so much scribbling on paper, words that don't mean *anything* and that no one *cares* about. Schoolwork that you don't want to write and the teacher doesn't want to read—so why are they forcing you to write it? Do you know what I mean?"

Max did not reply, but of course he knew.

"There's so much small talk, so much chitchat about things you don't want to say and the other person doesn't really care to hear. *So much* of life is like that. Isn't it?"

In his current state of hopelessness, Max felt all these things acutely.

Jean said, "I don't want to fill my life with that rubbish. I want to fill it with *experiences. Challenges. Triumphs.* And also with *failures.*"

Max was definitely listening now.

It seemed she could tell. "Yes, Max. I want failures, too. I want the biggest, broadest range of emotions that I can get. So you feel miserable and worthless, Max? Well, *good.* Because when you're older and you're sitting in a box scribbling words that you don't want to write and no one wants to read, you can think back on these powerful, tempestuous feelings you're having right now and smile."

I don't think I'll be doing that, Max told himself. Though he had to admit, he wasn't *certain* Jean was wrong.

"Shakespeare wrote, ''Tis better to have loved and lost than never to have loved at all.' Do you know what I think he *should* have said? ''Tis better to have *lived* and lost than never to have *lived* at all.'"

Jean became quiet.

Max pulled the covers down from his face.

Jean smiled at him with her crooked teeth and her deep dimples and her fawn-brown eyes. "Think about where we are, Max," she went on. "We're living in cottages on the Rothschild estate, with homemade bombs going off every hour, kangaroos and zebras wandering around just on the other side of the trees, while we train you in espionage for a mission to enemy territory to do your small part to help Britain defeat evil. And you're working your *arse* off, pardon my French, and you are *this close* to succeeding." Max didn't think he was *this close* to succeeding. But everything else Jean said was true. "Max, think about it. Is there *anyone* luckier than you?"

"You're luckier than me," said Max.

Jean shook her head and her hair tossed about. "No, I'm not. I have to stay here, on the home front, and assist a bunch of pompous old men. But *you*, Max. You're going to war. I'm sure of it. You're the luckiest one here."

"You think going to Nazi Germany as a Jewish child is *lucky*?" Berg cried.

Berg was right. *Lucky* was the wrong word. Max was as far from being the luckiest person as he was from his parents. He was as far from being the luckiest person as they were from safety.

He wasn't the luckiest person. But maybe he was the most *alive.*

"We've got two days of training left," Jean said. "How about I kick your butt in our cross-Tring race at *least* one more time?"

Max replied, "Jean?"

"Yes, soldier?"

"Thanks."

She showed him her crooked teeth again. "Don't thank me yet. I'm going to beat you *so very badly* this morning."

And she did.

CHAPTER
Thirty-Nine

After he'd finished training for the day, Max swung by Sergeant Thompson's guardhouse. The sergeant was preparing to go home for the night.

"How's life, Max?" he asked.

Max sighed. "Well, tomorrow's my last day."

Thompson closed the large ledger that sat on the little table in the guardhouse and placed it delicately into a leather briefcase. "You gonna pass your training?"

Max shook his head.

"Really? I'm surprised! You're such a smart boy!"

Max looked at his feet and said nothing. He couldn't think of anything to say that wouldn't make it hurt worse.

Sergeant Thompson latched the briefcase closed and locked it with a small brass key.

For no reason at all, Max asked, "Why do you take the book with you? You could just leave it here for tomorrow morning."

Sergeant Thompson lifted an eyebrow at him. "Are you joking? There's some secret stuff in here. Names of agents, comings and goings . . . I take it to the safe at the Mansion every night." As he closed up the guardhouse, he scoffed, "*Leave it here for tomorrow morning . . . ha!*"

Before he headed off for the Mansion, Sergeant Thompson shook Max's hand. "Good luck, young man. I'm sure you'll figure out something."

Max stared at the briefcase as he said, "Thank you, Sergeant."

And then, to Stein and Berg, he said, "I think I just did."

As Max warmed up beef stew for himself in a small saucepan, he thought about ledgers and kangaroos.

Meanwhile, Berg was talking to Stein: "Will you tell me what in the world is going on with you? You're acting . . . *nice!* Like you're a *garden gnome* or something! It's like I don't know you anymore!"

Stein played with his toes. After a space, he said, "I've been doing some thinking."

"For someone with your mental capacity, I really don't recommend that."

"What if . . . we're doing it all wrong?"

"What?"

"What if . . . we're not *supposed* to be heckling, or annoying, or haunting? The Boss didn't give us any directions at the beginning of time. I've just been *improvising!* What if I've been improvising . . . not right?"

Berg said, "But it *feels* right! Being a pain in the butt feels good, doesn't it?"

"Yes . . ." Stein admitted.

"So? It's clearly what we were meant to do!"

Stein looked up from his toes at last, peered around Max's neck, and made eye contact with the kobold. "But have you ever *tried* helping? It feels . . . good, too."

"I don't believe it," Berg answered.

Stein shrugged.

Berg shook his ugly head. "I refuse to believe it."

CHAPTER
Forty

On the last day of training, Max burst out of bed.

He knew what to do. He'd put it all together in the moments before he fell asleep last night. It had come to him. Like the pieces of a watch, assembled in just the right order, everything fitting just so.

Max did not meet Jean out in front of cottage number 3. She came in and found him in the small kitchenette, surrounded by half a dozen open jars of Marmite, shoving sandwiches into the rucksack she had given him.

"Are you running away, Max? On your last day of training?" she asked, perplexed. And then she added, "I thought you didn't like Marmite?"

Max zipped up the rucksack, shouldered it, and walked out of the kitchen.

"Max! What about our run?"

The door of cottage number 3 swung shut behind him.

Max waited in the woods on the far side of West Field, pacing warily. Unlike in his games with Chumley, he *wanted* to be found. What he *didn't* want was to be surprised. Because being *found* was not the same thing as being *caught.*

He shifted from foot to foot, peering around a large hemlock tree, trying to control his breathing. *Stay calm,* he reminded himself.

Suddenly, there it was.

Loping through the forest toward him.

The kangaroo.

Max started to jog away.

She kept coming.

Max picked up his pace.

So did the kangaroo.

Max began to run.

He ran down the dirt road, back toward the cottages.

The kangaroo hopped after, drawn along by the tangy, salty smell of Marmite.

It was *kind of* like racing Jean, except for once he was in front. Though he knew that if the kangaroo really wanted to catch him, she could.

Not yet . . . Max thought. *Not yet . . .*

He had passed the cottages and could see the guardhouse now.

He started shouting.

"Help! Sergeant Thompson, help me!" Max cried as he broke into a full sprint.

Sergeant Thompson stuck his head out of the guardhouse

just in time to see Max approaching, chased by a very large kangaroo.

"*What in the world—?*"

"*Helllllllllllp!!!*"

Max slid under the lowered arm of the gate, popped up, and kept running. He glanced over his shoulder. As if in slow motion, he saw the kangaroo effortlessly leap *over* the arm.

"*Holy heavens—*" cried Sergeant Thompson. Then he ducked into the guardhouse, pressed a button on his radio, and called for backup.

"The boy, Max, just left the main entrance! Followed by a kangaroo! Yes! Max and a kangaroo! I'm going after them! Somebody cover the gate!"

Max sprinted down the road outside Tring Park, the brick wall of the grounds on his right, woods on the left. He pumped his arms: *left up, right down, right up, left down.*

Come on. This was what he'd been training for all along. He simply hadn't realized it until just now. *Faster!*

But the faster he went, the closer the kangaroo seemed to get.

Sergeant Thompson was now running down the road after them, shouting, "Max! Max!"

With each of the kangaroo's mighty leaps, Max could feel her footfalls making the dirt road tremble.

She was ten feet behind him.

Eight feet.

Six feet.

"WHAT IN THE WORLD WERE YOU THINKING?" Stein screamed.

"HE IS GOING TO BE KILLED BY A KANGAROO!" Berg wailed. "IT IS GOING TO LOOK DISGUSTING!"

Come on, Max thought. *Just a* little *farther.*

Be extraordinary.

And then it seemed the kangaroo decided that this game was boring and that it *wanted the sandwiches.*

With one swift and terrifying leap, the kangaroo was on top of Max. She pushed him down with her arms, and Max slammed into the dirt. He rolled over, wriggling out of the rucksack's arm straps as he did.

He was staring up at the kangaroo. She loomed over him, looking crazed.

Next piece of the watch, Max thought, and suddenly he flung the sack wildly away from himself, toward the wooded side of the road.

The kangaroo's gaze followed the sack.

Then it returned to Max.

He wondered if she might kill him. Out of rage, or pure annoyance.

Max had no doubt that she could.

But then the kangaroo bounded off after the rucksack.

Sergeant Toby Thompson was sprinting down the road toward them. "I'm coming, Max!" he shouted. "Get away from the 'roo!"

Max did as he was told. He climbed to his feet, turned toward the six-foot brick wall that ran along the edge of the Tring Park estate, gave himself a running start, leaped, grabbed the top of the wall, hoisted his belly higher, swung his leg up, and rolled over the wall. Just like it was a hay bale.

Except that the wall was far narrower than a hay bale, so Max crashed down the other side, falling flat on his back.

"Ow," he moaned.

"That was cool!" Berg shouted.

"That was dumb!" Stein cried.

Max could hear Sergeant Thompson on the other side of the wall. "Max! Are you okay? What in the world is going on?"

Max pushed himself up and broke into a sprint again, ignoring Sergeant Thompson. Now he was running back the way he'd come, along the inside of the brick wall toward the little white guardhouse.

The door of the guardhouse was swinging open. A voice on the radio was saying, *Sergeant Thompson? Can you repeat that? What was that about a kangaroo? Thompson, do you copy?*

On the small desk in the guardhouse, the big ledger lay open. Max scanned the entries as he frantically flipped through.

He had to go back six pages, but he found it.

He stopped.

No.

It wasn't *possible.*

He stared a little longer than he should have. Someone would be coming any moment. But he had to be sure.

Then he slipped out of the guardhouse, walked along the brick wall to the dead letter box, paused, and then strolled back toward cottage number 3 as if nothing in the world had happened, and as if half a dozen Military Police officers were not running down the road between the cottages in a panic, toward Sergeant Thompson's cries of "Help! Help! This blasted kangaroo! Someone help me with this kangaroo! What is in this rucksack? Help!"

An hour later, Max was in his room, lying on his bed.

There was a hard rapping on his bedroom door.

He stood up and opened the door. In walked Uncle Ewen, Lord Rothschild, and Jean.

Lord Rothschild was red in the face. His owlish eyes were narrowed and dark.

"Sit down, Max," said Uncle Ewen.

Max sat down on the thin mattress of his bed. The three adults loomed over him.

Ewen inhaled slowly and deeply. "Am I to understand," he began, "that you lured a kangaroo *off the grounds* of Tring Park? Into a road used by *automobiles*? Prompting the *Military Police* to *abandon their posts* in order to save the poor beast? The whole command is in an uproar! Sergeant Thompson might be *fired*!"

Max looked at the brown wool blanket on his bed. He felt bad.

But he thought of the story Sergeant Thompson had told him. And the moral of that story.

"Max!" Max looked up. This was Lord Rothschild. "Kangaroos are *wild animals*! They can be *very dangerous*! Who *knows* what could have happened with her out there on a rampage? What if she'd made it to the village nearby?! Also, kangaroos are *creatures*! Made by *God*! Not toys! Kathy could have been *killed* by a car!"

"Kathy?" said Max.

"That's the kangaroo's name!" Lord Rothschild scolded him. "Kathy Kangaroo! And she might be dead right now, having bounded down a busy road, and then trying to eat Marmite sandwiches with the wrappers still on! The only reason she *isn't* dead is the heroic work of Sergeant Thompson and the other Military Police! I'm glad they saved her—I'm also glad there *apparently* wasn't any attempt by enemy elements to breach Tring Park *while* they were saving her, because it was left completely unprotected! The Military Police detail had to make a split-second decision between the security of some *highly* sensitive documents that are being stored in the Mansion, and the *life* of Kathy Kangaroo! All because of some puerile prank that you decided to pull! What on *earth* were you thinking?"

Max tried to open his mouth, but Uncle Ewen beat him to it. "Really, Max. I don't care if you think you had a good reason." He was shaking his head sadly. "Is it because training is almost over? Is this some ridiculous form of protest? Well, I'm sorry, Max, but if there was any doubt in my mind before that you would not be going on your mission, there is none n—"

Just then the door downstairs slammed open. "Max!" someone bellowed.

"Now what?" Lord Rothschild exclaimed.

"Max!" It was Lieutenant Chumley. "Max, where are you?"

"We're all up here!" Jean called.

Lieutenant Chumley stomped up the stairs, his footfalls as loud as antiaircraft gunfire. He appeared in the doorway—all but his forehead, because he was taller than the doorframe. "Oh!" he expostulated, on seeing the entire team crammed into Max's tiny bedroom. "What have I interrupted?"

"We were just upbraiding young Max here for about a dozen breaches of protocol," Uncle Ewen snapped. "From leaving the grounds without permission, to causing a serious lapse in perimeter security—"

"To endangering Kathy!" Lord Rothschild put in.

"Who?" said Chumley.

"The kangaroo!"

"What *else* did he do, Lieutenant?" Ewen demanded. "Why were *you* looking for him?"

"What did he do? What did he *do*?" Lieutenant Chumley bellowed. "*This* is what he did."

And he thrust a piece of paper into Uncle Ewen's hands.

Jean and Lord Rothschild and Uncle Ewen all bent over the small note.

It read: *Cholmondeley.*

"I'm sorry," said Lord Rothschild. "What does this mean?"

Lieutenant Cholmondeley replied, "It means he's passed bloody training, that's what it means."

Everyone turned and looked at the small boy sitting on the bed.

Very slowly, Max began to grin.

CHAPTER
Forty-One

Uncle Ewen parked his little blue sports car in front of an enormous hotel overlooking the Thames. Lieutenant Chumley (let's keep calling him that, because Cholmondeley is as impossible to read as it is to spell) pulled his junky Ford up right behind and then unfolded himself out from behind the steering wheel. Jean popped out of the Ford's passenger side, stretched her arms wide under the uncharacteristically blue morning sky, and asked Max, "Ready?"

The hotel was a busy, bustling place. Which surprised Max, because he didn't think lots of tourists were coming to London these days, with the Germans dropping bombs from the sky every twelve hours or so. But as Max looked more carefully, he realized that the people hurrying back and forth *weren't* tourists. No one had luggage. There were no crying children or bags from the fancy department stores. Everyone was rushing around like they were in the middle of a hectic workday.

Uncle Ewen, Chumley, Jean, and Max took the lift to the eighth floor, and then walked down a long, ill-lit corridor until

they came to room 818. Ewen rapped on the door. Two raps.
One rap. Three raps.

It was, Max realized with a thrill, a secret passcode. The first
one he'd ever heard.

A chain was undone from the inside and the door opened
to reveal Admiral John Godfrey, who immediately shouted,
"You're late, Montagu, blast it all!"

Uncle Ewen looked at his wristwatch. "We're early, John!
For God's sake! Calm down."

"Not early enough!" grumbled Admiral Godfrey.

They entered a cramped, smoky hotel room, which Max
noticed had no bed. "Come on," the admiral said, "let's get
bloody started!"

"Good morning to you, too," Ewen murmured.

"How are you, Admiral?" Jean said politely.

"Spiffing morning, isn't it?" Lieutenant Chumley added.

Admiral Godfrey barked, "A little less *spiffing* and a little
more *spying*, for God's sake! He'll be here in less than two
hours. Bloody sit down already and let's get started!"

Who will be here? Max wondered. But he didn't have time to
ask, because Uncle Ewen was saying, "Lieutenant, would you?"

Chumley sat down in one of four green, low-slung arm-
chairs that surrounded a small glass coffee table. He gestured
for Max to take the seat beside him. The admiral and Ewen took
the other two chairs, while Jean stepped back to lean against the

wall. Max glanced at her and she gave him a small head shake, which seemed to mean, *Don't worry about me. This is your show.*

Chumley had already begun. "During your time at Tring, when we weren't chasing you 'round the premises or watching you beat a hay-filled dummy half to death, we've been preparing your *legend*, your *cover*, your *reception*, your *targets* . . . all the operational details."

Max raised his hand.

Chumley was surprised. "Yes?"

"I don't know what half those words mean."

Admiral Godfrey shot forward in his chair. He pointed a finger at Max. "You don't have to raise your hand! This isn't primary school! Though for God's sake, that's probably where you should be right now. And you!" He fired a finger at Chumley. "Speak bloody plain English! So the boy *and* I can understand!"

"Right, sorry, Chief." Chumley started again. "We've been preparing your mission."

Max's hands slid down his thighs to his knees and he found himself gripping them tightly.

"You will be going to Berlin," said Chumley.

"YES!" Max shouted.

But only to Berg and Stein.

On the outside, Max remained as impassive as possible.

"*Pending* one last assessment," Chumley added, glancing

warily up at the clock on the wall. "But in the meantime, we have some photographs we'd like to go over with you."

Max wondered what the last assessment could be. Whatever it was, he would pass it. He was too close to going home to fail now.

Admiral Godfrey was handing Chumley a dossier. Chumley balanced it on his knees and looked inside. Then he removed a large photograph and placed it on the low table.

It was of a small German radio shop.

"Do you know this place?" Lieutenant Chumley asked.

Max looked carefully. It appeared to be in Berlin, but based on the trees planted along the sidewalk, it had to be located in a nicer part of Berlin than Max's neighborhood. Maybe it was in Steglitz. Yes. Max thought maybe he'd been there once with his father.

He told them so.

"Do you know anything about it?"

"Just that it's a radio shop," Max replied.

Chumley produced another photograph. This one was of a portly man with a bristle-broom mustache, sitting in a café sipping a small glass of schnapps.

"Do you know him?" Chumley asked.

Max studied the photo. "I don't think so."

Chumley said, "He owns the radio shop." He took another picture from the dossier. It was a photographic portrait of a boy about Max's age. He was chubby, with hair so blond that in the gray-tone photo it looked white. He was squinting at the camera as if he didn't see very well. He wore a Hitler Youth uniform, and he seemed proud of it, because his thick hands were gripping the lapels of the outfit like it might be taken away from him at any second.

"Have you ever seen this boy before?"

Max noticed that the adults in the room were all watching him carefully now. As if his answer mattered a great deal.

"Do you think they want me to say yes or no?" he asked Stein and Berg.

The immortal creatures shrugged. "Whatever they want," Berg said, "would you mind doing the opposite?"

Max, unable to guess the right answer, just gave them the real one: "I don't recognize him."

Very subtly, Ewen shifted back in his chair. And Max realized, *That was the right answer.*

Chumley wasn't satisfied yet, though. "What if I told you his name was Fritz? Now do you remember him?"

"No sir," said Max.

"He might have gone by Freddie," Chumley tried one more time.

Max looked up at the tweedy spymaster and said, "Sorry, I don't know him."

Chumley nodded and looked back into the folder on his lap. He pursed his lips. While he chose the next photo, Max stole a glance at Jean. She winked. Confidence surged through him.

Chumley placed a professional-looking portrait in front of Max. "Any idea who this is?" When Max shook his head, Chumley added, "I daresay you'd know his name if you heard him speak."

Max looked more closely. The photo was of a man with a wide mouth, a prominent nose, and a reassuring confidence in his eyes. They seemed to say, *Just listen to me and everything will be fine.*

"I don't know who it is," Max said.

"Are you sure? He's rather famous."

Max studied the picture again. What was the right answer this time? Yes? It didn't matter; he truly didn't recognize the man.

After another moment, Chumley told him: "This is Hans Fritzsche. Does that ring any bells for you, Max?"

"Oh! Of course! Hans Fritzsche, 'the most trusted voice in Germany,'" Max said. He added, "I listen to his programs all the time," and then he immediately regretted it. He didn't think he was supposed to listen to Nazi news reports. He glanced sheepishly at Admiral Godfrey. Godfrey looked thoroughly disgusted. Max went on quickly: "I just don't think I've ever seen his face."

Why is Chumley showing me a portrait of Hans Fritzsche? Max wondered.

Ewen had now picked up the photo of the blond boy in the Hitler Youth uniform. "Max, this is Fritz Fritzsche. Hans Fritzsche's son. His friends call him Freddie."

"Well, they would," said Lieutenant Chumley, "except, he hasn't got any friends as far as we can tell."

Max could see instantly how hard it would be for this chubby, insecure, nearsighted boy to make friends in the Hitler Youth, or anywhere in Nazi Germany. Max said, "He must look like his mother."

"Perhaps," Ewen replied. "But since his mother doesn't live in Berlin, we haven't got eyes on her."

So he's away from his mother, too, Max thought.

"His father works constantly," Chumley piped up, "since he's Germany's top newsman. So we guess that Freddie there is rather lonely."

The next photograph Chumley produced was not of a person, but rather of a building.

A building that made Max's whole body sing. He would have leaped out of his seat and stood on it if he didn't think that would make them instantly cancel his mission. Before Chumley could even ask, Max said, "That's the Haus des Rundfunks, also known as the Funkhaus. Where all of Berlin's radio stations are broadcast from. The most important broadcasting station in Germany."

Chumley glanced at Ewen and Admiral Godfrey. He even turned around to make eye contact with Jean, whose lips were curling up ever so slightly.

"Ever been inside, Max?" Chumley asked.

"No," said Max breathlessly. "But it's always been a dream of mine." He looked from Ewen to Chumley to Jean to Godfrey. "Is my mission to get into the *Funkhaus*?"

Chumley, apparently ignoring Max's question, said, "As you may or may not be aware, before the Nazis took power, there were roughly a million wireless sets in German homes. Now, thanks to the efforts of Dr. Joseph Goebbels and his Ministry for Public Enlightenment and Propaganda, we estimate there are over *forty* million. Nearly every household has one. And when the Germans listen to the radio—and they listen to the radio *a lot*—they are receiving *messages*. And all of these *messages* are coming from one place. The Funkhaus. The Funkhaus might not be the *brain* of Germany, but it *is* the *nervous system*. It is my personal opinion that, outside of the Reich Security Main Office, the Funkhaus is *the most important building in Germany*."

Max felt like he was about to burst out of his skin. *Say it,* he thought. *Say it, you breathing chimney broom.*

Chumley folded his long body forward to put his elbows on his knees. "Max, our mission for you is to infiltrate the Haus des Rundfunks. How does that sound?"

It was now *very* difficult for Max to speak. He simply managed: "It sounds . . . *really good.*"

"It sounds like a bloody death sentence is what it sounds like," grumbled Admiral Godfrey.

Max looked at Jean. She gave him a solemn smile.

Berg pointed at Admiral Godfrey. "I agree with *that* guy."

Ewen said, "If you do this, you must be *better* than you were at Tring. No messes like that Kathy catastrophe. Yes, it was clever and it got the job done. But it caused immense chaos and attracted far too much attention. From now on everything is clean, disciplined, *absolutely* following orders. Do you understand?"

"I understand," promised Max.

Admiral Godfrey, looking confused, said, "Kathy?"

"Kathy Kangaroo," everyone else replied, all at once.

Just then, a telephone rang loudly, startling them all.

Admiral Godfrey passed an ominous eye over the assembled spymasters. He stood. The phone kept ringing. He picked it up. He said, "Right. On our way." He replaced the receiver.

And the foulmouthed admiral, head of Intelligence for His Majesty's Royal Navy, sounded positively *nervous* when he croaked, "He's here."

CHAPTER
Forty-Two

"*Who* is here?" Max asked in the tense silence of the lift.

No one answered.

Once they reached the basement, Admiral Godfrey led them down a corridor of concrete walls and rubbish bins, to a steel door painted red. He pivoted toward Max. "Just tell the bloody truth and you'll do fine. All right?"

"What is happening?" Max demanded. But Godfrey was already turning the knob on the red door. Max tried to get an answer out of Ewen, or Jean, or Chumley. Or at least some reassurance. He got nothing.

"Why does everybody look so miserable all of a sudden?" Stein asked.

Berg replied, "Yah. I *like* miserable, but they are creeping me out."

Admiral Godfrey pushed open the door.

Max took in the room and swallowed hard. What had once been a basement storage room was now set up for a trial.

Along the left wall of the room were four empty chairs. In the center of the room, facing each other, were two more.

And at the far end of the room was a long table. Two men were sitting at that table.

One appeared to be a general in the army, given the decorations on his olive uniform. He wore a sour frown on his weather-beaten face, and when they entered, he was reading a dossier through preposterously small spectacles.

To the left of the general was a man who looked like an alumnus of St. West's School—an Old Wet—who sported long boyish hair despite being more than fifty years old. The Old Wet was watching them curiously as they entered.

There was a third chair at the long table. Empty.

"Come right in, please!" announced a high sharp voice. A little man stood to the right of the open door. He had a bald head that shone as brightly as his wire-rimmed glasses and his freshly polished black leather shoes. "We are waiting!"

Admiral Godfrey addressed the bald man: "Good morning, Dr. Brown. Is . . . ?" He left the question unasked, but he glanced meaningfully at the empty chair at the long table.

Dr. Brown appeared not to have heard the question. He directed Godfrey, Ewen, Jean, and Chumley to the seats along the wall.

Then he gazed through his wire-rimmed glasses at Max. After a moment of appraisal, he said, "Max *Bretzfeld*," and he pronounced Max's last name the way a fluent German speaker would, with a z that sounded like an s and a d that sounded like a t. Then he reverted to his perfect schoolmaster's English. "My name is Dr. William Brown. *Will* you please sit?" He gestured at the two chairs facing each other in the center of the room.

Max glanced at Jean. She smiled bravely. Max took the chair facing her and the rest of the team.

Dr. Brown snapped, "The *other* chair, if you please."

Dr. Brown's voice was so sharp Max felt like he'd been smacked across the ear with a ruler. He moved to the other chair. The little doctor sat down, too.

Berg said to Stein, "Do you recognize this man?"

Stein said, "No. Do you?"

Berg squinted at the bald doctor.

"Right," said Dr. Brown, slapping his hands on his thin thighs. "Shall we start your psychological assessment?"

One last test, Max thought, *before I see my family.*

"Now," said Dr. William Brown. "We'll begin with—"

Just then, a door opened. It wasn't the one Max and the others had come through. It was behind the long table, off to the right.

Dr. Brown abruptly stopped speaking. A man in a bowler hat and a long baggy black overcoat had entered the room.

Everyone except Dr. Brown looked in the newcomer's direction and then instantly looked away from him.

Max saw him, and then looked away like everyone else had. And then he looked back.

Prime Minister Winston Churchill walked over to the empty chair behind the long table. He was reading something from a long brown folder. He didn't look up, nor did he sit down. He just stood there, reading, as if he were alone in the room. His face was puffy and ugly, with a bulbous nose not unlike those on Berg and Stein.

Dr. William Brown maintained his gaze on Max the whole time, as if the prime minister of Great Britain entering the room was absolutely normal, something to be patiently endured and ignored entirely. Like the chiming of Big Ben—of no great consequence and right on time.

"I am," said Dr. William Brown to Max, attempting to recapture the room's attention, "a specialist in wartime psychology. My particular interest is trauma and fitness for deployment into combat."

Max thought, *Combat?*

Stein said, "COMBAT?!"

"It's typical that someone from my department would do an assessment of an agent before that agent was released into enemy territory. It is also typical that each of you would review our report before a final decision was made. What is *not* typical is that we are doing this review *in person*. But because of the *unique nature* of this agent, a higher standard of scrutiny has been set."

"I don't understand what he's trying to say," Stein admitted.

Max translated: "It's weird that I'm a kid, so they want to be extra sure before they send me to Germany."

"Extra sure of what? That you're going to die?" Berg asked.

"*Please,*" Max said to the kobold, "don't mess this up for me."

And Stein added, "Maybe, just this once, you listen to the kid."

Berg held Stein's gaze for a moment longer than usual. Then he went back to scowling at Dr. Brown like he *knew* him from somewhere.

"In addition to being a psychologist," Dr. Brown went on, "I'm an *expert* on Germany. I've written the *definitive* history of how that state came to embrace Nazism. I had a two-hour *private* meeting with former prime minister Neville Chamberlain before the Munich conference of 1938 to educate him on the German mindset."

There was a sudden guffaw from the long table. Max glanced at the Old Wet, who was covering his mouth like he'd let something escape accidentally. Max figured it was because Neville Chamberlain had returned from meeting with Hitler in Munich and announced there would be "peace for our time." Less than a year later, Hitler was at war with every nation in Europe and Neville Chamberlain had resigned in disgrace.

"*First,*" said Dr. Brown, "I'd like to ask you some basic questions." And off he went.

He asked Max where he'd been born, when he'd been born, who his parents were, what schools he'd attended in Germany . . . They were all questions that Dr. Brown already had the answers to. Max had no idea why he was asking them.

Winston Churchill was still standing, but the file folder was behind his back, and for some reason he was now glowering at a wastepaper bin in the far corner of the room.

And then Dr. William Brown said, "Now, Max, I'd like to play a little *game* with you. Would that be all right?" and he took a small notepad out of an inside jacket pocket. "It is a word-association game. I say a word, and you tell me *whatever* comes to mind. You can say a single word, or you can tell me your life story. *Whatever* occurs to you. Do you understand?"

Max replied, "I understand."

Dr. Brown said, "Germany."

Immediately, Max thought *my country.*

But that was not the right answer. Max was certain. So he said, "Enemy territory."

Dr. Brown studied Max for a moment. "Enemy territory?"

"Yes," said Max.

Dr. Brown frowned and looked at his small notepad again. He said, "The Gestapo."

Max didn't have to pause to consider what word he associated with Germany's secret police: "Scary."

"The SS," said Dr. Brown.

"Terrifying."

"Joseph Goebbels," said Dr. Brown.

"Evil."

"Adolf Hitler," said Dr. Brown.

Max paused, and then said, "Hate."

Dr. Brown stopped. "Yours or his?"

"Both," said Max.

The Old Wet nodded sagely. The general scribbled a note. Winston Churchill's stony frown deepened.

Dr. Brown said, "November 11."

Max furrowed his brow. "Um . . . I don't know. Two days after Kristallnacht?"

Dr. Brown looked at Max with undisguised disbelief. "November 11 is *Armistice Day*. The day Germany surrendered in the Great War."

"Oh!" Max said. And that was all.

Dr. Brown said, "How do you feel about *Armistice Day*?"

How was Max supposed to feel about Armistice Day? Good, because the English had won? Bad, because his country had lost? That was a decade before he was even born! Max shrugged. "Fine? I guess?"

Dr. William Brown continued to gaze at Max with a look of disbelief. Finally, he shook his head and went on with the word-association game with: "England."

For some reason that he could not explain, Max thought: *Sergeant Toby Thompson.*

But Max didn't think *Sergeant Toby Thompson* was the right answer. And clearly he was doing poorly, based on his Armistice Day response. So he said:

"Jean Leslie."

Dr. Brown looked at Max quizzically. *"Who?"*

"That'd be me," Jean said from the side of the room, raising her hand.

"YOU WILL NOT *SPEAK* DURING THE *ASSESSMENT!*" Dr. Brown shrieked. It was so loud and so high-pitched that the room seemed to keep ringing for several seconds.

Max looked at Winston Churchill.

He had turned his back on the proceedings and was studying the file again.

"*No one* will speak!" Dr. Brown snapped, having regained his composure only a little. "Or laugh!" he added, shooting a look at the Old Wet.

Berg said cryptically, "Yah, I've definitely seen him before."

Dr. Brown suddenly spat at Max, "Berlin."

And Max nearly said *home*.

But he stopped himself even though he saw his father bent over a black-velvet-covered table, and his mama sitting on the side of his bed, and himself leaning against his beautiful home-made wireless set as the rich horns of Strauss's *Ein Heldenleben* floated forth and his parents cuddled with each other on the threadbare love seat in their living room.

"Max?" snapped Dr. Brown. "What does 'Berlin' call to mind?"

Again, Max said, "Enemy territory."

And Dr. Brown peered through his small glasses at Max. For a very long time.

Finally, he closed the notebook.

"I was *asked,*" Dr. Brown said—and Winston Churchill turned around again—"to perform a psychological assessment of a *young man* who was bound for Germany to work as a spy." The little doctor took a deep breath. "And yet what I am met with is not a *young man* but a *boy.*"

Max's stomach dropped.

"He is a *boy* in appearance. He is a *boy* in his knowledge of the world. And he is a *boy* in his emotional makeup."

Max could hear his team shifting in their seats behind him.

"The idea of sending him to *Germany* is, to put it bluntly, *preposterous.*"

"I think he's saying no," said Stein.

It's not possible, thought Max. *I've come too far . . .*

"I must respectfully ask: Are you out of your *minds?* Does the Society for the Prevention of Cruelty to Children know what you're proposing? We don't let the coal miners in Newcastle send children into the mines! But you're sending this *boy* to *certain death!*"

"Yeah, he's definitely saying no," Stein concluded.

"To be a spy you have to understand the men and women around you! How could a child *possibly* do that? You have to have total control of your emotions! How could a child do *that?* You have to understand the ins and outs of the nation's politics and history. He doesn't even know the date of Armistice Day! And the pregnant pauses whenever I said 'Germany' or 'Berlin' were concerning in the *extreme!* No child is capable of this kind of task! And if one were, *this one* isn't!"

And Max thought, *I will never see my parents again.*

Stein was gazing at the side of Max's face. The Old Wet and the general were looking at each other. Max's team were whispering. Winston Churchill had the folder under his arm and was buttoning up his coat.

Max said to the immortal creatures on his shoulders, "What a worthless son I am."

And then Berg emitted the longest, heaviest sigh of his eternal life. And he said, "Ask that annoying little man if he has ever visited Munich."

CHAPTER
Forty-Three

"What?" Max asked the kobold.

"Ask him if he has ever visited Munich," Berg repeated.

"What are you doing?" asked Stein cautiously. "Are you trying . . . to *help* him?"

Berg looked very upset. With himself. He didn't answer.

Stein turned to Max. "I don't know what Berg is up to . . . but at this point, what do you have to lose?"

Which was exactly what Max had been thinking.

Dr. Brown was over at the long table. The general had stood up and was shaking Dr. Brown's hand. The Old Wet was waiting his turn. They were all studiously ignoring Winston Churchill, who was glancing at a golden pocket watch.

Quite loudly, Max said, "Excuse me, Dr. Brown."

Dr. Brown appeared to freeze. Then slowly, oh so slowly, he turned to face the boy he'd just dismissed. He said, with menacing innocence, *"Yes?"*

Speaking deliberately and very clearly, Max said, "Have you ever visited Munich, Dr. Brown?"

The doctor furrowed his otherwise perfectly smooth brow. "Certainly," he said.

The room had become very quiet.

Berg said to Max, "When was the last time?"

So Max said to Dr. Brown, "When was the last time?"

Dr. Brown looked uncertainly at Max's team and then at the general and the Old Wet. "It was 1936. October."

Berg said, "Did he have any of those huge pretzels?"

"Uh, what?"

"Okay, forget that one. Did he meet any other doctors there?"

So Max said: "Did you meet any other doctors in Munich?"

Dr. Brown snapped, "What is the *meaning* of these questions?"

"Any Nazi doctors?" Berg added.

"Any Nazi doctors?" repeated Max.

Every person in the room suddenly seemed to have stopped breathing. Even Churchill had looked up from his timepiece and was gazing at the little doctor.

Dr. Brown stammered. "I—I spoke with . . . with *colleagues*. With *eminent* doctors in various fields."

"Like who?" Berg said.

"Like who?" asked Max.

"Um, well . . . *actually*, I don't see what *business* this is of *yours*."

But everyone in the room was waiting for an answer.

Finally, he expostulated, "Yes! Fine! I had dinner with Dr. Ernst Rüdin!"

"You don't say," Ewen murmured from behind Max.

And, for the benefit of the Old Wet, who looked thoroughly lost, Chumley said, "Head of the eugenics and euthanasia projects for Hitler. Murdering disabled people in the name of 'purifying' Germany's gene pool."

The Old Wet's baby-blue eyes opened very wide.

"He wasn't *then!*" Dr. Brown objected. "I mean he wasn't *murdering* anyone then! He was just *discussing* it! And I *disagreed* with him, I'll have you know! Absolutely disagreed! And I told him so!"

"Over a beer at the *Hofbrauhaus,*" said Berg.

Max said, "Over a beer, Dr. Brown? Just two doctors, having a beer at the *Hofbrauhaus,* discussing murder?"

Dr. Brown began to stammer.

"Ask him about the pretzels now," said Berg.

"Did you eat one of those enormous pretzels?" said Max.

"What?! No!" Dr. Brown expostulated. "I mean *yes!* But it wasn't like that!" Suddenly, Dr. William Brown was spitting, "*How* did you know that?" He spun toward Ewen and Max's team. "Did *you* put him up to this? Is this some bloody spy trick? Well, I won't *stand* for it! I advised Prime Minister Neville Chamberlain in 1938!"

"Yes, you mentioned," Admiral Godfrey drawled.

Dr. William Brown's very clean face was now also very, very red. He stuck out a finger and wagged it at everyone. "This is *outrageous* . . . and *irrelevant* . . . and . . ." He was aiming his finger at Max now. "*How* did you know that?"

Max didn't reply.

The general was smirking at Dr. Brown. "Does anyone have follow-up questions for the good doctor?" he asked.

No one seemed to.

"In that case," said the general, "I vote yes to the mission."

Max caught his breath. Dr. Brown looked like the shiny top of his head was about to blow off. Maybe it had streamers inside.

The general turned to consult the Old Wet. The boyish man with the floppy hair looked almost surprised to be asked. "Well, I say yes! Absolutely!"

And then everyone looked to the far end of the long table. To Winston Churchill. He was still standing, but he'd gone back to scowling at the file folder. He hadn't bothered to open it, though. He was just scowling at the cover.

"Prime Minister?" said the general. "You have the final word, of course."

Dr. William Brown was practically begging now. "Prime Minister, you can't *possibly* think this is an appropriate thing to do . . . really, it's out of the *question*, isn't it?"

For the first time, Churchill slowly swiveled his large, jowly frown toward . . .

Max.

The first and only words the prime minister uttered were "Good luck, young man. And . . . thank you."

Then he nodded curtly at Admiral Godfrey, tossed the file folder onto the table, and left the room.

Max and his team were alone in the basement of the hotel on the Thames. Admiral Godfrey said to Max, "How on earth did you *do* that?"

And Max smiled. "I could tell you. But you would never believe me."

Jean and Ewen and Chumley and Godfrey were all gazing at Max in wonder. Ewen said, "Could you do it again?"

Max silently asked Berg, "Could I?"

Berg shrugged. "Maybe."

"How did it feel?" Stein asked. "To *help* for once?"

Berg shot back, "How do *you* think it felt? You've been helping for *weeks* now, you traitor!"

Stein said, "I told you already. Strange. But not bad."

Berg grumbled, "Yah. It's very *confusing.*"

Max kept all that to himself. He just answered, "Yes, I could."

Jean was rubbing her head in wonder. Lieutenant Chumley was grinning like an idiot.

"So . . ." said Max. "Can I go to Berlin now?"

CHAPTER
Forty-Four

Lieutenant Chumley was driving, Uncle Ewen was in the passenger seat, and Jean and Max were sitting in the back. The military-issued Humber Snipe—Britain's Jeep—rattled over the dirt road, through a wide heath as the sun set. Bare bushes were pushed around by strong gusts of wind. Which made Max very nervous, because he was about to get in an airplane.

He'd never been in an airplane before.

Neither had Berg or Stein. They were *not* thrilled.

"Flying is for birds! And angels! And fairies!" Stein was saying. "Look at my face! Do I look like a fairy to you?"

"I don't want to do this. I can't do this. Please don't make me do this," Berg pleaded. Max had never heard him sound so earnest. Or scared. It was kind of sweet.

But Max wasn't really paying attention to the panicking passengers on his shoulders, because a conversation he'd overheard between Admiral Godfrey and Uncle Ewen was banging around in his head.

Max had spent the last week studying the details of his mission. He'd studied the photos of every important person who might walk in or out of the Funkhaus. He'd learned his cover identity upside down and inside out. He'd been drilled over and over again on where to go and what to do if he suspected his cover had been blown. At the end of it all, Admiral Godfrey had wished Max good luck. And then he'd taken Uncle Ewen aside.

"Listen here, Ewen. How much does the boy know? Worst case, what can he tell the Jerries about us?"

Lieutenant Chumley was showing Max the photographs of his targets for the hundredth time. The people Max would need to befriend, or manipulate, or use and discard in order to infiltrate the Funkhaus. The shop owner with the push-broom mustache. Hans Fritzsche's son, Freddie. Max's upstairs neighbor, Pastor Andreas Maas.

But Max was only pretending to look at the pictures again. In fact, he was eavesdropping on Admiral Godfrey and Uncle Ewen.

"All he knows about," Admiral Godfrey went on, "is what he saw during training and at the hotel, right? And his mission. Nothing else?"

"Nothing else, Admiral."

"So the worst that can happen"—Admiral Godfrey threw a look over his shoulder at Max—"is that they catch him, torture him, and dump him. He can't give them anything they don't already know."

Even from the corner of his eye, Max could see Ewen's face turn pale. "Let's hope it won't come to that, Admiral."

"But worst case?"

"Yes. Worst case, he is merely caught, tortured, and killed. No harm done to us."

"We're not giving him a cyanide pill?"

Uncle Ewen nearly choked on his own tongue. "*No*, Admiral, we are *not* equipping a twelve-year-old child with a pill for committing suicide."

"Thought it might be prudent."

"It would *not* be prudent. If he gets caught he is to tell the Germans everything he knows. Which is nothing compromising."

"Fine, fine," Admiral Godfrey said, nodding vigorously. "He's not even English, after all. Just a foreign refugee who came to stay for a while." Then he turned and smiled at Max while still speaking out of the corner of his mouth to Ewen. "All right, then. Let's see what the little freak can do."

"Max." Uncle Ewen had turned to face him in the back of the Humber.

"Yes, Lieutenant Commander?"

"There's one more thing I need to tell you before I let you go."

Max swallowed and waited.

Uncle Ewen said, "You'll be making your way back to your apartment building in the Kreuzberg neighborhood of Berlin, as we discussed."

Max nodded.

"And you're certain you know how to get there?"

"I lived there for eleven years. I know how to get there," Max assured Ewen for the fifth time that day.

"Right. Well, when you arrive, you'll want to ring the *fourth* bell."

"Of course," lied Max.

The fourth bell was Pastor Andreas Maas's apartment. Max would be living with the pastor, pretending to be his nephew from the countryside, and taking on the name Max Maas. That way he could pretend to be a Lutheran Christian—not a Jew.

But his parents lived right below Pastor Andreas, and secretly Max was planning to spend as much time with them as possible. Every night, of course. And even during the daytime, when he could get away with it.

And he would *not* be ringing the pastor's bell first.

He had already imagined the whole thing. Ringing his parents' bell in the dead of night. Them being terrified that it was the Gestapo. They would look out the window, and Max would step back into the street and wave—and they wouldn't be able to believe it. They would rush downstairs, and open the door, and he would leap into their arms. His mother's first, certainly, and then his father would wrap them both in an embrace, and they would whisper, *Family hug!* Like they always used to.

Max had thought about it every two minutes for the last week.

Uncle Ewen interrupted Max's daydreaming. "Be sure to ring the *fourth* bell . . ."

"I *know.*"

"Because the people in your old apartment are *not* to be trusted."

Suddenly, there was a very loud sound in Max's ears.

"Oh no," Stein murmured.

Max said to Uncle Ewen, "What do you mean 'the people in my old apartment'?"

"They're called the Persickes. They moved in after—" Suddenly Uncle Ewen stopped speaking. "Max," he said. "Max, you didn't think your parents were *still* living there, did you?"

The Humber was still driving, still rocking from side to side, but it was as if all sound had been stripped from a film and had been replaced by a loud noise that seemed to be coming from *everywhere.*

"Max, your parents haven't been in that apartment for *months.* We don't know where they are. I told Stuart—Mr. Montagu—as soon as we found out. I thought he had told you."

All Max could hear was the sound of Ewen's voice and that loud noise, which he had begun to suspect was coming from inside his own head.

"Max, can you hear me?"

You are all I can hear. You and this noise—this infernal screaming—inside me.

"Is Max okay?" Berg asked Stein.

"What do you think?" Stein replied.

"I think no?"

Jean put a hand on Max's shoulder. "Max, you didn't think you would be living with your parents, did you?"

Max didn't answer. He couldn't have even if he'd wanted to. The screaming in his head was too loud.

"Max," Chumley cut in. "You *must not* go looking for them. Do you understand? Wherever they are, it would put them in grave danger—because it would mean their child is a British spy. And it would put *you* in grave danger, because it would mean you are a Jew. And then they'd be dead. And you'd be dead. You don't want to be dead, do you, Max?"

I don't know. It might quiet this screaming.

"Max!" Ewen pressed him. "Max, do you understand? Max, can I trust you? I can't send you on this mission if I can't trust you *not to go looking for your parents.* Please tell me now."

Suddenly, the sound came back, and that weird screaming inside Max's head stopped. He looked at Jean, and then over to Uncle Ewen, and he said, "You can trust me. I won't look for them. I promise."

Berg asked Stein, "Is he lying right now?"

Stein answered, "I can't tell."

Ewen was saying, "You'll be in one of the most important buildings in the entire German war effort. Our eyes and ears. This is *crucial work.* So please, for the love of God and all that is good—focus on that."

Jean still had her hand on Max's shoulder. "You can't help us if you go looking for your parents. And it won't help them either. It's more likely to get them killed. Really, Max. Are you hearing us?"

Max nodded.

Ewen said, "Do you promise me, Max?"

"I promise you, Uncle Ewen."

And then Max promised himself:

I will find them if it's the last thing I do.

CHAPTER
Forty-Five

The sun was down and the sky was gray-red. Ewen, Chumley, Jean, and Max seemed to be in the center of a sea of gorse bushes, and, like any sea, the wind whipped up waves across them.

A dozen aircraft were stationed in the middle of the heath. Three large bombers, and the rest smaller fighters. "You'll go in one of the big boys," said Ewen as they walked across the tarmac. "The Spitfires here are your escort."

"This is all for me?" Max wondered.

"Oh no. This is a bombing run. You're a stowaway."

Lieutenant Chumley saw someone ahead in the red dusk and began waving a ridiculously long arm above his head. The man started toward them.

"I don't get it," said Max. "One of these planes is going to land during a bombing run? Without getting spotted?"

"Land?" said Uncle Ewen. "None of these planes is going to *land*. At least, I certainly hope they don't. That would mean something has gone terribly wrong."

"I don't understand."

Jean linked arms with Max as she said, "You're going to *jump*."

"WHAT?!" Berg screamed.

"That's a joke," said Stein. "Trust me. I make sarcastic, *sick* jokes all the time. I know one when I hear one. She's joking."

Uncle Ewen pointed to the man Lieutenant Chumley had waved to. "That's Johnny Jameson. Commando. First rate. You'll be strapped to his chest. When he jumps."

"So *you* won't be jumping so much as *falling*, attached to someone who's jumped," Jean said.

"No, no, no, no," said Berg. "Walk away, Max. Get out of here."

"Just run!" said Stein. "What are they going to say? They can't force you to do this!"

But Max couldn't have run if he'd wanted to. His legs had turned to jelly. He was surprised he was still walking and hadn't collapsed in a puddle. Suddenly, the propeller of a Spitfire started up, very nearby. Max should have been startled—but his heart was beating so hard and so fast that he didn't have any more capacity for fear.

Major John Jameson greeted Ewen and Chumley and Jean. He had a thin mustache and a big chin and a broad smile with many golden teeth. When he and Max shook, he crushed Max's little hand. But not maliciously. On the contrary, he was in high spirits.

"Well, this is *really* spiffing!" he said. "Certainly a first for the RAF!" That meant the Royal Air Force. "A tandem jump with a child!"

"I'm glad *he's* excited," Berg said. "I am about to throw up."

"Have you ever seen kobold puke?" Stein asked Max. "It's awful."

"He's not a *child*," said Jean to Major Jameson. Then she added, "Well, *legally* he is, but he's *very* mature."

Max tried not to faint as Major Jameson told him what to expect. Jameson was shouting because more and more of the planes around them were starting their propellers. "Nothing to it, Max! Not to worry! We'll get in the bomber, sit down in the bomb bay, and I'll strap you to my chest! I'll have the parachute on my back, of course! Our pilot and navigator will get us within spitting distance of Berlin, and at the right speed so we won't die on impact with the ground!"

He grinned. Max was trying very hard to hide that he was on the verge of crying.

"Once we're over the target," Major Jameson continued shouting, "I'll open the bomb bay door! And then one, two, three, Bob's your uncle! What do you say!"

Max opened his mouth and tried to speak, but all the sound was strangled in his throat. Half an hour ago, Max would have told himself, *Just get in the plane and jump out. Your parents are waiting for you in Berlin. The quicker you do this, the sooner you see them.* But now he *couldn't* tell himself that. And did he *really* think he could find them? Were they really even still *alive*?

He looked at Uncle Ewen.

"Just tell him you've changed your mind, Max," Berg said.

Stein added, "No one is gonna blame ya, kid."

Max decided to tell Uncle Ewen he'd changed his mind.

And then Jean smiled at him. His Mother.

And he thought of his mama.

And his papa.

So Max turned to Major Johnny Jameson and said, "What are we waiting for?"

CHAPTER
Forty-Six

The bomber's bay door was trembling. Or maybe that was just Max.

He was sitting on Major Johnny Jameson's lap. Which was weird. He hadn't sat on anyone's lap for a really long time. The last person was his mother, the night before he'd left for England.

He hadn't, he realized, even been this physically close to another person in over a year—except for that one hug from Uncle Ivor. How Max wished he were with Uncle Ivor right now.

They'd been in the air for a couple of hours, and Max was freezing. The air whipped through the bomb bay, turning the sweat that was covering Max's body into frost.

"I hate this I hate this I hate this I hate this," moaned Berg.

Stein was whimpering incomprehensibly.

The navigator turned and looked over his shoulder. He and the pilot were just visible in the cockpit through the dark machines and wires. "Ten minutes to drop point!"

Johnny Jameson gave the man a thumbs-up. "Righto!"

"WRONGO! THIS IS WRONGO!" Berg screamed.

Max agreed. He did not want to jump out of a plane. What had made him think he could do this? You were not *supposed* to jump out of planes. You weren't even supposed to jump out of *trees*. And this plane was probably as high as a *hundred* trees. This was stupid.

"Five minutes!"

Max started wondering if he could tell Major Jameson that he'd changed his mind. He began planning what he would say: *I'm sorry, Major. I don't want to do this. I don't think I can really be much help to the British. I'm just a kid. Could we just turn around? Or I'll stay here and you can jump, if you need to. It's really no problem for me. I'll just unstrap myself from you. Okay?*

But none of these words passed through his teeth, which were chattering hard. He couldn't tell if it was the cold or his fear. Probably both.

Max thought back to his goodbyes with Ewen and Chumley and Jean. Jean had almost brought him in for a hug. He thought. But instead, she'd just pulled him close and said, "Remember your training."

And he'd said, "Everything is training."

And she smiled sadly with her beautiful crooked teeth and said, "Not anymore."

Suddenly, the pilot shouted, "GO!"

Major Jameson kicked the bay door and it swung open.

Max heard himself shouting, "I don't want to! Please!"

"Listen to the kid!" Stein pleaded. But either the plane was too loud for Major Jameson to hear, or he was ignoring Max.

The dark ground was far below, tiny trees and hills and towns, appearing and disappearing in moments.

"I wasn't made for this . . ." Berg wept softly.

Then they were sliding through the bomb bay door, and Max's legs were dangling in the air, and his stomach was pressed up against the edge of the bomber's floor, and he was about to—

"BLAST!"

"What?!" Max cried.

"BLAST IT ALL!" Major Jameson shouted. "WE'RE STUCK!"

I'm going to die I'm going to die I'm going to die, Max was thinking.

"He's going to die he's going to die he's going to die," Stein was saying.

"I don't even like the kid that much," Berg was sobbing. "I just don't want to see his skull pass through his lungs."

"CHAPMAN, GIVE US A HAND!" Jameson screamed.

Max saw the navigator look back through the darkness, unbuckle himself, and then hurry toward them, crawling through the machines and wires. His eyes were wide and panicked. He took in the situation—Max and Major Jameson wedged in the bomb bay door, Max pressed against one side, the parachute pack pressed against the other, neither the boy nor the commando able to drop or to climb up. And then Max saw the navigator raise one boot high in the air and bring it down hard on Major Jameson's parachute pack.

Max's chin slammed into the steel edge of the bomb bay door.

And then there was nothing pressing against Max's stomach, and wind was lashing his cheeks, and they were in free fall.

CHAPTER
Forty-Seven

It was very fast, and then there was a violent jerk, and then it was very slow.

They hung in the air, Major Jameson's stomach pressed against Max's back, floating gently over the sleeping German countryside.

Stein and Berg were both weeping.

Max wanted to ask where they were, because Berlin was nowhere in sight, but Major Jameson had warned him not to speak while they were floating to the ground, lest their voices carry and alert someone down below. Even after they'd landed, Max was to wait until he was spoken to—so Major Jameson could determine that the coast was clear.

They floated through the frigid night air, over trees and fields and dark houses with lit windows. It was peaceful.

Until it was not.

Max had had no idea how fast they'd been going until the ground was right below them, and Major Jameson put his legs out to steady them both—but they were going too fast, and suddenly they were both somersaulting, heads crashing into the frozen ground, parachute cords wrapping around their necks and arms.

Finally, they came to a stop, and everything was still.

Max hurt all over. But the adrenaline coursing through him reduced the pain to a distant ache.

Max waited for Major Jameson to speak. Or move.

"Uh, Max, is that guy okay?" Stein asked.

Berg was hugging the earth, crying and kissing it and crying some more, saying, "Sweet earth! Sweet, sweet earth! I swear I'll never leave you again."

Max said to Stein, "Major Jameson is keeping still until he's sure the coast is clear."

They lay there for a few more minutes.

"I think," said Max.

An owl called in the distance.

It was very cold.

"He's not moving, Max," said Stein.

"Yah, he is totally still," Berg agreed.

Max started undoing his harness very quickly. Trying not to panic. He was so tangled in the cords he couldn't untie them and they scratched his neck and face as he slid out from their grip.

Finally, he was free, panting German air and kneeling over Major Jameson.

Major Jameson's eyes were open.

Under his head was a pool of black blood that reflected a slim crescent moon.

Major Johnny Jameson was dead. Max was alone.

"What now?" Stein asked.

Well, not totally alone.

"Wasn't this guy supposed to get you to safety?" Berg asked. "I'm pretty sure about a thousand Nazis are going to start looking for you any second."

"Yeah, Max." Stein sounded nervous. "What's the plan?"

Max stared down at the dead commando.

The plan was . . . to put the watch together, one piece at a time.

HOW MUCH OF THIS STORY IS REAL?

Max in the House of Spies is a work of fiction. Obviously. The British did not send a twelve-year-old boy to Nazi Germany as a spy. Also, we don't have any evidence that invisible, eternal kobolds and dybbuks exist. Though they could. I hope they do.

But even though the story is fiction, nearly every element of it was inspired by fact. Many of the characters are real people, most of the settings are real places, and all the significant historical events really happened.

The *Kindertransport*

Both Max's journey and my personal connection to his story begin with the *Kindertransport*. In 1938 and 1939, ten thousand Jewish children were taken out of Germany to escape the Nazis. They were sent away from their parents to live with families in Great Britain. Why didn't their parents go with them? Because they weren't allowed to. Great Britain, like the United States and just about every other country in the world, said they had too many Jewish people already. Even the countries that didn't have any.

Michael Steinberg having just boarded the train in Berlin that would take him to Holland, where he would get on a ferry bound for Harwich, England.

Michael Steinberg, aged 55, with the author (me), aged one.

I became aware of the *Kindertransport* at a young age, because a close family friend was one of those children. When he was ten years old, Michael Steinberg was sent by his mother to live with a family in England. His story was very much like Max's: He was put on a train to Holland with other Jewish children and a few adult chaperones; they got on a ferry that took them to England; then they waited anxiously at the dock to see which family would take them home. Many children never saw their parents again. Some were luckier. Michael was one of these relatively lucky ones—his mother was able to join him in England after the war.

Kobolds and Dybbuks

Kobolds and dybbuks may or may not be real—but I certainly didn't invent them. *Kobold* is a German word that became *goblin* in English. Kobolds were thought to be mischievous spirits who typically lived in homes or in mines under the earth. In fact, the blue stone cobalt got its name because when it's mined it releases a poisonous gas, and when German miners got sick they blamed the kobolds. So if you ever hear someone describe the sky as "cobalt blue," they are actually referring to Berg. Kinda.

Dybbuks come from Jewish mythology. They have historically been thought of as evil spirits that take possession of a person and torment them. The term *dybbuk* has its roots in the

Hebrew phrase "a case of attachment," and the verb "to cling." Which describes Stein pretty well, I think.

The Montagu Family

I am very pleased to report that there really was a Montagu family. Ewen Montagu really did work for British Naval Intelligence, and he really was the boss of Ian Fleming—the man who invented James Bond. Ivor Montagu really was the founder of the English Table Tennis Association. (But he was actually a rather accomplished filmmaker—I wasn't quite fair to him in that regard). Mr. and Mrs. Montagu really did have two sons, David and Anthony (and also a daughter, who was older). They did live at 28 Kensington Court, and the family patriarch really was born Montagu Samuel, but his family changed his name to Samuel Montagu when he was a child in an attempt to protect him from the antisemitism that was rampant in England in the nineteenth century (and continued unabated into the twentieth).

And while Max is fictional, Ivor and his wife really did take in a child from the *Kindertransport*. I don't know if that child became a spy or not—but we can always imagine.

Radios

In 1939 and 1940, radios were a bit like computers were in the 1980s and early 90s (I realize that reference is only helpful if you're ancient like me): radios of the time were expensive but becoming less and less so; most families had them—but never more than one; and there were people, like Max, who built their own radios, took them apart, and kept close tabs on this cutting-edge technology.

Portable radios like the one Max uses by the river were not common in 1939, but nearly all radios could run on a battery—and kits for making radios at home were available from specialty stores and mail-order catalogs. Of course, Max wouldn't have needed a kit. He would have ordered individual parts and built a custom portable set.

Because European nations are so physically near one another, listening to radio broadcasts from other countries was easy. This meant that nations at war often used radio to spread information, propaganda, and misinformation to their neighbors. In Nazi Germany, listening to foreign broadcasts was illegal, though people did it anyway. Some German radios were even manufactured to prevent listening to broadcasts from other countries, but a radio wiz like Max could usually find workarounds.

St. West's School

St. West's School is inspired by real schools in England, particularly the Westminster School, which has a marvelous online catalog of historical archives. I don't know if the pigeon prank was ever pulled off there, or anywhere, but it's an old urban legend that's been told about schools from Oxford to MIT.

Harold Wadia is an invented member of the real Wadia family, a Parsi family from India who became wealthy building ships and dyeing cotton. In the early twentieth century, the Wadias had a major presence in both India and in England, including quite a few children in England's exclusive private schools.

The disgusting taunting of Jewish students by placing a fist at the end of one's nose and cooing "groo groo" is, sadly, taken verbatim from an account of a Jewish student who attended an exclusive school in England a few years after Max would have.

The Blitz

In 1940, Hitler directed his air force to bomb London and other major cities across Great Britain, in an attempt to break the spirit of the British people and convince their leaders to give up on the war effort. Forty thousand civilians died, two million homes and many other buildings were destroyed, and an untold number of people were injured and traumatized. Like the Montagu family, many Londoners fled the city during the Blitz—it is, in fact, the event that sent Susan, Peter, Edmund, and Lucy to the house of the old professor in *The Lion, the Witch, and the Wardrobe*.

But instead of breaking Britain's spirit, the Blitz ultimately had the opposite effect, strengthening the British commitment to defeating Hitler and uniting the population in the war effort.

The World of Spies

During World War II, British spying was divided between different groups—the codebreakers at Bletchley Park; the Security Service (sometimes called MI5) who defended Great Britain from foreign spies; the Secret Intelligence Service (sometimes called MI6) whose job it was to spy overseas; and the intelligence services of different military branches, including Naval Intelligence, run by Admiral John Godfrey. The work of these various groups overlapped, and they often worked together—though not always smoothly.

But they were often quite effective. For example, despite constant worries that Great Britain was crawling with German spies, we now know that the British intelligence services had found and neutralized *every single* German spy in the British Isles within the first year of the war. Even more impressive, Germany *didn't know*. The British made the Germans believe that their spies were still operating, while in fact feeding the Germans false or trivial information.

Within Naval Intelligence, Charles Cholmondeley (pronounced *Chumley*) really did work with Ewen Montagu on some of the most exciting and unorthodox intelligence operations of World War II, Jean Leslie really did assist them, and Admiral Godfrey really did curse his way through the whole ordeal. Tring Park really was used for storage of sensitive documents during World War II; and Lord Victor Rothschild, who owned the place, really was in charge of explosives and anti-sabotage measures for MI5—including dismantling German bombs in his own personal laboratory.

Sergeant Toby Thompson is invented, but the Trinidadian Labor Revolt he describes is one of the seminal moments in Caribbean history, and should be widely known and studied. Toby Thompson calls the indigenous people of Trinidad Caribs, which was the common word at the time. He wouldn't have known that that term was used by the Spanish to identify Amerindians who they targeted for enslavement. The tribes of Trinidad would have referred to themselves as the Nepoya, the Suppoya, and the Yao.

Camp 020 was a real place. It was likely George Orwell's inspiration for Room 101 in his novel *1984*. Captain "Tin Eye" Roberts is based very closely on a real interrogator—Lieutenant Colonel Robin Stephens—who really did hold awful viewpoints on racial and national superiority. Dr. William Brown was a specialist in battlefield trauma and also a prolific author on the mindset of the German nation; his officious attitude and relationship with Nazi doctors was entirely made up for dramatic purposes. My apologies to him.

I am deeply indebted to the many researchers who have uncovered the hidden histories of World War II. The sources that most influenced *Max in the House of Spies* are listed in the bibliography that follows.

But I am equally indebted to an author of fiction: John le Carré. John le Carré perfected the form of the literary spy novel: He wrote of richly real, deeply flawed people trying to navigate a world where motivations are unclear and morals are murky at best. He wrote page-turners that break your heart.

I once wrote to Mr. le Carré, to point out a neologism that has since become ubiquitous. He is widely credited with introducing, or reintroducing, the word "mole" into English as a synonym for "double agent." But in his book *A Small Town in Germany*, I believe he also introduced the modern meaning of the word "stalking"—in the sense of following someone in a creepy way. After receiving my letter, Mr. le Carré very kindly wrote back:

"Well, it never occurred to me that I was breaking fresh ground with 'stalking' and I'm tickled by the notion, even if I suspect it may not hold. To be truthful, I no longer know what may have been original to me, and what not. As a fellow writer, you will know that we invent everything we write, even if someone has done it before."

That is particularly true of this book. *Max in the House of Spies* is a work of fiction, fabulation, and invention—even though much of it had been done, in real life, before.

ANNOTATED BIBLIOGRAPHY

Perhaps no period in history has had more written about it than World War II, so it can be daunting to know where to begin researching it. Here are a few of the sources that were instrumental to me in writing this book, with notes—to help you decide if they might be useful to you, too.

Harris, Mark Jonathan, and Deborah Oppenheimer. *Into the Arms of Strangers: Stories of the Kindertransport*. London, New York: Bloomsbury, 2000.

This book should be required reading for any educator who teaches the Nazi period. It is a collection of first-person accounts of the *Kindertransport*. The participants remember their experiences as children: life in Nazi Germany and Austria; *Kristallnacht*; the flight to England; and their lives once they got there. It is so rare, in primary sources, to find details this specific to and appropriate for young people.

Macintyre, Ben. *Operation Mincemeat*. New York: Broadway Paperbacks, 2011.

Macintyre, Ben. *Agent Zigzag*. New York: Three Rivers Press, 2008.

Ben Macintyre is probably the most respected writer of nonfiction spy stories working today. He has been granted special access to the archives of the United Kingdom's Secret Intelligence Services, and he has used that access to write deeply researched, hilarious, thrilling, shocking, and moving accounts of the world of espionage. Both of these books are utter joys to read. For adults and young people aged thirteen and up.

Welch, David. *The Third Reich: Politics and Propaganda*. London, New York: Routledge, 2002.

Bergmeier, Horst, and Lotz, Rainer. *Hitler's Airwaves: The Inside Story of Nazi Radio Broadcasting and Propaganda Swing*. New Haven, London: Yale University Press, 1997.

These two books give a detailed look into the propaganda program in Nazi Germany, and the use of radio in that program. *The Third Reich* is an excellent overview of how the Nazis thought about and implemented propaganda, and was the very first book I read in the process of creating Max's story. *Hitler's Airwaves* is a remarkably researched deep dive into the *Funkhaus* and the specifics of Nazi radio programming. Recommended for adults.

British SOE. *How to Become a Spy: The World War II SOE Training Manual.* New York: Sky Horse Publishing, 2015.

Hoare, Oliver, ed. *Camp 020: MI5 and the Nazi Spies: The Official History of MI5's Wartime Interrogation Centre.* Richmond: Public Record Office, 2000.

These are remarkable primary sources about the training of British spies and the interrogation of suspected enemy spies. Crack them open, see the typewriter typeface, and you just might feel like you're an intelligence officer in 1940 yourself. Recommended for adults and teens who are excited about primary sources printed in courier font.

Kaplan, Marion A., ed. *Jewish Daily Life in Germany, 1618–1945.* Oxford: Oxford University Press, 2005.

Meyer, Beate, Hermann Simon, and Chana Schütz, eds. *Jews in Nazi Berlin: From Kristallnacht to Liberation*. Chicago, London: Chicago University Press, 2009.

Pine, Lisa, ed. *Life and Times in Nazi Germany*. London: Bloomsbury Academic, 2016.

These books are scholarly collections of academic essays on various elements of life in Germany. If you want to understand a specific aspect of everyday German life during these periods, these are excellent sources. Recommended for adults.

———

Cohen, Roger. "A Jew in England," *New York Times*, November 30, 2009.

Lezard, Nicholas. "On Being a Jew-ish Schoolboy," *New York Review of Books*, November 21, 2018.

These two essays provide moving, and distressing, windows into what it was like growing up Jewish in England in the middle of the twentieth century. For adults and teens.

———

Fraser, Tony. "The Sidelining of Trinidad's Indigenous People." *Caribbean Intelligence.* https://www.caribbeanintelligence. com/content/sidelining-trinidads-indigenous-people Retrieved September 18, 2023.

Høgsbjerg, CJ. "'A Thorn in the Side of Great Britain': C.L.R. James and the Caribbean Labour Rebellions of the 1930s." *Small Axe: A Caribbean Journal of Criticism* 15, no. 2 (35) (July 2011): 24–42.

Newton, Melanie J. "Counterpoints of Conquest: The Royal Proclamation of 1763, the Lesser Antilles, and the Ethnocartography of Genocide." *The William and Mary Quarterly* 79, no. 2 (April 2022): 241–282.

Three vital articles on the history and present of the Caribbean. The Newton piece details the way the British racialized the natives of the Lesser Antilles and used that racialization to exploit, cheat, enslave, and murder both the indigenous people and Africans. The history is sickening—but also an eye-opening must-read for anyone who wants to understand the history of colonization and slavery. The article on C.L.R. James, on the other hand, paints an inspiring portrait of the sophisticated and heroic struggle of Trinidadian workers for fair treatment and, ultimately, independence from

Great Britain. And Fraser reports on the current indigenous population of Trinidad's attempts to gain some small measure of the respect and recognition that they deserve. Newton and Høgsbjerg are for adults, Fraser can be read by students as well.

ACKNOWLEDGMENTS

Every novel requires a battalion of friends, readers, supporters, and editors to bring it to fruition. But historical novels, it seems to me, require an entire army. I am indebted to so many people for helping bring this book into the world that I am terrified that I have forgotten someone—if you helped me make this book, and your name isn't here, know that I am deeply grateful to you.

First, while he is already included in the bibliography, I need to make clear that the work of Ben Macintyre was a prerequisite for the existence of *Max in the House of Spies*. His books *Operation Mincemeat* and *Agent Zigzag* introduced me to the historical figures who make up most of my characters. If you enjoyed this book, please go read one of Mr. Macintyre's books right away.

Professor Steven Remy very kindly allowed me to audit his course at Brooklyn College on the history of Nazi Germany, and then he took time away from his work on *Adolf Hitler: A Reference Guide to His Life and Works* to consult with me. For Professor Remy's time, his openness to my questions, his generosity of spirit, his deep well of knowledge, and his sense of humor—I am deeply grateful.

Professor Remy was an early reader. So was Katherine Locke, the brilliant author of *The Girl with the Red Balloon* and *This Rebel Heart*, among many other books. Other invaluable early readers were Zachary Gidwitz, Marissa Honma, and Lauren Mancia. All gave me feedback that helped this novel become richer, funnier, faster, and kinder to its readers. (If you don't think this book is any of those things, you should read the earlier drafts.)

I am very grateful for the careful and diligent work of Chandra Wohleber in copyediting the manuscript. She found a million small and not so small errors, thus making this book enormously better.

I read this book aloud to my mother, Patricia Lewy. She has a keen ear and a withering wit, which she only turned on me occasionally.

Sensei Masahiko Honma has burned the phrase "it is all part of training" into my brain over the last decade. I was very pleased that Jean could echo a small part of his great wealth of wisdom.

Professor Rosamond Black and Professor Raquel Otheguy both provided guidance on Sergeant Toby Thompson, directing me to C. L. R. James and the incredible history of the Trinidadian labor revolt. Professor Otheguy also shared eye-opening resources on the history of the indigenous people of the Lesser Antilles.

Sayantani DasGupta read the passages about Harold Wadia—my gratitude to her, both for that and for her hilarious and thrilling books, such as *The Serpent's Secret* and *The Chaos Monster: Secrets of the Sky.*

Mike Watson runs a brilliant website called TheCodeMachine.co.uk which has schematics and manuals from thousands of old radios, amps, and televisions. Mike was a little bemused by my initial request for the service manual of the 1939 Murphy A46, but when I explained what I needed it for, he generously volunteered advice and guidance on my exploration of late 1930s radios, both their outsides and insides.

My cousins Aaron Parrott and Erin Cole Parrott, their children Jackson and Emma Grace, and my daughter Ellie, participated in a March Madness–style bracket to help determine the name of this book, which was both hilarious and extremely helpful. The idea was Lauren Mancia's because, as she regularly points out, all of my good ideas are actually originally hers.

I owe the brilliant authors of the Hotel Bar a deep debt of gratitude for their encouragement, advice, expertise, and love.

I have so many loyal friends who have helped me hash out this book and survive the process: John and Raquel, Ryan and Jesse, Julian, Brandon and Tina, Yoni and Jane, Tony, Erica . . . without you, neither this book nor I would be here.

I have published with Penguin Young Readers since 2010, and I don't express often enough how lucky I am to have this relationship with such an extraordinary group of people. Anna Booth, Venessa Carson, Christina Colangelo, Rob Farren, Carmela Iaria, Trevor Ingerson, Bri Lockhart, Jen Loja, Shanta Newlin, Emily Romero, Olivia Russo, Jocelyn Schmidt, Jenna Smith, Natalie Vielkind, and the best marketing, production, publicity, and sales teams in publishing—your commitment to my books over the years puts me in a position that other authors can only dream of. Thank you.

Ally Horn has worked with me in various capacities since she graduated from college—from assistant to, now, full-fledged writing collaborator. It is a partnership that elevates my work at every turn.

My agent, Sarah Burnes, has been supporting me with fierce intelligence and deep kindness since I was her daughter's first grade teacher. Thank you, Sarah.

And Julie Strauss-Gabel, my editor and big sister, who holds me to a higher standard than I hold myself—to my great suffering and much greater joy. This book—and its unpublished predecessors—represent a very hard five years that has made us stronger as a partnership and as friends. I am in awe of our strength and our enduring love for each other.

Finally, to the three most important authors in my life: Mama, Lauren, and Ellie. I admire you almost as much as I love you.

THE MISSION
CONTINUES IN

MAX in the
LAND of LIES

COMING SOON